*Something's rotten in the Riverglow pack.*

Still learning more about each other as bond mates and adjusting to their new roles as Advisors to a Councilor, Constance Newcastle and Liam Murphy must deal with the ghosts of their past.

A quiet weekend in Boston is anything but that, when Constance comes face to face with the betrayal of those she considered the closest to her. Everyone has secrets, and wherever Constance goes, she has a knack for uncovering them. The only problem is that some secrets are deadly.

# Books by Amy Lee Burgess

*The Wiolf Within Series*
Beneath the Skin, Book One
Scratch the Surface, Book Two
Hidden In Plain Sight, Book Three
Inside Out, Book Four
About Face, Book Five
Across the Line, Book Six

**Published by Kensington Publishing Corporation**

# Scratch the Surface

*The Wolf Within Series*

## Amy Lee Burgess

**LYRICAL PRESS**
Kensington Publishing Corp.
www.kensingtonbooks.com

Lyrical Press books are published by
Kensington Publishing Corp. 119 West 40th Street New York, NY 10018

All Kensington titles, imprints, and distributed lines are available at special
quantity discounts for bulk purchases for sales promotion, premiums, fund-
raising, and educational or institutional use.

Special book excerpts or customized printings can also be created to fit
specific needs. For details, write or phone the office of the Kensington
Special Sales Manager:
Kensington Publishing Corp.
119 West 40th Street
New York, NY 10018
Attn. Special Sales Department. Phone: 1-800-221-2647.

First Electronic Edition: March 2012
eISBN-13: 978-1-61650-349-9
eISBN-10: 1-61650-349-1

First Print Edition: March 2012
ISBN-13: 978-1-61650-853-1
ISBN-10: 1-61650-853-1

Printed in the United States of America

*This one is dedicated to one of my best friends, Leslie Johnson Bevis. I've known Leslie since I was born. Really! She is a whole month and a half older than me and our parents are friends too. She listened patiently to my endless stories as I read them aloud to her all through junior and senior high school. Thanks, Les. This one you can read on your own!*

# Acknowledgement

As always, thanks to Nerine Dorman, for her sharp editing eye and merciless grasp of grammar. She says working with me is like herding cats, but I think wolves would be more like it.

# Chapter 1

*Wind in my face. I happy! Friend with me! We look at strange water.
No move now. Stuck. Put paw on it. Cold! Want to walk on strange
water. I scared! Strange water make noise—Crrrack! Paw wet and cold.
Friend has tongue out, Friend laugh. Friend look at strange water. I not
understand. Water moves. But strange water does not move . Why? Why?
Want word for strange water. Want know why it not move. Think! Think
hard. Strange water there when it very cold. Me seen it with Him and Her
before they go away and not come back. Us run on it. Run, run, run. Me
not want run now, me want word. I. I want word. I want word for strange
water. Think. Think. Friend watch over me. Think. Think. I so mad. I
want word! I want word! No. No get mad. Can't think for mad in head.
Go away, mad. Stop. Think. Strange water not move. Cold. White. Water.
Not water. Think. Think. Want word. Word for strange, cold water that
not move. Word is...word is...ice! Yes! Ice, ice, ice, ice! I see ice! I see ice!
Friend, I see ice! Friend, I happy! I see ice! I lick Friend's face. Friend
lick me. I happy. I see ice!*

* * * *

The shrill ring of the phone dragged me out of sleep. Murphy and I
had shifted the night before and we'd exhausted ourselves in wolf form.
By the time we'd shifted back, shivered into our clothes and driven home
to Boston, it had nearly been dawn. The sky above my condo had been
a pale shimmering pink as I'd fallen onto the bed, my hair still wet from
the shower. I didn't even remember Murphy coming to bed but he was
there with me. The ringing phone had roused him too. He was snuggled
up against my back, his arm across my waist and he rolled over into a

defensive ball, swearing colorfully in Irish under his breath while he tried to shield his ears with one of the fluffy down pillows.

"Goddamn it," I muttered. I could tell it was frigid outside. Well, naturally, it was January. Barely. "Happy fucking New Year, Murphy."

His only response was more Irish swearing. The phone stopped ringing and I let my eyes drift shut again but that's when the damn answering machine kicked on with an earsplitting beep.

"Fuck." Murphy's curse was muffled by the pillow.

"Constance," said someone familiar. We both scrambled up on our elbows, wildly shifted the covers and tried to get the phone before it disconnected.

Since the phone was closer to my side of the bed, I won the mad race and scooped it up, panting and out of breath.

"Hello, Councilor Allerton," I gasped into the phone while Murphy performed some sort of strange-looking war dance on the cold hardwood floors. I didn't feel much sympathy. I had told him to wear socks to bed and he had refused.

"Is there no frigging heat in his place?" He hopped from one foot to the other.

"Good morning, Constance, did I wake you?" Jason Allerton was a Councilor on the Great Pack's Council. The Council oversaw all of the packs spread out across the world. Murphy and I were his newest Advisors. He sent us on assignments to other packs to investigate accidents, murders and disputes that could not be worked out by the Regional Councils and other projects as he desired. So far, we'd only been on one assignment for him and that one had been unofficial, before we'd affiliated with Mac Tire—one of the largest, continuous packs in the world. They were based in Dublin, Ireland, but we had yet to go there. I'd only met two people from my new pack—Murphy and the Alpha male, Padraic O'Reilly. The rest were amorphous strangers I supposed I would eventually meet.

At the moment Murphy and I were in Boston, Massachusetts. I owned a condo and we were in the process of cleaning it, packing up the stuff I wanted to keep and getting it ready to act as rental property. When all this was accomplished, we would go to Belfast to clear out Murphy's cottage there before we went to Dublin to meet the rest of our pack.

After Councilor Allerton had asked us to be his Advisors, Murphy and I had been asked to join Mac Tire. In Murphy's case it was rejoin since he had been born into the pack and had left after the death of his bond mate, Sorcha, but it was a new pack for me.

Murphy had bought a car in Houston and we'd spent the past two months leisurely driving to the East Coast, stopping at all the major cities that interested us so we could sightsee. I'd seen more of my native country in the past two months than I had the previous thirty-two years of my life.

We'd arrived in Boston the day before New Year's Eve, so we'd barely even begun to tackle the condo. Murphy didn't want to be on a time table. He wanted us to go slowly and explore. I think he meant each other as well as the cities we visited. We'd been thrown together and bonded under extreme circumstances and now that the dust had settled and we were still standing, we had a lot of getting to know each other to do.

In the three months I'd known him, he'd rapidly become my best friend and confidante. My teacher and my guide.

After my first bond mates, Grey and Elena, had died in a car crash two and a half years ago, I'd been kicked out of my small pack in Connecticut. Although the Councils had cleared me, my pack had never stopped believing I had been drunk the night I drove that car over the embankment and my bond mates died.

It had been later proved that it was Grandfather Tobias, another member of my old pack, who had tampered with the brakes of my new Mustang. He was part of an underground movement made up of some of the oldest members of the Great Pack who resented the new ways we were adopting that brought us closer into interaction with the Others—those who were not Pack—and brought money and prestige into our packs by way of this involvement.

The new direction was integration, although not going as far as to reveal we were Pack and could shift into wolves. The old way was behind the scenes, on the fringes. Jobs in retail were common, but some of us were con artists or magicians as well. The trick was to avoid attention and interaction with the mainstream world as much as possible.

This movement saw to it that certain young Pack members, who flouted tradition, met with fatal accidents. It was meant to scare us, stop the flow of revenue and destroy the ones with the closest ties to the Others.

Murphy and I, with Councilor Allerton's assistance, had discovered and unmasked this movement. We had not stopped it because it could not be halted simply by announcing to the Pack it existed. That would have caused chaos and panic. They had to be stopped one and two at a time— quiet arrests and detainment.

We'd barely scratched the surface and I knew a lot of work was yet to be done, but after what we'd gone through in Paris and Houston, I wasn't sure I had the stomach for it.

This was the other reason for the long road trip—it was a chance to regroup and get myself together.

Allerton had checked in on us a few times along the way, but I wondered if this phone call heralded the end of the vacation and was a wake-up call in more than one sense of the word.

However, his next sentence blasted everything out of my mind.

"We've arrested Tobias Green and he's confessed."

Murphy stopped hopping and swearing when I pulled out the desk chair and fell into it. My legs felt hollow, as if all the bones had melted.

Tobias Green. I called him Grandfather Tobias. I'd loved and respected him. I'd looked after him more than anyone else in my pack and, although I'd had a sense of duty because he was old, I'd done it more out of genuine love. He was not my blood grandfather, but he might as well have been. I loved him that much.

Ever since that moment in Houston when I'd realized the grandmother in Paris had deliberately put a lethal overdose of narcotics in the homemade pill she'd given Murphy, it was an easy, yet devastating, intuitive jump to understand that Grandfather Tobias was guilty of killing my bond mates. Once we'd uncovered the grandmothers' and grandfathers' plot, it had been horrifyingly clear he'd done something to the car. I'd brought it to him that afternoon and he'd gone beneath it to inspect it because he was a mechanic and he told me he wanted to see for himself that his dear girl and her bond mates were in a safe, reliable vehicle. Yet he'd tampered with the brakes so they'd fail and I'd lose control.

Without being able to prevent it, I flashed back to the accident.

\* \* \* \*

*"The Comet or Blue Moon, Grey? Which club do you want to go to?"*

*I see Grey laughing in the dashboard lights as he fiddles with the CD player. Depeche Mode's Strange Love morphs into Billy Idol's White Wedding. Grey has an addiction to eighties music. Sometimes I find it endearing. Sometimes I find it annoying as hell.*

*"I don't care. It's your birthday, Stanzie. You choose. The Comet or Blue Moon, it doesn't matter to me." He turns his head to smile at me. The love he feels for me is written all over his face. His shaggy, dark hair falls into his blue eyes. He's got the back part confined in a rubber band. When it's loose, his hair brushes his shoulders. Right now it's about two inches longer than mine. I'm experimenting with a bob. I'm not sure I like it.*

*He needs a haircut. He has an appointment on Monday. I wrote it on the erasable calendar stuck to our fridge. I made it for him yesterday.*

*"Elena?" I glance into the rearview mirror to see her beautiful face. She is putting on eyeliner and her bright red purse is open on the seat beside her—a compact in one hand, the eyeliner stick in the other. She frowns at her reflection, with concentration, not because she finds fault with her appearance.*

*"Oh, you know I don't care, I just want to dance with you, Birthday Girl."*

*The Comet is closer and I have a sudden desire to be out of the car. I want to feel the summer breeze and hear my new metallic gold stiletto heels click against the soft, warm pavement of the August night. I want to hear music from this decade. I want to dance, to feel Grey's hands on my hips as we move together beneath the strobe lights and Elena guards our drinks at the table.*

*I make a decision. I take the exit. The road climbs over a small crest then dips sharply. I brake because we've been traveling at seventy miles an hour and now we need to slow down. We'll still be above the legal speed limit, but this is a Mustang GT, metallic gold like my stiletto heels, with an ink-black leather interior. My dream car is a present from Elena who has just signed a lucrative contract with a company that develops PC games. Elena is a whiz at designing games. We have six different PCs and laptops set up in our house in New Britain and she is always perched in front of one of them, sucking absently on her bottom lip as she contemplates the scenarios in front of her on the screen.*

*Yesterday she made an important deliverable to the company and they extended her contract for another game, this one even more ambitious— about werewolves. It is slated for tentative release October of 2010, which is two years and two months into the future.*

*I put my foot on the brake, but it doesn't seem like we decelerate. Confused, I press harder then we hit the dip and I see a shadow or a bird or something that distracts me then the wheel is a traitor beneath my hands. Elena screams in the backseat as the guardrail looms closer.*

*I have time to think to myself,* This is just a dream. This is not happening. This is not—

*The Mustang's front end smashes into the guardrail with a terrific bang. It crumples with a metallic grinding and tearing. The engine screams in protest.*

*"Stanzie!" Elena shrieks. Grey is stiff and terrified beside me. The whole car reeks of our extreme fear. It pours out of our skins like invisible sweat and the mad stink of it paralyzes my muscles and vocal cords. I am a mute statue. I cannot even blink.*

*As Billy Idol sings the Mustang turns up and over. Wind rushes in when Grey's door flies open. I see a blur of movement when he falls out and my paralysis breaks. I reach out for him, but the airbag hits me in the face and something hard smashes the back of my seat. Elena stops screaming. She stops screaming because her neck breaks under the force of her body slamming into the back of my seat. She, like Grey, never wears a seatbelt.*

\* \* \* \*

Pressure brought me out of my trance. Murphy squeezed my shoulder reassuringly.

Allerton said my name, probably not for the first time.

The car crash was so vivid in my head I could still hear Elena's screams and the jagged sound of tearing metal.

"I'm here." I swallowed an obstruction in my throat. It was two and a half years ago. It was time to let go and get over it.

I'd been doing a good job of that, thanks to Murphy, but one sentence made me realize that maybe I would never truly be free. It was not a pleasant thought.

"I'm sorry if I've upset you." Allerton's voice was rich with sympathy. I visualized his handsome, distinguished face and his dark black hair he wore as fashionably cut as his designer suits. "I thought you should know. There's something else as well."

My stomach sank even though I had no idea what the something else could be, only that it wouldn't be good.

"He wants to speak to you. Privately."

My mouth dropped open in protest. Sick bile burned my throat and I must have twisted in my seat because Murphy put both hands on my shoulders. I was absurdly grateful for his touch.

With his Pack-enhanced senses, he could hear what Allerton said, and he could smell my distress. I know I reeked of it.

"Do I have to?" Tears clogged my sinuses and, if not for Murphy, I would have been bawling like a baby, I knew it.

"Of course not," said Allerton at once, and there was just a tinge of disappointment in his voice that I strove to ignore, but it was impossible. Damn him. Damn me for wanting to please him because he was a Councilor.

"Where is he?"

"He's being held in the safe house in Hartford. I'm here with him, along with one of the Regional Councilors. Riverglow is not being told the whole story. Just that he confessed to doing it not why."

Riverglow was the name of my former pack—Jonathan, Nora, Callie, Vaughn and Peter.

"Aren't they even curious?" I couldn't disguise the bitterness in my voice.

"He's saying he accidentally put a hole in the brake lining, causing the brake fluid to leak out, and he realized it when he went over the car after the accident but was too ashamed to admit it."

"An accident? And do they believe it?" My voice shook with outrage. "They didn't believe me. Are they going to believe him?"

"Constance, he had to say something. We need to keep the knowledge that people in the Pack are murdering others under wraps. He can't tell them the truth." Allerton was sympathetic but firm. "And you can ask them yourself what they believe if you come to Connecticut. They want to see you too."

I wanted to throw the phone into the wall and stomp on it. I wanted to spit in Allerton's arrogant face. What I didn't want was to ever see any of my former pack again—especially Grandfather Tobias.

"How am I supposed to face them? How am I supposed to look Grandfather Tobias in the eye after what he did to Grey and Elena? To me!" It was disrespectful to say the least to shout at a Councilor, but I rarely paused to think before I reacted. Allerton took my tirade in patient silence which is what made me stop shouting. My cheeks burned with humiliation.

"I'm not telling you what to do, Constance. I'm giving you the opportunity to hear the man out. It might provide some closure." He didn't say it, but I knew damn well he thought I could use a huge, heaping dose of it.

I squeezed my eyes shut and heard Elena screaming in my head again. "When do I have to be there?"

"As soon as you can make it." Allerton paused then said, "He's not going back to Riverglow. The Council will acknowledge his cover story and accept it, but he won't return to the pack. He's going to go to sleep one night very soon and he's not going to wake up. If you want, you can hand him a glass of warm milk or hot chocolate to help him go to sleep. If you want." Allerton's tone was deceptively nonchalant but what he offered was the chance to administer the fatal poison. That would be closure for sure.

I didn't answer because I couldn't. A part of me wanted to kill that old man, not with poison, but with my claws and fangs—in wolf form. I didn't know if I could be such a civilized murderer. Or maybe executioner was a better word.

"Can I speak to Liam, please?"

I thrust the phone at Murphy and he took it, but when I tried to get up, he frowned at me.

"I want to take a shower." I had to get out of the room and away from the phone and Allerton and the sound of Elena screaming.

His dark gaze searched my face for a moment before he let go of my shoulder. He watched me as I stumbled for the bathroom. He acknowledged Allerton then went grimly silent as he listened. I smelled the anger that escaped from his pores and clouded the air around him—protective anger.

# Chapter 2

I cried in the shower—bitter, painful tears that ripped my guts to shreds. Intellectually, I had known Grandfather Tobias had done something to the car. He was a mechanic. He'd been under the car. I remembered how the car hadn't seemed to slow down. When I told my story to Councilor Allerton and the Regional Councilors after the accident, I'd told them I didn't think the brakes had been working. There were no skid marks on the road and that supported my theory. Grandfather Tobias had stood in front of them all and declared that the car had been mechanically sound. It was suggested I'd hit the gas instead of the brakes and that I'd been drinking. I'd panicked and my judgment was impaired.

A breathalyzer test had been administered but, because it had not been done immediately after the accident, I'd passed it and there was no real way to say whether I would have failed it if it had been done sooner.

It had been my word against theirs. The Regional Council had wanted to rule against me. My punishment would have been expulsion from my pack and a mandatory two-year prohibition against attending Great Pack events and bonding with someone—plus the everlasting and eternal shame.

Allerton, as a member of the Great Council, had persuaded them it had been a tragic accident that was no one's fault. He did this I now knew because even back then he suspected something was wrong within the Great Pack. There were too many of these tragic accidents and something didn't feel right to him.

So I had been cleared. However, my pack was free to sever ties with me anyway, and that's what they'd done as soon as they could. I was told to get the hell out of Connecticut and never come back.

As a non-voting member of Riverglow due to his advanced age, Grandfather Tobias had not been formally involved in my former pack's decision, but when I'd gone to his home, desperate and grieving, wanting him at least to comfort me, he had refused to answer the door.

His front window blinds had been up when I'd knocked on the door. I'd seen him peer out and when he'd recognized me, the blinds had gone down with a whoosh and the last, dim speck of hope and self-esteem I'd had left had been extinguished. Up until that point, I'd let myself believe I was a victim of a tragic, horrible accident, but after that the doubt had started to creep in and the blame I had struggled not to give in to had swept across me and drowned me.

I'd always known Elena and Grey would not have blamed me—even if I had been drunk. They had loved me. I'd thought Grandfather Tobias had loved me too.

Technically, I was free to join another pack whenever I wanted, but after Grandfather Tobias rejected me, I'd wanted to punish myself. The worst I could think of was exile from the Pack.

I'd gone to the safe house in Hartford, where Allerton had been staying, and he'd invited me up to his room on the second floor so he could finish his packing. His expression had been grave and full of compassion, and I'd followed him up the stairs. Saturated with guilt, I'd barely been able to lift my feet from one stair to the next, wanting only to curl up in a ball, go to sleep and never, ever wake.

* * * *

"*I think, Councilor. I think maybe I was drunk. I think maybe I did kill them. Not on purpose, but it's my fault.*" *I look at him, full of shame and self-hatred, wanting him to punish me even though I am already punished.*

*He stares at me and doesn't say anything.*

"*Elena has left you nearly three hundred thousand dollars,*" *he says after a moment.*

"*I don't want it.*" *My lips are numb. My body is too and I want to sit but this is not my room and, anyway, I deserve no comfort.*

"*Nevertheless, it's yours. She wanted you to have it.*"

"*Before I killed her. If she could do it over, she'd leave it to somebody else,*" *I say.*

*"She left it to you. Not Grey. You. I think that says a lot about your bond."* Allerton zips his suitcase shut and straightens the cuffs of his Dolce and Gabbana ice-blue button-down shirt. A dark gray suit jacket is draped carefully over the back of the chair in front of the desk in the corner. His pants match the jacket. They are perfectly creased and fit him as if they had been tailored. His shoes are shiny black Gucci loafers. Even though I love shoes, today I feel nothing when I look at them except that one of the tassels is crooked. I long to fix it but I stand still.

*"I need to be punished,"* I whisper in a dreadful voice. I will not cry. I promise myself I will not cry in front of this man.

He lifts his suitcase off the carefully made bed and puts it down beside his feet. The leather tassel is still crooked. He does not notice. Maybe these things don't bother him.

*"What more can I do that hasn't already been done to you by your pack?"* His voice is neutral and I can't tell what he is thinking. He smells only of Armani cologne. He hides his emotions well, but then he is a Councilor.

*"I killed them,"* I insist.

*"On purpose?"* He fixes me with keen blue eyes that see everything.

*"No,"* I falter. I squeeze my hands together in front of me. I feel sick and disconnected.

*"So I cannot punish you any more severely than your pack has already done."* He allows a small amount of impatience to creep into his voice. He glances at his watch—a quick gesture, but I am meant to understand he is in a rush and has other places to be. I am wasting his time. Shamed, I look down.

*"You could make it official,"* I tell him. I lift my gaze from the crooked leather tassel on his shoe to stare him full in the face.

*"If I do that—"* All the impatience left his voice. *"—chances are you'll never find another bond mate. You'll never find a new pack. You'll be an outcast all the rest of your life, Constance."*

*"Yes."* I nod rapidly. Finally, he understands. *"Exactly!"*

*"I can't do that,"* he says as the tears of shame and grief ignite in my eyes like acid. *"I won't do that. Take that legacy, Constance, and go live somewhere by yourself. In two years I want to see you at the Great Gathering. Time has a way of giving you perspective and..."*

*"I don't need perspective!" I shout. I tremble so hard my bones ache. "I have nothing left because I killed what mattered most. Time won't change that or bring them back!" I do cry then, cursing myself, and with an inarticulate noise, I whirl to run away.*

*That's when I feel Allerton's arms go around me and he hugs me, murmuring vaguely comforting things to me as he rocks me and I ruin the front of his Dolce and Gabbana shirt with my tears and snot.*

*Until then he has been this looming, authoritarian figure. Bigger than life. Bigger than me. Untouchable and remote. Now he reveals himself as human. I cry like I am being destroyed and he is the only thing between me and annihilation.*

*I take the three hundred thousand dollars. I use most of it to buy a condo in Boston where I live by myself for two years until the next Great Gathering.*

*I remember his words when I receive my invitation in the mail—on thick parchment paper inked with the date and location. My self-imposed exile is over if I want it to be and two years into the future, just as he'd predicted—I want it to be.*

\* \* \* \*

The mouthwatering scent of frying bacon permeated the entire condo when I emerged, red-eyed and shaky, from the bathroom. Murphy was making breakfast. He always fed me when I was in crisis mode. It was endearing. It didn't hurt that he made scrambled eggs and bacon in the style of the best greasy spoon diners.

I pulled on a pair of jeans and a black turtle neck sweater and went in search of gustatory bliss.

I couldn't decide which to drink first, coffee or orange juice, but the coffee needed milk and sugar so I went for the OJ. Two gulps and it was gone. The resultant sugar rush made inroads on the empty feeling inside me. It felt as if I'd been hollowed out by a huge ice cream scoop from hell.

He piled my plate high with eggs from the pan and gave himself a noticeably smaller portion. When he turned his back to get the bacon, I scooped some of my eggs onto his plate to make it a more even distribution.

He knew I did it, but he didn't say anything—just gave me twice as much bacon as he gave himself.

Wheat toast popped up in the toaster and when he was busy buttering it, I gave him half my bacon.

"Stop giving away all your food and eat some of it," he suggested, the butter knife scraping against the toast. Melted butter smelled like childhood to me—breakfast from the past—being little and my feet not reaching the floor.

"Come sit down and eat with me." I helped myself to the bottle of ketchup and doused my eggs with it. I adored ketchup. Elixir of the gods.

"The toast won't butter itself, woman," he told me, and I stuck out my tongue. I poured milk into my coffee and spooned in two teaspoons of sugar. The spoon clacked against the side of the pottery mug and that was a sound that comforted too.

"Is there peanut butter?" I shoved back my chair so I could search in the cupboard. We'd bought a ton of groceries the day before, but I couldn't remember if I'd put a jar of peanut butter in the basket.

"Sit down and eat." Murphy put the plate of toast on the table. He went to the cupboard to look for me. I devoured one slice of bacon then another.

I had one left by the time he came to the table with the jar of peanut butter. Total elapsed time—thirty-five seconds.

"You make the best damn bacon," I said around a huge mouthful. I swallowed and gave a contented sigh.

Murphy pulled out his chair and sat. His hair was tousled and needed to be brushed and razor stubble dotted his cheeks, but he was sexy as hell in spite of it, or perhaps, because of it. He had a long, narrow face with a chin more pointed than round. His cheek bones were high, his mouth dreamy and sensuous. His brown eyes were penetrating and full of intelligence and lively humor. Right now his expression was pensive. The look he gave me measured my mood and, while I think he was pleased I was eating, I don't believe he was entirely satisfied I was all right.

I crunched up my last piece of bacon and he reached out and transferred half of his to my plate, never glancing away from my face.

"I'm going to get fat," I predicted, but I ate one of the pieces A small smile quirked the corners of his mouth.

"Never happen," he drawled. "Your wolf will keep you in shape."

I thought back to the night before. After my wolf had come up with the word for ice, Murphy's had led us off on a wild chase through the winter woods. We'd had such fun.

Instead of champagne at midnight, we'd thrashed through fallen leaves, churning up wet cold clumps of them stuck together. We'd tussled in a clearing, ringed around by pine trees forty feet tall. The wind had blown through the pine needles creating a rattling, wintry sound. That's what we'd heard instead of *Auld Lang Syne*.

My wolf had bared her throat to his and he'd taken it in his jaws, exquisitely gentle. My wolf had infinite trust in him. She adored him. I think his wolf adored her. At least I hoped so. He was very, very kind to her and patient as she blundered through lessons most Pack's wolves had learned the first ten times they'd shifted.

I'd never learned, had never wanted to learn. My wolf was headstrong and stubborn. Free and innocent. She loved to run and play and exist without much coherent thought.

Well, she used to. Now she hungered for words, for the names of things. Running and playing were things she did after she taught herself words. Most times now she forgot about running and playing until Murphy's wolf reminded her.

She always had been an obsessive creature who fixated on one thing. Before it had been pleasure, now it was knowledge.

"She taught herself the word for 'ice' last night," I told him with pride. "She's getting so much smarter thanks to your wolf, Murphy. And you, telling me how to do it before we shift."

"She still getting mad at herself when she can't think of the word right away?" He sounded both indulgently pleased and concerned. He didn't like her to push herself too hard.

"She was furious and frustrated for a while last night," I admitted. I selected a piece of toast and spread it with peanut butter. It was the creamy kind. Damn. I'd meant to pick up chunky.

"I know." His eyes were sad for a moment. "She was pawing at her head. You've got a scratch on your cheek right now." He frowned as he looked at it.

I put a hand up to my cheek and my fingers encountered the thin, rough outline. It stung a little and I made a mental note to put peroxide on it.

"She was trying to scratch the mad out of her head so she could think," I said with a rueful smile. "She's so literal. The mad was taking up all the space in her head and there was no room to think about the word for ice."

"Constance," Murphy said, and I knew he was gearing himself up to lecture me again about pushing too hard.

"It's not use talking to me about this." I raised a protesting hand. "She's the one who gets that way."

"Where does she get it from? Who's telling her she needs to think so hard to find the words?"

"Me?" I shook my head. "I'm so far buried in her psyche when we're shifted that I doubt I have much influence over what she does."

"Bullshit." He dumped a teaspoon of sugar into his coffee and stirred. The spoon hitting the sides of the mug was pure frustration expressed in sound. "You persist in thinking there's such a separation between you and her and there's not."

"I don't see it. I am not me when I'm her." This was a well-worn, frequent discussion between us. He could tell me a hundred million times that I was my wolf and she was me, but I thought of us as distinct entities. While I was inside her and she was inside of me, when I was in human form, she did not influence me and I damn sure didn't have any influence over her when she was wolf.

Murphy drummed his fingers on the table top and drank his coffee. He kept his gaze fixed to the cupboards to the side of the table and not on me.

I took a bite of eggs but I wasn't hungry anymore. I managed to swallow what I had in my mouth but I knew I was done. I hated to disappoint him, but I couldn't see it his way and I couldn't lie to him.

"I'm sorry," he said. The drumming ceased. I got up and brought the coffee pot to the table and refilled his mug. Mine was still full, but I put a little bit in anyway to warm it up and then crossed the room to put the pot back on the burner.

"I push you harder than anybody, don't I?"

I couldn't agree with him, but if I did he'd argue and I didn't want to. My wolf frustrated me, but I didn't want him to know how much because he'd blame himself since it had been his idea to work with her.

I sat back down without answering and picked up my mug.

"When do we leave for Connecticut? You're coming with me, aren't you?" The idea that he wouldn't be with me made the bacon in my stomach roll over queasily. I needed him.

"Of course I'm coming. You don't have to face that bastard alone." Outraged shock spread across his face. "Besides, I'm dying for a chance to punch that asshole, Jonathan Archer, in the nose. You think I'd miss that opportunity?"

I gave him a suspicious look because I couldn't tell if he was serious. He probably was. Jonathan was the Alpha male of the Riverglow pack. He'd never liked me and he'd led the crusade against me after Grey's and Elena's deaths. I'd told Murphy a few stories about him and, as a result, Murphy hated the man like poison.

"Don't punch Jonathan in the nose," I said. Then I grinned. "Kick him in the 'nads. It'll hurt more."

Murphy burst into laughter as I'd intended and I joined in too. This was one of the shittier mornings of my life, but I least I could still laugh about it.

# Chapter 3

It had been Murphy's idea to take the road trip from Houston to Boston. Instead of renting a car, he'd bought a used charcoal-gray Honda Prelude from a Houston CarMax. He'd surprised me with it at the hotel where I'd been packing our things. I had been in one hellish hurry to leave Houston after Murphy's near-fatal overdose.

After he'd been released from the hospital, we'd rested in the hotel for three days. Well, he'd rested. I'd paced around until that drove him crazy and he sent me out shopping where I bought seven pairs of shoes only to return five of them the next day. Murphy hadn't said one word, but his expression had spoken for him. He thought my shoe fetish was bordering on clinically insane. This from the man who would wear the same pair of shoes for an entire week in a row. *That* was just plain weird, if you ask me.

On our trip east, at the beginning of each new week, I'd sneak a new pair of shoes for him into our hotel room and substitute them for the pair that was driving me nuts. The man never even noticed the difference until I pointed it out to him in exasperation twenty miles down the road.

"It was dark in the room when I got dressed," was his most used excuse, closely followed by, "As long as they fit on my feet, what do I care?" That pronouncement usually threw me into a sputtering fit of incredulity which he laughed at as he continued to serenely drive down the interstate.

Today we drove down the Mass Pike, each wrapped in a cocoon of our own thoughts and, for myself, fears of the unknown and yet to come.

It was a gray, overcast day. Dirty, salt-encrusted snow crouched on the sides of the interstate interspersed with bald patches of muddy, winter-brown grass. I had the Prelude's heat cranked up because I was perpetually cold. I think it had something to do with how often I was shifting. I got so damned chilled when I shifted back naked in near freezing temperatures. It took me hours and a long hot shower to shake the cold and the next day it seemed as if I could never get comfortably warm.

Murphy didn't seem to suffer the way I did. As the interior temperature of the car crept higher, he unbuttoned his black pea coat and loosened the gray scarf around his throat. After we merged onto I-84, he peeled off his gloves and stuffed them into the compartment between the seats.

He'd shaved, and brushed his hair, and his expression was introspective as he drove, his mouth almost as tight as his fingers clenched around the steering wheel.

He drove well, but I was always jumpy in the car, even after two months on the road.

Another reason for the road trip was to get me comfortable riding in a car again.

After the accident I had avoided cars, taxis and buses—anything on four wheels with an engine. I'd made sure to find a job within walking distance of my condo and, if I really had to, I took the bus as it was the least like a car, but I sat there in rigid fear until my stop, where I couldn't get off fast enough.

I still wouldn't drive, although Murphy asked me if I wanted to at least three times a week. I always refused. It was the one thing I wouldn't do to please him. I did everything else I could think of that I knew or suspected would make him happy. I wasn't ready to drive. I wasn't sure I ever would be.

It was a two-hour trip and I wished I could read in the car, but I couldn't relax enough to do that. I constantly scanned the road ahead for obstacles and accidents.

Murphy and I sometimes got lost in conversation and that's the only time I really even slightly relaxed. Today we didn't talk. Instead, we sat side by side as the miles melted behind us like dirty snow.

I played with a strand of my hair, winding it around one finger and letting it spring free, before repeating the process.

Things started to look familiar just past the state border.

"Want to stop for a minute?" Murphy asked. He was always quick to find a rest stop for me to stretch my legs when he thought the road was getting to me.

A large sign welcomed us to Connecticut, and off the exit, a small brick building had been erected that contained rest rooms, vending machines and brochures about attractions. This was typical across the country. We'd stopped at many of these just past the border rest stops from state to state.

I nodded and Murphy merged onto the exit, guiding the Prelude off the interstate into the parking lot.

Snow stacked up in a grubby pile at the end of the lot where the plows had pushed it. Some of the parking spaces were covered with patches of black water that would ice over at night but now, at just past one in the afternoon, were melted, cold puddles.

Murphy parked the car over one of them, but left the space where we'd exit the car clear.

The cold air invaded my nostrils and throat the second I opened the door. Murphy waited for me on the sidewalk. It was dotted with bits of sand and salt put down so people wouldn't slip on ice on their way to the rest room.

Our car was one of three in the lot. The other two were filthy and old. Ours was a prince among paupers. Murphy took good care of that car. He washed it every week, vacuumed it out and patiently picked up all the fast food bags and wrappers I carelessly let fall to the floor mats.

I'd heard once that Irish men treated their cars the way their forebears had treated their horses and I could believe it. If Murphy could have fed the Prelude oats and mash, and curried it down in the stall at the end of each day, he would have. Instead, he took it to by-hand car washes and spent two hours buffing, waxing and scrubbing dirt and grime from the hubcaps and windshield.

I helped him, but my help was half-assed, at least according to him, and so most of the time I sat on a bench or in the car and read a book or a magazine. Murphy was about the car the way I was about shoes. He didn't see it that way but it was true. Nobody needed to wash their car every damn week. Or spend two hours doing it himself instead of going through an automatic car wash where it would have taken ten minutes. Only suggest to him that we do that and it was enough to send him into a fifteen minute tirade about how those automatic car washes were for shit and scratched the paint job and didn't get the undercarriage and *how the hell can you even suggest a thing like that, Constance. Don't even think such sacrilege, please.*

I did suggest it about once a week because I secretly laughed my ass off at how frothed at the mouth the man would get. Like clockwork. Every single time.

He was waiting for me by the vending machines outside the ladies' room. The day after shifting was hell on the bladder. We drank tons of water before we shifted because if we didn't, the muscle cramps the next day were severe.

Instead of walking to the car, I went in the other direction, toward a small stand of maple trees and what, in spring and summer, would be a flower bed. Right now it was a sullen brown pile of half-frozen mud.

Murphy fell into step with me and we walked together without speaking. I wanted to hold his hand because I wanted the contact and the comfort but I was too fragile. Murphy didn't like to be touched first. When I forgot and did reach out to him, he invariably froze for a second before relaxing. He wouldn't take his hand away from mine, but he would freeze at first and I knew I'd take it way too personally today so I didn't risk it.

Instead I kept as close as I could get to him without touching him. Our coat sleeves brushed, but our hands never met.

We avoided the grubby snow bank by common consent. The bottom edges of it were liberally stained with dog piss. If I concentrated I could smell it. If I really focused I could tell which stains belonged to different dogs and which were made by repeat offenders. I had some dubious talents as Pack and that was one of them.

The whole damn snow bank depressed me, just like the whole damn thing with Grandfather Tobias and our trip to Connecticut.

"This sucks," I announced, apropos of nothing.

"At least you have the vindication, the satisfaction, of knowing for sure," he remarked. He'd carefully and considerately avoided talking about the situation, allowing me to go first. The entire hour and a half we'd been in the car, he'd wanted to talk about this but he wouldn't bring it up unless I did. He'd learned over our road trip that silence drew me out better than direct confrontation.

"You know the grandfather in your pack rigged Sorcha's accident too," I said in a low voice.

He shrugged and the wind blew his straight blondish-brown hair around. He'd cut his hair very short since Houston, but there was still enough for the winter wind to play with.

"He hasn't confessed yet."

"Has he been questioned?"

Murphy looked at me from the corner of his dark eyes. He was hunched against the biting wind and had his hands shoved deep in his coat pockets. His expression was a baffled mix of despair and rage.

"He's disappeared. Nobody knows where he is and nobody can find him."

I chewed on that for a moment, wondering how long he'd known this fact and hadn't told me.

"Since when?"

"Almost right after the incident in Houston." His mouth turned up wryly. He was referring to his near-fatal overdose.

"Someone gave him the heads up?" A cold sliver of disquiet slid down my spine then back up again as the implications hit me.

"Looks like it." We stopped where the sidewalk ended, facing each other. The ground beneath the maple trees looked muddy. I had on boots— black winter boots with sheepskin lining. I'd bought them on sale last spring and this was my first chance to wear them. They would have been okay in the mud, but Murphy didn't seem inclined to wander off the path. He had a pair of dark brown Timberland boots. They were waterproof but, ten to one, he didn't know that. He hadn't bought them—I had.

He saw me examine them critically and shook his head.

"Don't even think about it. I like these boots and if they go missing I'm going to hunt them down."

"You've been wearing them for two weeks, Murphy."

"And I'll be wearing them for two weeks more and two weeks after that probably. I like them."

"At least wear one of your other pairs once in a while? Couple times a week? Please?" I begged. The frigid wind blew a strand of hair into my eyes and I brushed it away with impatient fingers.

He gave me an ironic smile, one that tugged at something inside me. Sometimes when he looked at me, my heart gave a strange little flip.

"Only if you leave these alone and let me wear them in peace," he said.

I lifted a hand in a solemn oath. "I swear," I said in a serious tone that made him roll his eyes.

"Why didn't Grandfather Tobias get a warning the same as Grandfather Mick?" We were halfway back to the car when I posed the question. Murphy gave an eloquent shrug.

"Maybe he did and he chose to disregard it."

The Prelude's lights winked as Murphy unlocked the car with the button on the ignition key. He opened my door for me and I hesitated before getting all the way in.

"You know something I don't?" I knew I sounded suspicious, but damn it, sometimes the man could be an oyster.

He flashed me an enigmatic smile and waited for me to get all the way in before he shut my door. I watched him through the windshield as he crossed in front of the car and got behind the wheel.

Before he turned the key in the ignition he looked at me and said, "Wanna drive?"

"Get the hell out of my face, Murphy." I pulled at the seat belt.

"Just thought I'd ask." He turned the key. The Prelude's engine purred into life.

"I will never drive this car." I crossed my arms mutinously as he looked over his shoulder and backed out of the parking space.

"You are going to drive again someday."

"Don't hold your breath," I advised, and he gave me another ironic smile before putting the car in drive and moving forward.

We were back on the interstate in less than forty-five seconds. Traffic was sparse—it was New Year's Day and most people were sensibly sleeping off their hangovers and binging on junk food. Not us. We were almost to the safe house in Hartford where I'd have to confront the man who had murdered my bond mates. Happy fucking New Year indeed.

# Chapter 4

Hartford was a relatively small city dominated by tall buildings which housed insurance companies. The safe house was in the Asylum Hill neighborhood—which was rather apt, I suppose. Located on Farmington Avenue, the Great Pack owned it in conjunction with the Regional Council of New England. It dated back to the late 1800s and had five bedrooms and three baths upstairs, while the downstairs was divided into a large front room, a small kitchen, a half bath, a dining room stuffed with Colonial furniture and two conference rooms, one rather larger than the other.

I remembered the larger conference room vividly. I'd spent hours there going over the accident with Councilor Allerton and the Regional Council. One awful day had been spent with my pack—and one and all said vicious and hateful things about me. Even Callie, my best friend besides Elena, had not defended me. She had not added any vituperative fuel to the fire, but she'd sat there in a silence that indicated she did not disagree. She had studiously avoided my gaze.

My pack had painted me as the quintessential party girl, someone who didn't give a shit about anybody but herself or about anything except the next opportunity to have fun. They said my contributions to the pack funds were minimal because I refused to get a steady job and instead only wanted to play my harp for money. I wouldn't even go to the parks and play for tips. No, I was too superior for that. I would only play for weddings and business parties. I wouldn't even deign to teach.

It didn't matter that when I did have a gig, which wasn't as sporadically as Jonathan made out—I brought in more money for four hours' work than most of the pack brought in for a week's. They were all in retail, except for Grey and Elena. Elena had gotten Grey a job with the game developers. He had been a beta tester and she, a designer. They had both worked from home. The company was based out of California. I could have been a beta tester too, but Elena and Grey wanted me to spend my time practicing the harp. We'd talked about me teaching, but as Elena had indignantly said every time Jonathan made a snide comment about my work ethic, between us we brought in more than three times than the rest of pack.

In exchange for my flexible work hours, I was the one who had cooked for our triad and I'd been responsible for most of the housework and laundry. I'd run errands and done the shopping.

But the way Jonathan characterized it, I had been a lazy-ass bum supported by my hardworking bond mates and the rest of the pack.

Even Vaughn hadn't stuck up for me. Vaughn was the only other member of the pack who knew his way around a musical instrument. He was pretty good on the piano and the two of us used to spend many Sunday afternoons playing duets. Sometimes he'd gone on gigs with me and I'd arranged that, but he'd never said a word in my defense. He'd even agreed that my musical contribution to the pack had been negligible. Playing music wasn't work. It was an indulgence—a hobby.

I hadn't played the harp since the accident. I didn't even own one anymore.

After the funeral the pack had gotten together for a somber gathering. I had definitely not been invited. I'd taken a cab home, wishing we'd get into an accident even as I'd clung to the little strip of leather above the passenger door, skin coated with a cold sweat of terror. All I'd thought about during the funeral was how I'd wanted to go home and play my harp. I'd wanted to channel my grief and anger through the strings and release some of the more toxic elements of it through the notes. I'd wanted to mourn through music.

The front door of our rented house in New Britain had been yawning open and inside the living room and the bedrooms had been a shambles. My harp had been strewn around the living room carpet in hacked-up pieces along with Elena's computers, Grey's CD collection and nearly everything else we'd owned.

Upstairs in the master bedroom, the bed pillows and the mattress had been slashed with a knife, stuffing and feathers everywhere. Someone had taken ketchup and mustard and squirted both all over the walls and ceiling. The stains had still been wet and dripping. The damage had been done during the three hours I'd been gone for the funeral.

My clothes had been ripped to shreds. Even worse, so had been Grey's and Elena's.

I remember sinking down to the ketchup-encrusted floor with one of Grey's flannel shirts. It had been in tatters, but it had still smelled like him. I could smell his hair on the collar and his cologne in the sleeves. I'd rocked and cried like a fucking baby.

* * * *

All of this flashed through my mind as we stood on the front steps of the safe house and waited outside the imposing white door with the brass knocker in the shape of a wolf's head.

One of the Regional Councilors, a woman named Kathy Manning, answered the door. She was a petite brunette with gray-blue eyes that tilted seductively. Her hair was cut pixie short, lending her a sort of elfish quality. Arrestingly attractive rather than conventionally pretty, she wore a pair of gray wool pants and a white blouse with a gray vest. A long gold chain looped several times around her throat and hung between her breasts. Tiny gold studs winked from her earlobes.

"Hello, Stanzie," she said with a real smile. I smiled back, but mine was strictly cordial. Although she'd been one of the more sympathetic members of the Regional Council during my ordeal, she'd voted against me when the time came. I wondered if she regretted that now, although she evinced no guilt, merely friendly welcome.

She introduced herself to Murphy when I failed to do so and he shook her hand with reserve, obviously taking his cue from me. Nevertheless, he still charmed her. Women usually fawned over him. All he had to do was smile and they were hooked. She came up to the hollow of his throat and had to tilt her head to meet his eyes.

"Councilor Allerton is in the small conference room. I'm making a pot of coffee. Do you want some?" Her gaze traveled between the two of us.

I was cold, and coffee did sound good, so I nodded and once I did, Murphy did too.

An elaborate coat tree stood in the foyer decorated with winter outerwear and Murphy and I hung ours up too. We made sure to wipe our boots on the prim mat in front of the door so as not to track prints on the spotless parquet floor.

In the front room to the left of the hallway just past the foyer, a massive Christmas tree twinkled with lights in front of the bow window. It was adorned with silver and gold glass balls and a stiff, curled gold bow sprinkled with silver glitter held pride of place on the top.

Red poinsettias, six deep, were arranged artfully under the tree and along the shallow shelf beneath the bow window.

The room was filled with the scent of fresh pine and sap. I also smelled the coffee brewing down the hall in the small kitchen.

Murphy followed me down the hallway to the open second door on the right just before the formal dining room which, in turn, led to the kitchen.

Inside the small conference room, three of the four walls were covered with off-white wallpaper flecked with gold. A small crystal chandelier hung suspended over an oval-shaped cherry wood table with carved, scrolled legs. Ten cherry wood ladder-back chairs were arranged around the table. Each had a plush gold cushion for the seat and the back.

Dark, built-in bookshelves lined the far wall, broken only by a large multi-paned floor to ceiling window that overlooked the side yard and a parking lot for the small, brick office building on the next lot. Massive red velvet curtains were looped back with gold-braided tassels to allow access to the wintry sunlight.

Flames crackled and leaped behind the grate of a dark-green marble fireplace. Above the mantel hung a somber oil painting depicting a whaling schooner setting off to sea. The sky in the painting was the same ominous gray as the sky outside the house. It was a compelling painting, but it was not comforting.

Councilor Jason Allerton sat the head of the table with his back to the window. A hardcover book was propped on the table in front of him and his dark head was bent so he could read.

When he heard us at the door, he deliberately finished the paragraph he'd been absorbed in before he lifted his head to smile at us.

"Constance, Liam, it's good to see you." He rose to his feet, impeccable in a dark-gray Ralph Lauren suit with a white shirt and a subdued, yet powerful red tie. The jacket to the suit was draped across the back of his chair and his tie was loose. His shirt sleeves were rolled to just below his elbow.

In contrast, I wore a pair of faded Levi's paired with a black turtleneck sweater I'd bought at Target for twenty bucks. My hair was pulled back into a messy bun. The wind at the rest stop had tugged several strands free and I'd pushed most of them behind my ears rather than redo the bun.

Murphy also wore jeans, only his were Armani, paired with a cashmere crew neck sweater of a burnished copper color. The wind had mussed his hair but he'd combed it in the car before we got out. Even though we were both casually dressed, I think he pulled it off with way more style and elegance than I managed. For one thing, he never shopped at Target. From Houston to Boston, he'd pushed the bright red cart around the various stores for me and turned up his nose at every men's shirt or sweater I'd held up for his inspection. He wouldn't even buy underwear there, the snob.

Allerton grasped Murphy's hand and gave his forearm a meaningful squeeze. It was a handshake that expressed more than simply business. It was also a gesture of amity and fondness.

For me he had a hug, but I was stiff in his embrace. He gave my back a gentle pat before releasing me.

"Sit down." He waved at the chairs around the table and resumed his original seat.

Murphy and I sat next to each other, facing the fireplace. Its radiating heat was warm on the side of my face as I turned my head to look at Allerton.

"I've arranged a dinner tonight here with Riverglow," he informed us. My stomach knotted at the thought of having to eat with them. I'd seen them nearly three months ago at the Great Gathering in Paris, but they had snubbed me.

I still burned with humiliation at the way Callie's, Vaughn's and Peter's eyes had glazed over and they'd pretended not to see me when I'd called out to them in the reception area at the chateau. It had been an instinctive greeting, born of past familiarity. For a second the two intervening years had been wiped away and it had been like seeing family.

I'd expected to be snubbed by Jonathan and Nora, but not the others. I don't know why, because they'd been explicitly clear after the accident that they'd blamed me, but somehow I'd hoped that they'd had second thoughts, that maybe when they saw me they'd think family too.

"There have been some changes in the pack membership and leadership since you've left them, Constance." Allerton's blue eyes met mine across the gleaming conference table. When I refused to be drawn, he smiled a little and continued as if he'd never paused to allow me an opportunity to participate.

"The main reason they went to the Great Gathering was to find some new blood for the pack. Nora had a stillborn son last year and Callie's had several miscarriages since she, Vaughn and Peter took Alpha status. It was the same thing the first time they were Alpha, when you and Grey joined the pack. You remember. It was after one particularly bad miscarriage that the triad stepped aside as Alpha. You and Grey were approached but I recall being told you turned it down."

Beside me, Murphy shifted in his chair so he could stare at me. Passing up an opportunity to be Alpha was probably not something he'd ever contemplated before. In big packs such as Mac Tire, the position was highly coveted and campaigned for because not every female would get the chance before her fertility cycle ceased. Bigger packs tended to have shorter Alpha timeframes—five years was the usual span. However, smaller packs such as Riverglow tended to rotate the Alpha status. It wasn't unheard of for duos and triads to have multiple opportunities. Grey had turned down Alpha status because of Jonathan's jealousy. He'd known the position would eventually come to us and we were young, in our early twenties, and had plenty of fertility time left.

Pack women could only give birth once. Live or stillborn, if they carried a pregnancy to the end, they would become barren after the birth. Twins were slightly more common than singles.

While triads could be made up of two men and one female, most of them consisted of two women and one man in order to give two women the opportunity to bear a child at the same time. Only Alphas could have children. All the other women in the pack took birth control or had to have abortions.

I think it was both evolution's and our own cultural way to avoid detection by the Others. Our population stayed small and underground. Secret.

Again Councilor Allerton waited for me to say something. I admit I felt a surge of sympathy for both Nora and Callie. Callie was over forty, near the end of her childbearing years and Nora, who was three years older than me, was now barren.

They were at risk, of course, of losing their bond mates, who still had the chance to bond with a fertile female and become Alpha so they could procreate. A lot of us created such strong connections with our bond mates, very few left in search of a chance to be Alpha and to have a child. The ambitious ones would, but normally love conquered ambition.

I knew Peter would stick with Callie. He loved her with a steady and deep adoration. I wasn't sure about Vaughn. I was never quite sure of his feelings for her. He and Peter were close as brothers, but I wondered if that was enough to keep him bonded.

Jonathan, the bastard, I could see him ditching Nora in a millisecond if someone better came along. He was such a coward, he wouldn't do it until he was sure. I'd bet he'd spent the better part of the Great Gathering looking for just such an opportunity. The fact that he was still a member of Riverglow proved he'd failed. That afforded me some small satisfaction.

Again, after he was sure I was declining his invitation to make a comment, Allerton continued. "They were able to convince a pair from Mac Tire to leave that pack and join this one with the understanding they'd be Alpha when it was quite sure Callie was past her childbearing window."

"Mac Tire?" Murphy stirred in his chair. "Paddy never mentioned that."

Allerton held up a hand. His nails were professionally manicured and he wore an expensive Cartier wristwatch with a chased silver band around his wrist. I could hear it ticking if I tried hard enough.

"They're from the English branch."

For some reason Murphy's eyes darkened and he went very still. I was confused because, while I expected Murphy to know the members of his pack in Ireland, I didn't think his personal knowledge would extend all around the UK. Mac Tire was a huge pack, but each country had separate

Alphas who presumably knew each other and interacted, but I hadn't thought it trickled down to the entire membership.

"I believe you know them. Him at least," said Allerton, his expression bland enough, but something in his voice made me come to alert.

Murphy's gaze was flat and hostile.

"Colin Hunter and Devon Talbot."

Murphy reacted to the names like gasoline poured on fire. "Oh hell no," he snarled, pushing back his chair. "Oh, fucking hell no. You could've told me this on the phone, Allerton, leaving me the opportunity to decline your invitation. Now I'm just gonna have to friggin' walk out."

I leaped to my feet too, grateful for an opportunity to escape.

Murphy saw me and snapped, "You sit back down. I'll be back for you tomorrow, Stanzie."

He'd promised to stay with me. He told me he would be with me when I had to confront Grandfather Tobias and listen to what he wanted to tell me. Now he was halfway out the damn door all because of some man named Colin Hunter, and I hadn't the slightest clue who he was or why Murphy despised him so much. Hatred was all over his face and in the barely controlled violence of his movements. He was one step away from breaking something. He would have attacked Allerton if he'd dared, but he was putting distance between them instead.

I'd never seen Murphy so furious. The tone of voice he'd used on me was unfamiliar too. He'd never spoken to me so angrily, as if I didn't matter, as if I were just one more obstacle in his way out the door.

I had nowhere to go if Murphy walked out. I didn't even have my purse or any money. All of that was in the trunk of the car with our luggage.

The door slammed behind Murphy then five seconds later the front door slammed too. Absurdly, I wondered whether he'd taken his coat. It was bitter cold outside.

I stood there like an idiot, clutching the back of my chair. I struggled against bursting into cheated tears of frustration and betrayal. The weight of my bond pendant was heavy around my throat. The peridot and pearl hung suspended from a long chain I'd tucked under the edges of the turtleneck sweater.

The peridot was my birthstone; the pearl Murphy's. Together they symbolized our bond and were the Pack's version of a wedding ring.

Murphy had one too. He wore it beneath his sweater and never took it off unless we shifted.

"I'm sorry, Constance. I knew he'd be upset, but I'd hoped he'd handle it better than this. Please sit down." Allerton's tone was gentle and kind, and I responded to it obediently.

The conference room door opened and I spun around in my chair, ridiculously hoping it was Murphy. Instead, it was Kathy Manning with coffee and cookies.

"Is something the matter?" She hesitated at the door, her expression uncertain, but moved forward when Allerton gestured her inside.

"It's all right, Kathy. How's dinner coming along?"

"Under control." She flashed him an attractive grin. "I'm making a seafood casserole. You might want to look at the wine we've got on hand and choose some. Oh, and for dessert, your favorite. Creme brulee."

"That sounds delicious." Allerton reached for the carafe of coffee so he could fill the china cups. He filled all three and invited Kathy to sit with us.

She unhesitatingly pulled out the chair opposite mine and regarded me with bright curiosity. "You've come up in the world, haven't you?" She sounded as if she were personally responsible for it. I suppose she'd had an indirect hand in it, helping pave the way for me to be expelled from Riverglow. "Isn't it exciting to be an Advisor? I was an Advisor for seven years back in my twenties. Gave it up when Matt and I were named Alpha. Then I had my son, served as Alpha for a few years, and the next thing I knew, I was invited to join the New England Regional Council. I imagine you're in line for some of the same." She took an appreciative sip of the coffee. She drank it black with no sugar. "Quite a difference from being the bottom of Riverglow, I would think. And now you belong to Mac Tire. Well done, Stanzie."

I felt as if I were a character in an absurdist play and all communication was slowly being rendered meaningless while everything I thought I knew crumbled and became distorted and weird.

I remembered how this woman had judged me. She'd sat in silent disapproval as she listened to my pack condemn me. The entire Regional Council of New England had voted against me and it was only Jason Allerton, with the power of his personality and the weight of the Great

Council behind him, who had been able to turn the tide and change their votes.

Now she sat across from me, her head tilted like a bird's, and grinned at me as she congratulated me for becoming an Advisor and a member of Mac Tire. It was as if she'd always been on my side of things and believed in me, when she absolutely had not.

"It's all because of Councilor Allerton," I managed to choke out. I wanted some sugar but was afraid to reach for it. In this strange world of contradictions and about-faces, I thought my arm might fall off or something equally bizarre.

She tilted her head to the side and smiled at me as if I were a well-behaved dog. "I believe you must have done something to attract his attention. You don't get to be an Advisor simply because of happenstance."

I wanted to argue, because that's exactly how I'd done it, but instead I watched Allerton pour cream into his cup and when he offered the pitcher to me, I took it, fully expecting to drop it or have it turn into a rubber chicken or something else totally unexpected.

It remained a pitcher of cream firmly in my grasp and I managed to pour some into my cup.

"I believed you were drunk the night of the accident, Stanzie. I was wrong. Please accept my apologies. This whole new chapter has thrown me for a loop, I'm afraid. I've had to reconstruct many of my previous beliefs and I hope that if I'm ever involved in a case like yours again, I will have more compassion as well as discernment." Kathy Manning's tone was sweet and sincere. She couldn't reach across the wide expanse of the table to touch me, but she settled for giving me a very warm smile. "Your pack was so vehement and I thought they were the best judges of your character. I tended to believe you at first, but the more they talked, the less I trusted my initial judgment. That's not a good trait for a Councilor to nurture, I'm afraid. Forgive me?"

Nervously, I wiped the backs of my fingers across my mouth. My lips were dry and chapped from the wind and shifting the night before. I'd forgotten both lip balm and lipstick. I did have on eye makeup. I seemed to always remember that, but sometimes I forgot my lips.

"You did what you thought was best," I allowed. I was feeling more and more unreal and agitated the more I realized how alone I was without Murphy.

"That's very generous of you. In your place, I'd want to spit in my coffee," said Kathy Manning, as she winked at me. She swallowed the rest of the liquid in her cup and rose gracefully to her feet. "I'd better see to that casserole. Do you like Brussels sprouts? I have this wonderful recipe for Brussels sprouts Parisian that I hope everyone will like. Normally, you say Brussels sprouts and everyone's first reaction is to grimace and pass the platter without taking any, but I swear if you try these, Stanzie, you will like them."

"Do you need any help?" I didn't know what to do with myself. I didn't want to sit here at this enormous table and stare at Allerton for the rest of the afternoon. That was for sure.

A pleased smile lit up her face. "No, but thank you so much for the offer. I've got a certain way I like to do things in the kitchen and it's best if I do it alone. Helpers tend to get in my way and then I feel awful for snapping at them. You enjoy your coffee with Councilor Allerton. Have a cookie—they're homemade. Sugar cookies, a grandmother's secret recipe." She gave us both a rueful smile. "I'm not quite a grandmother yet, but I managed to cadge the secret out of one. She was happy to pass it along, actually. Made her feel useful and wanted, I suspect."

The topic of grandmothers and grandfathers was a sore one with me and although she knew what was going on in the Pack, apparently she still managed to be able to separate the good and innocent grandmothers and grandfathers from the corrupt ones.

The mere thought of them made me shudder. I didn't trust any of them anymore.

She left the door open on her way out and I heard her cheerfully humming to herself in the kitchen. It was only a few feet away from the conference room in the back of the house.

Allerton helped himself to a sugar cookie in the shape of a mitten. It was glazed with green frosting and dotted with red M and Ms. It looked damned good but I refused to give in and eat one.

He consumed the green mitten and half of a red stocking before he said, "Aren't you going to ask me why Liam has such an issue with Colin

Hunter?" His voice was mild and completely casual which made me doubly determined not to ask. If Murphy wanted me to know, he'd tell me. I didn't need to hear the gossip behind his back, even if it came from a Councilor.

"No." I took a sip of my coffee. I grimaced because I'd forgotten the sugar and hastily remedied that overlooked necessity.

Allerton smiled and took another bite of the red stocking. "These are really very, very good, Constance." He pushed the plate invitingly closer to me but I resisted.

He waited until I had the cup raised to my lips before inquiring, "How are things going with you and Liam? Everything working out?"

I swallowed wrong and only by sheer force of will avoided going into a coughing fit. "We're fine." I hoped my tone encouraged him to change the damn subject.

"Do you like him?" He was deliberately oblivious. And sadistic, I decided grumpily.

"I said we were fine." A note of truculence crept into my voice.

"But that's not an answer to the question I asked." He finished the red stocking then looked wistfully at the plate and the remaining six cookies— three more mittens, one stocking, a Christmas tree and a snowman, and resisted.

"You know I can't help but feel partially responsible for the fact you two are together." He poured more coffee into his cup and into mine.

Partially responsible? I thought with an inward snort. Try completely. Totally. Under normal circumstances Murphy's and my orbits would never have crossed at the Great Gathering.

"Councilor, I would have thought it was obvious I liked Murphy from the way I fell apart when he nearly died." I sounded waspish and my fingers reached for the snowman without my permission. My stomach and my brain did not always listen to each other.

"That could have been guilt." He stirred in cream and sugar. The silver band of his wrist watch gleamed in the firelight.

The sun outside had gone behind a cloud and the dim lighting of the chandelier cast an almost melancholy glow over the table.

The snowman crumbled into three pieces between my agitated fingers. "I didn't do it," I denied through numb lips.

"I know that," he agreed with a patient smile. "But you did bite him and that was the reason he took that pill in the first place."

I swallowed against a sudden obstruction in my throat. The scent of vanilla and sugar clogged my sinuses and I wanted to be anywhere else but where I was at this moment.

"We've been working on my wolf," I confessed in a low, distressed tone. My words came in a rushed, defensive tumble even though I knew he wasn't judging me. "We shift every chance we get and my wolf knows words for things now that she never knew before. She doesn't run and play, she listens and learns. She would never bite him now. Never bite anybody."

Allerton put a fatherly hand over mine. The rest of the cookie disintegrated into crumbs.

"Constance, I know you've been working hard. Liam has nothing but praise for your efforts. If anything, he thinks you're trying too hard. And I know most of your motivation stems from that bite. But aside from working together on your wolf, how are you finding each other? In this form? Easy to live with? Annoying? I'm curious, indulge me."

The fact that Murphy had been reporting to Allerton about my wolf's progress should not have been a surprise to me, but it was. A deep, visceral jolt of betrayal surged beneath my skin, but it cleared. Of course he would talk to Allerton. Why wouldn't he?

It was humiliating as hell that Allerton would be in contact with Murphy to talk about my wolf. He didn't talk to me about Murphy's wolf. It made bitter sense. Murphy didn't need to do the work I needed to do. His wolf was adult and responsible. Mine was still childlike.

"We had fun on our road trip," I said in a small voice. "We saw so many places. My favorites were New Orleans, Atlanta, and Knoxville."

"How long are you planning to stay in Boston? I wonder that you don't want to go to Dublin and meet the rest of your pack." Allerton pushed the cookie plate toward me and I caved and took one of the mittens. Eating it gave me an opportunity to not answer him for a moment and I'd take all the time I could get.

The cookie melted in my mouth. The tastes of vanilla and sugar combined with the chocolate of the candy into sheer brilliance. Kathy Manning was a baking genius.

I remembered there had always been baked goods on the conference room table two and a half years ago when I'd been questioned. I hadn't eaten any of them, but when I thought of the conference room I associated it with the smell of sugar and flour and chocolate—a weird dichotomy.

"Well, we just got to Boston two days ago. I want to show the city to him. We're packing up the stuff I want and getting rid of the rest of it. We're going to rent the condo out to tourists, in weekly blocks. We've got to talk to a rental agency to manage it for us. It'll be a good source of income for the pack."

"Your pack is being handsomely compensated for the time I take you away from them," Allerton remarked. "Plus there's some for you both personally. I've paid you for two months, have you not noticed your bank balance lately?"

I shrugged and debated a second cookie. Goddamn, they were good.

"I don't bother with checking the balance. I use my debit card sometimes, but mostly Murphy pays for everything. He's rich."

Allerton's smile was fond.

"I know, Constance. Quite a switch for you. You've always counted your pennies. I'm glad you feel comfortable enough not to check your balance nowadays, but just so you know, Advisors are well paid." He casually mentioned a whopping sum that I took to mean at least six months' salary, but no, that was just for one month.

"The Council's rich," I remarked, astonished. I wouldn't exactly be a millionaire off my salary, but I would be comfortable. I was earning more than Elena had earned for her games.

Allerton laughed. "I'm personally well off. I pay my Advisors slightly more than the going Council rate. Mine deserve it."

I wasn't afraid of hard work, but I was a little remorseful for accepting two months' salary for doing not a damned thing but gallivant through American cities.

"I'm ready to work whenever you want me to," I told him, guilt pricking at my conscience.

"What you're doing here right now is working," he said

"Does it have to do with Grandfather Tobias?" I whispered. My mouth was dry and I took a sip of the coffee.

"I want to know what he tells you," answered Allerton evenly.

I nodded.

"I want you to interact civilly with your former pack as well," he added.

I bit my lip. "I wasn't planning on making a scene, Councilor."

"That's very good." He got to his feet and I followed suit. My gaze happened on the book he'd casually moved to the side to allow room for his coffee. It was the latest John Grisham. I gaped a little because I'd expected someone like him to read something a little more highbrow or intellectual.

He saw me looking and a smile quirked his lips. "It's quite riveting. I intend to spend the rest of the afternoon consuming it. I hope to be finished by dinner. Would you like to choose a book to read while you're here?" He gestured to the bookcases, which were crammed with both paperbacks and hardbacks. "You're welcome to browse after you're settled in your room. Are your bags in the hall? We can bring them up on our way."

I flushed. "Murphy has them in the trunk of the car."

Allerton steered me to the door, his hand hovering at the small of my back.

"No matter. There are toiletries supplied in all the bathrooms. I'll see what Kathy can do for pajamas for this evening."

"I guess I'm not really dressed for dinner," I said.

"You'll be fine," he assured me as we walked down the hallway toward the front door. A wide staircase painted gleaming white with red-and-black carpeted stairs was just to the right of the hallway, making up part of the wall.

We ascended it and came out on a large landing that branched off into a hallway. The door to the master suite was at the end of the hall. It was obviously in use by Allerton. He'd used it two and a half years ago as well. There was a bathroom en suite. The other two bathrooms were located between the bedrooms on either side of the hall and were accessible through the rooms on either side of them as well as by the hallway.

All the doors, including Allerton's, were open, except for the second door on the left-hand side of the hallway and the bathroom door between that room and the other bedroom. I knew immediately that's where they held Grandfather Tobias. Both doors were locked against him, but allowed him access to the bathroom.

The windows in the house were electronically monitored by an alarm system, so if he were so foolish as to try to leap out the bedroom window, they'd know downstairs in a heartbeat.

Grandfather Tobias was old and frail. No match for Kathy Manning, let alone in combination with Allerton. If the fall didn't kill or injure him, they would not let him get far.

Allerton showed me to the door of the first room to the right.

It was a small room dominated by a fireplace with gas logs. The mantelpiece and surrounding woodwork were painted a creamy white. An old-fashioned armchair was placed just to the side of the fireplace.

A mahogany four-poster bed was covered with a white down comforter with a Colonial patchwork quilt in reds, yellows and blues folded across the bottom. The pillow shams were also quilted. An old cedar chest crouched at the foot of the bed. A tray with a carafe, two mugs, and a plate of the sugar cookies wrapped in red plastic wrap decorated with a green bow sat atop it.

Bright yellow-and-red curtains hung across the window to the left of the fireplace.

A mahogany dresser with an oval mirror was placed against the wall opposite the bed. On either side of it was a door. One led to a small closet, the other to the bathroom which was tiled in white and dark blue. The toilet and spa tub were also dark blue, as were the two sinks in the granite-topped counter. A separate shower stall with glass doors stood to the side of the spa tub.

Every toiletry imaginable was arranged artfully on the countertop, including a wicker basket filled with travel-sized toothbrushes, mouthwash, soaps, shampoos and skin lotions.

The towels were royal blue, thick and fluffy. Two white waffle-knit spa robes hung on pegs on the door leading to the hallway. A motion sensor air freshener scented the air with vanilla when we walked by it.

Candles and bubble baths were arranged on the window sill above the spa tub. The window itself was glazed in a diamond pattern which alternated in blue and white glass.

Allerton made no mention of when I was supposed to talk to Grandfather Tobias and I didn't bring it up because I wasn't ready.

"Please make yourself at home. Dinner's at seven thirty, but we're having cocktails in the front room at six." Allerton checked his watch. "That gives you about three hours. Is there anything you can think of you might need?"

*Murphy*. I mustered a smile from somewhere and told him I would be happy to curl up on the bed and take a nap. I'd stayed up late the night before.

He left me alone then, but not before he took my hands in his and gave them a gentle squeeze.

# Chapter 5

With the door shut and the only sound the forced air from the central heating, I found myself unable to fall asleep.

Instead, I switched on the gas fire, poured myself a mug of coffee and drank it while I ran a hot bath liberally dosed with peppermint-scented bubbles.

I lit the candles, turned off the lights, wrapped my hair in one of the fluffy blue towels and relaxed beneath the bubbling water.

The warm swirling water produced a soporific effect, which washed away the early morning wakeup call, the stress of the trip, Murphy's defection and the unnerving thought of having to face my old pack.

I dozed off into an amorphous dream, but woke with a start when I heard a noise in the bedroom. I'd shut the door to the bathroom and I wondered if the sound had been in my dream and not really in my room, but then I heard it again. Someone had slid open one of the dresser drawers. Was it Kathy Manning with pajamas?

The bubbles were gone in the tub and I was beginning to prune so I figured I'd been soaking long enough. I pulled the stopper on the drain and climbed out, drying off with the towel I'd used as a makeshift turban.

As I tied the sash of one of the waffle knit robes around my waist I ventured back into the bedroom, hoping I'd given Kathy enough time to vacate.

Murphy was sprawled moodily across the four-poster bed. One arm was curled around his head defensively, the other straight down at his side and he looked morose and frustrated. He'd taken off his boots, but he was fully dressed still and his mouth had a certain tightness that, over the past months, I'd learned to tread around carefully.

Our suitcases were half in, half out of the open closet door. My purse was on the dresser with his wallet and cellphone.

"I suppose that Allerton told you all about Colin Hunter," he spat at me before I even got the chance to say hello.

He made it sound as though I had eagerly lapped up the story and the unfairness of it took my breath away.

"It's none of your business, Constance, so I don't want to hear one word out of your mouth about it."

When he called me Constance, he was pissed.

"I don't—" I began to deny any knowledge at all, but he interrupted me.

"Shut the fuck up, I told you. I don't want to hear it."

If I had been wearing anything but a goddamn robe, I would have left the room, left the house and him and his fucking attitude with it, but I couldn't.

So I retreated into the bathroom and slammed the door, locking it for good measure.

I thought about taking another bath, but ended up sitting on the toilet, head in my hands, crying as silently as I could. Not since the night Murphy had nearly died had I felt so acutely displaced and alone. I wished I could go back to Boston. I wanted the Murphy who didn't snarl at me back. How could I face Grandfather Tobias or my former pack, with Murphy in this foul mood?

For the first time in ages I wanted Grey so badly I could smell his hair and his cologne in my memory. The way he'd looked at me with love written all over his face, the way his hair had been dark and long and I could run my fingers through it while we lay tangled in bed together.

I could never touch Murphy like that—in bed or out.

I'd thought I was okay, I'd thought I was good, actually, but no, I was a frigging mess, fragile and weak and rapidly disintegrating.

The door knob rattled then, encountering the lock, Murphy was forced to knock. "Stanzie, let me in." All the rage was gone from his voice. Frustration was still present, but there was also remorse.

"Go away," I tried to disguise that I was crying, but it was no use.

*Amy Lee Burgess*

"I want to talk about Colin." He made his voice gentle and kind but that only served to make me feel worse about crying and terrible about missing Grey.

"I don't," I yelled. "I didn't want to talk about him with Allerton because I wanted you to tell me if you wanted to. But now I don't want you to. I don't care." That was a lie, I did care.

"You don't know anything? You don't know who he is to me?" Murphy sounded incredulous and dismayed, which boggled my mind because he'd obviously resented like hell the thought of Allerton telling me.

"No, I don't. And I don't care. Leave me alone!" I swiped at my leaking eyes with the sleeve of the robe. It was very soft. I left a trail of mascara and dusky rose eye shadow in my wake.

"Please unlock the door."

After a moment I got up off the toilet, stalked to the door and twisted the lock. I stomped to one of the sinks where I began to scrub my face free of makeup. My goddamn hair kept getting in the way, so I held it back with one hand and washed my face with the other.

The door opened and Murphy walked in. I saw his remorseful expression reflected in the mirrors above the sinks and counter. He handed me a towel and waited for me to say something.

Silently I dried my face, threw down the towel and walked past him into the bedroom, forcing him to step aside to let me pass.

He dogged my footsteps. I dug my brush out of my purse and began to savagely pull it through my snarled hair.

"That looks painful." He winced as he watched me.

"It is," I agreed wrathfully, brushing harder. Guilt swamped me—guilt and anger.

"What time is this goddamn dinner?" He made a disdainful face and retreated to the window, pushing aside the curtain so he could look out. While I'd been bathing, the sun had set. It was pitch dark outside and I doubted he could see much of anything but he still stared out as if fascinated.

"Seven thirty," I told him. "Cocktails at six in the front room. The one with the Christmas tree. I think we need to dress in something other than jeans."

He let the curtains fall. "I really shouldn't be here," he remarked, almost to himself.

"Nobody asked you to come back," I snapped, terrified he was going to leave me again.

"Allerton must have a reason for doing this to me."

"To you," I whispered sullenly. How did this suddenly get to be about him? I guess I was supposed to drop all my anxiety and terror around facing my former pack, including the one who'd murdered my bond mates, and cater to him and whatever the fuck problem he had with some guy from England I didn't even know.

How bad it could be? I was pretty sure it couldn't compare to my situation, but I was supposed to feel bad for Murphy and jolly him along even while I silently went to pieces.

"It's complicated," he said. He glanced at me and sighed. He looked so desperately unhappy I felt a little bit like a selfish asshole.

He was always there for me. He'd stuck up for me and protected me at the Great Gathering. He'd bonded with me to keep me out of Councilor Celine Ducharme's clutches. He guided me and my wolf, he'd brought me on a two-month road trip to allow me to sort myself and various issues and nobody was more sympathetic to those various issues than he.

Now here he was, beside himself, angry and desperate, with nowhere to turn. I had him to turn to, but he didn't have anyone. He was trying to turn to me and I was being a baby.

"You don't have to tell me," I said softly. "It's okay, Murphy. It'll be all right. And you don't have to stay tonight if you don't want. I'll be fine. I know you only came back because you were worried about me."

He gave me a small, relieved smile. The skin stretched tight around his eyes and mouth relaxed slightly.

"That and the fact that Allerton must have a reason for this bullshit."

I snorted laughter despite myself.

"You are always so curious about what that man is thinking and what he's up to."

"I have to be because lately what's he been thinking about and what he's up to somehow ends up deeply impacting my life. You're a prime example." His smile was sardonic, but his voice softened when he got to me.

"He asked me if I liked you," I confessed in a guilty rush.

His dark eyes searched my face.

"What did you tell him?"

"The truth," I said.

"That bad." He mock groaned.

"I do like you. A lot," I said and he became serious in an instant. "I told him we were having so much fun on our road trip and all the cities we'd seen and then he asked me why I wasn't in a rush to see Dublin and meet my new pack members and I didn't know what to say."

"Because now you're thinking I'm deliberately keeping you away from Dublin and the rest of the pack. Aren't you?"

It killed me, but I nodded. Every time I'd brought up Dublin, he'd adroitly changed the subject. I'd thought he'd wanted me to relax and not rush through every experience as though I were eating ice cream in ninety-degree weather, but this afternoon after Allerton asked me, I'd begun to wonder.

His reaction to the fact that this man from the English branch of Mac Tire was going to be here tonight made me wonder if there was some sort of secret being kept that he didn't want me to know. I didn't like thinking that way. It made me nervous and guilty, as if I were the one keeping the secret and not him.

"We'll go to Dublin soon. Especially now that Colin's in the picture." The way he spat out the man's name, as if it burned and disgusted him, made me shiver. I wouldn't want to be Colin Hunter.

I waited for him to say more, but he didn't. He turned back to the window and I put down my brush and went to my suitcase.

Forty minutes later we were both ready. My dress was a metallic burgundy sheath with a matching bolero jacket edged in dark red sequins. I wore my new Jimmy Choo black platform pumps—a Christmas present from Murphy.

I stood before the mirror fixing my bond pendant to the short silver chain I wore for evening events while Murphy stood just behind me making last-minute adjustments to his tie.

He had on a pair of black wool trousers and the white button-down shirt with blue pinstripes I'd gotten him at the Armani store in Houston. A black Giorgio tie with a tiny silver triangular pattern completed his look.

He had a gray jacket tossed across the bottom of the bed. Thankfully he'd put aside his Timberland boots for a pair of black wing tips.

When I went to fasten the chain around my throat, he was there to do it for me and I gazed at us both in the mirror. He was so attentive and the way his eyelashes brushed his cheeks as he concentrated on his task, produced a strange longing inside me.

I'd rolled my hair into a sleek French knot held in place with a rhinestone clip. I looked far more sophisticated and at ease than I actually was.

"You are so beautiful." Murphy sounded wistful as he stared at both of us in the mirror. "I look at you sometimes and I can't even breathe, Stanzie. That's how beautiful you are. I remember the first time I saw you coming to the table that night at the Great Gathering and I thought, Jaysus God, she's gorgeous."

I flushed. Every time he complimented me I had no idea how to take it. None at all.

"I thought you were so handsome," I said. "And bored," I added with a laugh. "And I seemed to bore you even more than you already were."

"I wasn't bored with you, I was intimidated," he said with a grin.

"Oh, hell, Murphy, you and your Irish blarney. That's such bullshit." I clasped a silver chain link bracelet around my left wrist. Now I doubted the fact he'd thought I was gorgeous that first night. I hadn't intimidated him the first night. He'd left the table the minute it had been revealed my bond mates were dead because everyone believed I was drunk behind the wheel. I'd made no effort to defend myself and I knew he'd been disgusted. He'd as much as told me later during the Gathering.

His dead bond mate, Sorcha, had been a fiery-haired red head and I'm sure she had been really, truly beautiful and people didn't just tell her she was beautiful to compliment her, they actually meant it. I wished I could see a picture of her, but then again I didn't. She was already stiff enough competition without me feeling absolutely hopeless in the face of her beauty.

"There's not enough Irish blarney in the world to convince you I'm not using any when I compliment you." He gave me a rueful smile then moved to switch off the gas fireplace.

I slid a few rings on my fingers and waited for him to put on his jacket. It was five minutes to six and time to run the gauntlet.

# Chapter 6

We found Kathy Manning and Councilor Allerton seated together on a light brown sectional sofa beneath a large framed picture of the Hartford skyline at night. The photo had been artificially enhanced and tiny electrified lights had been inserted around the buildings with a realistic and modernist result.

The long, low coffee table in front of the sectional sofa was spread with plates of cheese and crackers, bowls of mixed nuts, an olive-and-pickle tray and a plate of three different kinds of handmade canapes—slices of cucumber topped with smoked salmon and cream cheese, cheese and olives topped with maraschino cherries speared to small round pieces of homemade sourdough bread with toothpicks, and ham, cheese and stuffed olives on cracked wheat crackers.

A drinks cart had been wheeled in and left in a strategic corner. It held iced buckets of champagne and white and red wine, gin, whiskey, rye and mixers.

Allerton had a plate heaped with all three kinds of canapes in one hand, a glass of chilled Riesling in the other.

Kathy had swapped her conservative wool trousers and vest for a severe, high-necked black halter dress with velvet bands around throat and waist, sheer black stockings and patent leather pumps. Silver bracelets were laddered up one arm, a diamond tennis bracelet on the other. Her bond pendant, a duo of a diamond and an emerald, dangled on a long silver chain below her small breasts. She nibbled on a piece of Gruyere and a tumbler with rye and soda on a cocktail napkin rested on the end table beside her.

Classical music, one of Mozart's sonatas for flute and harp, played softly from a CD player housed within a discreet cabinet with glass doors.

In a small alcove at the back of the room was a beautiful thirty-six string Celtic harp. My heart did a little queer thud against my ribcage. Surely, they wouldn't.

Kathy noticed my stare and smiled.

"We were hoping, Stanzie, that you might play for us tonight. Possibly after dinner."

Murphy gave me a look of surprise. I had never mentioned I could play the harp.

"I haven't played in over two years, Councilor. I'm sorely out of practice." Remarkably, my voice remained calm but really I wanted to shriek in outrage.

"I'm sure you'd play beautifully. Isn't this harp almost like the one you had?" she wondered.

"The one I found hacked into a million pieces along with the rest of my stuff after the funerals?" I snapped before I belatedly tried to get a grip on myself

Murphy's face took on a thundercloud expression of outrage, while Kathy winced delicately and reached for her rye and soda.

Allerton said nothing. He continued to munch on his damned canapes.

"Your stuff was hacked to pieces?" Murphy demanded. "By who? That bloody bastard of an Alpha?"

"I don't know," I returned in as calm a tone as I could muster. "Whoever did it, did it during the funerals. Jonathan was there the whole time so I don't see how it could have been him."

"But I bet he ordered it done," said Murphy balefully.

I wasn't so sure. Vaughn was the one who had truly known how much my harp meant to me. I'd always had the sneaking suspicion that most of the wreckage was camouflage for the destruction of my harp.

Vaughn had been my duet partner, and, he'd been in love with Elena. He'd confessed as much to me one Sunday night when we'd gotten drunk together after practicing most of the afternoon.

She'd never returned his affection, save as fondness for him as a pack mate. Her love was unreservedly for me and Grey.

I'd felt sorry for Vaughn until I saw my harp in shattered pieces. He'd been late to the funeral, arriving agitated with his tie crooked and the appearance of having thrown on his clothes in a terrible rush. He hadn't even combed his hair.

He'd given me one malevolent, resentful smile that had chilled my blood and made me glad he was on the opposite side of the caskets. Everyone was, except Councilor Allerton who had made it a point to stand close beside me.

Murphy stalked to the drinks cart while muttering imprecations in Irish under his breath, and made a gin and tonic. He poured me a flute of champagne and handed it to me, still cursing.

"It was a long time ago," I said gently. I could smell his anger. His face was flushed and I thought he might crush the glass containing his gin and tonic if he didn't fling it at the wall first.

"It's the goddamn principle of the thing, Stanzie," he argued with me in a low, growling tone. "I can't believe these people. Are they animals? Because that's what they act like in every story I hear about them. I saw it myself at the Gathering. Those two arseholes went out of their way to knock into you and spill red wine all over your dress that night. I saw the whole damn thing. I only wish I'd kicked the shit out of that bastard when I'd had the chance."

"I hope you'll restrain yourself tonight, Liam," said Allerton mildly, but his blue eyes held a distinct warning.

Murphy made a snarly noise I guessed meant he would try not to lose control.

Allerton continued to gaze at him for a moment then picked up his wine glass.

"And you'll not be forcing her to play that damned harp if she doesn't want to," Murphy snapped at Kathy Manning, gesturing at her with his glass. It was really rather rude, but Kathy simply smiled at him the way one would smile soothingly at a snarling dog and kept her prudent distance.

I gulped at my drink and wondered if getting drunk would be good or disastrous.

The doorbell chimed and I nearly doused myself with champagne.

Kathy Manning leaped gracefully to her feet and when she walked away, I saw her dress was just as severe in the back as it was in the front. That woman gave nothing away but smiles and baked goods.

I heard familiar voices in the foyer. A gust of cold air blew into the room, making me shiver. Murphy moved closer to me.

A moment later Kathy returned to the room. Behind her were Callie, Vaughn and Peter.

Vaughn and Peter wore dark blue suits. Vaughn had a white shirt and blue tie, Peter, always more flamboyant, had on a pink shirt and blue tie. He had his blond hair slicked back in 1940s gangster style and a pink handkerchief peeped out of the breast pocket of his suit jacket.

Vaughn had grown a goatee since I'd last seen him and let his hair grow out. It was nearly as long as Grey's had been and the same dark brown. His eyes were brown too and he was clearly nervous, scanning the room as if looking for hidden assassins, his narrow mouth clamped tightly shut.

Callie's strawberry blond hair was piled high on her head and, even though she had on lots of makeup, she looked pale and unwell. Her dress was emerald green, skimming her knees in a silky froth. Its thin spaghetti straps sewn with rhinestones glittered under the soft glare of the Christmas tree lights.

Allerton had mentioned she'd suffered a series of miscarriages since becoming Alpha last year. I suspected she'd recently had another one. Her blue eyes were puffy and all the makeup in the world couldn't conceal how tired and dispirited she looked.

Despite myself, my heart went out to her. We had ten years of history between us and it was hard to forget she wasn't my friend anymore.

Peter and Vaughn hovered close to her. They all stared at me and Murphy, stopping a few feet away from where we stood.

There was an awkward silence, made even worse by Murphy's unfriendly glower.

I was damned if I would break it. Murphy would kill me, for one thing, and they were the ones who should be ashamed of themselves for another.

Like a curious elf, Kathy looked between us all, waiting to see who gave in first.

It was Peter. Vaughn still clearly held a grudge and Callie looked as if she might burst into tears if she tried to speak.

Peter stepped forward, his face scarlet, and held out his hand to me.

"Hello, Stanzie. It's goddamn apparent we were wrong and we owe you a big apology. You don't have to accept it, but I wish you would."

He was not a handsome man, but he had a definite appeal. He was built like a bull and he worked out all the time, which only enhanced what he already had naturally. I remembered the way he would lift me up and pin me against the wall with my legs wrapped around his muscular waist when we'd slept together. He'd made me feel as though I weighed nothing and he was two inches shorter than me.

Vaughn wasn't classically handsome either, but he had pretty boy looks, as if he could have been in a boy band when he was fourteen. He was tall and thin and had a natural agility that turned heads when he walked into rooms. All the teenage girls at gatherings tended to flock around him and follow him around, giggle over him in corners. He'd been asked more than once to initiate girls through their first shift so they could participate in the Great Hunt at the Regionals. He always treated the girl with sensitivity and style, and watched after her in wolf form, guiding her through her first time with finesse.

I remembered him as a gentle lover, who always took care of me.

Peter and I had only had five encounters in ten years, but Vaughn and I had slept together several times a year. I liked to give Elena some space with Grey. We made an awesome threesome, in and out of bed, but I'd thought they'd both deserved some dedicated time together without me, just like Peter and Vaughn deserved one-on-one time with Callie.

"Hi, Peter." I took his hand and, for a moment, tears burned my eyes. He was also affected. He had to clear his throat before he spoke again and he squeezed my hand more than he actually shook it.

"Stanzie, I'm sorry," he repeated, his voice husky and shaking.

"You damned well should be," muttered Murphy from beside me, and Peter flushed scarlet to the tips of his ears.

"I know," he said, turning to him. "I'm Peter Gardiner, one of the Alphas of Riverglow. You must be Stanzie's new bond mate."

"Yeah," allowed Murphy. He even shook hands, which was more than I thought he'd do. "Liam Murphy. Mac Tire."

"Our new pack mates, Colin and Devon, come from Mac Tire. The English branch of it. Do you know them? I guess it's an off chance considering the size of the pack, but maybe you do?" Peter was desperate to make a good impression and some kind of connection with Murphy, but he could not have tanked more spectacularly. I winced as Murphy began to glower and I thought it could only be a matter of seconds before steam burst out of his ears and nostrils.

"Him I know," said Murphy and, amazingly his voice was controlled. No steam appeared. He was visibly hanging onto his temper, but that was no doubt because Jason Allerton had moved to stand behind the Riverglow pack mates, ostensibly to greet them, but also, I'm sure, to keep an eye on Murphy.

The doorbell chimed again and Kathy tripped off to answer it, cocktail glass in hand.

For some reason Peter either didn't notice Murphy's reined-in rage or was deliberately ignoring it, maybe in hopes if he didn't acknowledge it, it would go away. He obviously didn't know Liam Murphy.

"Well, that's awesome. You'll get a chance to hang out with him again tonight. He should be here any minute. That might even be him at the door."

"I can't wait," deadpanned Murphy, and Allerton cleared his throat.

Everyone turned to him and he shook Peter's hand then Vaughn's.

Callie approached me, her blue eyes huge in her pale, unwell face. "Hi, Stanzie," she all but whispered. "I've missed you."

Murphy didn't say a word, but I could just about read his mind. I knew he was cursing her out in Irish. Of course, I don't understand Irish, but I could still get the gist.

"Hi, Callie," I said. She moved forward as if to embrace me, but I held out my hand. I didn't think I could bear to hug her.

She half grimaced, half smiled, and shook my hand.

"This is Liam Murphy, my bond mate. Murphy, this Callie Olstrom, one of the Alpha triad in Riverglow."

"Evening," said Murphy. His jaw had to ache, the way the muscles bulged from him grinding his teeth.

"Nice to meet you, Liam," whispered Callie. "You're very lucky to have a woman like Stanzie for a bond mate."

"I know," he agreed, and he even thawed enough to take her hand and halfway smile as he did. "Your loss was my gain, it seems." Allerton cleared his throat again.

My heart did a sick little stutter in my chest as Jonathan and Nora walked in, trailed by Kathy.

Jonathan swaggered, and I heard Murphy mutter something foul beneath his breath. Allerton moved to stand beside him and I took a step closer to Murphy myself.

He surprised me by putting his arm around my waist. I took advantage of that and pressed myself against him, so close I could smell his cologne. And his anger.

Jonathan was dressed to the nines in a navy blue pin-striped suit with a blindingly white linen shirt and a fancy black tie. His shoes were cheap, though. Cheaper even than his suit, which was off the rack, probably the clearance rack at that. Obviously, he thought he made quite the debonair figure in it.

He was attractive, but his looks were cheap as his suit and I knew when he moved into middle age and beyond, he'd get jowly and rough. Now, in his prime, he had an obvious sort of handsomeness but he knew it and that killed most of his appeal for the majority of women.

His hair was so black it had blue highlights and it was evident he had some Native American blood in his ancestral tree. He was tall and almost as muscular as Peter, with a barrel chest and a narrow waist. He had a flashy silver wolf's head belt buckle that he wore with every pair of pants he owned. I hated that damn wolf buckle. It was as bargain basement obvious as he was.

By contrast Nora was emaciated, her collar bone jutting out so sharply it hurt to look at it. Her cheekbones were hollowed and prominent, her wrists so thin I could have encircled them with my thumb and forefinger and had inches to spare.

She tried to disguise how painfully thin she was with a geometrically patterned black-and-white dress in an Empire style. It swam on her, and I wondered how long it had been since it had fit. Her legs were like sticks and her dark hair looked brittle—in need of a deep, penetrating conditioner.

There was hectic color on her pale cheeks and she clung to Jonathan's arm as if she might fall if not supported.

As she wobbled closer and I saw her unfocused gaze and slack mouth, I realized she was well on her way to being shitfaced drunk.

I'd be damned if Jonathan wouldn't have embraced me in a bear hug if not for Murphy's arm around my waist. Instead he gave me a great big wet kiss on the cheek and boomed, "Hello there, Stanz! Long time no see, eh? Guess we were wrong about you, weren't we? I have to say though, things looked pretty black against you and all along it was my senile old grandfather who fucked everything up, not you. Well, shit happens, huh?"

Murphy cocked his head as if he were trying to replay the words Jonathan had just uttered because he couldn't possibly have heard right the first time around.

Nora tittered a high-pitched yelp of laughter, which only made things worse.

I wiped my cheek with my fingers, disgusted and pissed off.

He'd been drinking too. Stupid asshole. One of them had driven a car here and they'd been damned lucky to get here unscathed. The irony, of course, was not lost on me but I took the high road and held my tongue.

Murphy's grin was absolutely terrifying. It made me nervous as hell even though it wasn't directed at me.

"Liam Murphy, Stanzie's bond mate." He took the initiative to introduce himself but did not hold out his hand.

Jonathan held out his but Murphy made no move to take it and, after an awkward moment, Jonathan let it drop to his side.

"I guess you know me," he said and Murphy grinned ferociously.

"Narrow squeak you had getting out of that thing with that German guy at the Great Gathering, huh, Stanz?" Jonathan made matters even worse with that statement.

Jonathan referred to Rudi Grunwald who I'd promised to bond with at the Great Gathering in Paris three months ago. He'd been poisoned by the grandmothers and grandfathers involved in the conspiracy. I'd been blamed at first but Allerton and Murphy had rescued me. His death was pretty much the whole reason why Murphy and I were bonded.

Murphy's maniacal grin almost gobbled up his face and I slipped my arm around his waist to hold him back. Although I would have dearly loved to see Jonathan's face beaten to a bloody pulp, Murphy was an Advisor and had to be above such petty actions, deserved or not.

"His name was Rudi. Funny how that should escape your memory, Jonathan," I said. He'd opened himself up for this and I intended to eviscerate with words and spare Murphy from having to do it with his fists.

"Is it?" Jonathan blustered. Yeah, right. As if the bastard couldn't fucking remember. The shifty way he kept glancing out of the corners of his eyes and never at me gave him away.

"Well, the way you came up with that nickname for him at the Great Gathering in New Orleans, I thought for sure you'd remember him."

"That was him?" Jonathan said with unconvincing astonishment.

"Please." I shook my head.

Everyone in the room hung on our exchange with varying degrees of fascination and dread. They all thought Jonathan and I had met for the first time when Grey and I had joined Riverglow. Instead, we'd met as teenagers when we'd both belonged to our birth packs. For a decade we'd pretended the meeting had never taken place, but I was damned if I'd stay silent one night longer. What did I have to lose anymore?

"Rudi the Cutie, remember?" I said with a saccharine smile. "You came up with that and hounded him with that name until everyone else in our group called him that too. Except me." I stopped smiling.

"Well, he was one of those asshole pretty boys and he couldn't speak English for shit. There was more to it than that as well. He obviously pissed me off about something only I can't remember now what it was. He deserved it, and anyway, we were kids, Stanz. What were we? Eighteen? Nineteen?"

Murphy's ferocious grin became positively gloating. I'm sure he halfway suspected the reason behind Jonathan's animosity. Everyone else also had a fair idea, so I almost didn't have to say it, but I'd come this far and I'd waited years to do this. In the past, I'd always held back because I hadn't wanted to jeopardize my chance to join Riverglow. Then later Jonathan had been named the Alpha of my pack. I had no further allegiance to him or to his pack and I was free to say what I wanted. And I wanted to say this. It explained everything, the whole reason why

Jonathan hated me and had made my life in Riverglow as miserable as he could.

"You were nineteen," I replied. "And you didn't like him, Jonathan, because he stole me right from underneath your nose. Remember?" I gave him a nasty grin and his eyes became very black.

"Oh, yeah," he said, obviously pretending it was all coming back to him after all. By everyone else's expressions, he fooled absolutely no one. "You were really into me, Stanz. I remember that now. Always trying to drag me into corners to make out. And then that goddamn pretty boy pulls the wounded, 'I'm a foreigner and I'm lost and lonely' act and you fell for that. You always were a sucker for the pretty boys with moody eyes." He looked at Murphy and grinned insinuatingly. He also managed to ding Grey's memory with that pronouncement too, the asshole.

"I prefer to think I came to my senses. I dragged you into corners to make out with you in the vain attempt to teach you how to kiss. I thought with practice you'd get a little better. I can only hope the intervening years have taught you the lesson I never could," I said with a rueful shrug.

Nora uttered another one of her drunken high-pitched yelps of laughter. I couldn't have asked for better timing.

"You weren't exactly a pro yourself," said Jonathan in a vain attempt to regain some of his lost dignity.

"Aren't we supposed to be letting bygones be bygones?" Callie wondered.

Peter chimed in with a heartfelt, "Please, let's."

"Ha. You two knew each other before Riverglow. I always knew you had the hots for Stanzie," declared Nora with a little smirk.

"For Christ's sake, go sit down and put something in your stomach," snapped Jonathan. He tried to lower his voice but did not do a very good job. He looked at all of us appealingly.

"Look at her," he said. "Skinny as a walking skeleton. I keep telling her to eat but she's got a screw loose or something. Thinks she's fat."

"I do not," huffed Nora with a drunk's haughty self-assurance. Her gaze sought out and found the drinks cart and she made a beeline for it, but Allerton got there first and adroitly steered her to the canapes and cheese platters, helpfully piling a ton of all of it on a small, clear glass plate before he sat with her on the sectional sofa.

Jonathan muttered to himself, as he stalked to the side of the sectional farthest from his bond mate. Kathy offered to mix him a drink but he asked for Perrier. He apparently had at least a little common sense left.

"Were you two really an item at a Great Gathering?" Peter drew closer, his expression both fascinated and repulsed. "I cannot even fucking believe it. I had no idea you'd known him before you joined Riverglow. He's always had it in for you, Stanzie, and I never could figure out why. Why didn't you ever say anything?"

"Well, for most of my time in Riverglow he was my Alpha," I said and Murphy's arm tightened around my waist.

"Alpha my ass," whispered Callie, twin spots of color staining her white cheeks. "If I were you I would have said something. I wish you had. It explains everything. And if I'd known that, I don't think I would have sat there during your interrogation and not said anything in your defense." Her voice dropped and her eyes became pleading. "I never said anything against you, Stanzie, you remember, don't you?"

I remembered her condemning silence. It had been twice as loud as words would have been.

"I want you to sit down, Callie." Vaughn put a sheltering arm around her frail shoulders. "I'm going to get you something to eat. What do you want? The salmon and cream cheese looks good. You want some? And how about a drink? Some wine? Champagne?"

He led her away, his head bent protectively close to hers. Peter watched them go, effectively stranded.

"She just had a miscarriage last week." His voice was soaked with pain. "The third one since we became Alpha last June. I don't even think she should be out. Vaughn and I didn't want to come tonight, but she wanted to see you, Stanzie." He glanced at Nora seated on the sofa with Allerton. He had persuaded her to eat one of the cucumber-and-salmon canapes on her plate and I hoped she wouldn't get sick later in the evening. Peter followed my gaze and grimaced.

"Don't mind Nora. Her baby was stillborn last April. She hasn't been the same since."

I wanted to harden my heart against both of them, but it was impossible. Even Murphy, quiet as he'd been, looked concerned, and I suspected he was thinking about Sorcha and their lost baby, suffering his own grief even as he sympathized reluctantly with Nora and Callie.

"I'm sorry, Peter," I said and he flashed me a grateful smile. "Besides all this shit, how have you been? Okay?"

"I'm fine. Just worried about Callie. I want to step down as Alpha so badly. She just can't carry a baby and she refuses to acknowledge that. She won't take birth control and Vaughn and I are even talking about secretly putting it in her food or something. Anything so she won't have another miscarriage. It was the same damn thing when we were Alpha the first time. She blames it now on her age, she turned forty last year, but it was the same when she was twenty-five." His eyes filled with tears. "Some women just can't have babies and she refuses to believe she's one of them. Vaughn and I don't give a shit about being Alpha, we just don't want to lose her, but do you think she'll listen to us?"

Before the tears could leak out of his eyes, I put my hand on his arm in a gesture of sympathy and compassion.

"I thought this new duo were supposed to take over," I said. Murphy's arm slid away from my waist and he took my empty champagne glass as well as his gin and tonic glass, and went to the drinks cart for a refill. I cursed myself, but I had to get Peter's mind off Callie.

Peter grimaced and put his free hand over mine for a gentle, grateful squeeze before he let go.

"Yeah, they are." Peter blew out his breath. "Only Callie wants to wait until she's sure she's past being able to get pregnant. Goddamnit, Stanzie, it's a shit mess with Riverglow, I'm telling you. Vaughn and I only took our pack to the Great Gathering so we could maybe find new Alphas and you'd think we'd knifed her in the back to hear her tell it. We're only trying to protect her." His voice shook and more tears filled his eyes, but luckily Murphy reappeared. Not only did he have a new glass of champagne for me and refill on his gin and tonic, he also had one for Peter.

"Not sure if you like gin, mate, but I thought you could use it." He thrust the glass at Peter. It was a gesture of reluctant acceptance, if not outright amity, and Peter was astute enough to grasp that. I was pretty sure he did not like gin but he drank it as if he loved the stuff.

"Stanzie, why don't you get something to eat?" Murphy suggested and I looked at him, wanting to make sure he didn't mind being left alone with Peter. He gestured at the food-laden coffee table and, with a shrug, I left them.

With a plate piled high with cheese, crackers and lots of the canapes with the olives, cheese and maraschino cherries, I sat next to Nora, who had managed to eat half the food on the plate Allerton had made up for her. I was impressed.

"I'm thirsty," declared Nora. She gave me a plaintive look as if I would take pity on her and jump up and get her a whiskey sour.

"I'll get you a Perrier," declared Allerton, as he rose gracefully to his feet.

To our left, Jonathan and Kathy seemed deeply involved in conversation, mostly from her side. To our right Vaughn hand fed Callie a cracker and she laughed a little.

*Go, Vaughn*, I thought with a small inward cheer.

I stole a look at Murphy and Peter, as they conversed. I'm sure it was small talk and nothing of great import, but Murphy was making an effort.

"Perrier," said Nora with a pout. "I want a scotch on the rocks."

"There isn't any scotch," I told her. "Damn, these maraschino cherry things are good. You wouldn't think olives and cherries would taste good together, but it's actually kick ass. You want one?" I held my plate enticingly under her nose and her eyes crossed as she tried to focus.

"I guess I could try one," she allowed.

She gnawed her way up the toothpick and would have tried to eat that, but I hastily removed it from her skeletal fingers and set it aside.

"These crackers are excellent too." I offered her one piled high with a wedge of Vermont cheddar.

She obediently opened her mouth like a baby bird and I popped the cracker and cheese in, hoping like hell she didn't choke.

She had to chew an awfully long time, but she didn't choke.

I began to feel more and more resentful of Jonathan. If I could get her to eat and if Allerton could, he damn well could if he halfway tried. She loved him, the poor deluded soul.

"Sorry I spilled that red wine on your party dress in Paris, Stanzie." Nora's voice wobbled with a drunk's all-consuming contrition.

Allerton sat beside her and held out a blue-tinted glass filled with bubbling water and a slice of lime. She took it tearfully and gulped half of it down.

"You forgive me, don't you? I was drunk. I didn't know what I was doing. I'm drunk a lot, you know." Her voice lowered to a conspiratorial whisper. "My baby died."

She looked at me with huge brown eyes and waited for me to sympathize.

"That was last year," I said in a deliberately nonchalant voice. Allerton met my eyes over the top of her head and he gave me silent approval to carry on.

Nora's mouth dropped open in protest.

"You're supposed to be sorry for me, goddamnit," she cried and, for a moment, all talk ceased as everyone stared at her. "Shut up!" she yelled at them, although no one had said a word. "I'm talkin' to Stanzie. None of your damn business." She all but smashed her glass down on the coffee table and glared at the whole room.

Murphy was the first one to look away. He said something to Peter, who responded, then Vaughn whispered something in Callie's ear and she nodded, lifting her face to his for a gentle kiss.

Jonathan scowled fiercely at his bond mate, who blithely ignored him. Kathy Manning gallantly tried to recapture his attention by leaning close and whispering something in his ear.

"My baby died. Say you're sorry about it," Nora hissed at me, but her voice was barely above a whisper and the classical music drowned it out for everybody's ears but mine and Allerton's, unless they really strained to overhear.

"Say you're sorry for treating me like shit and kicking me out of the pack then," I retorted. Allerton smiled behind his wine glass, but quickly schooled his features into blandness when Nora turned to him for support.

"She's supposed to be sorry for me. My baby died." She clutched the lapels of his jacket and he gently took both of her hands in his.

"I'm sure she's sorry, Nora," he told her, his expression kind and patient.

Nora's eyes filled with easy tears. "She's the lucky one. She got out of this damn pack. I know Grey and Elena had to die for that to happen, but she was lucky. I voted to kick her out because I felt bad for her. She didn't need our sorry asses. I knew she'd do better if she got out and I was right." She struggled to free her hands from his grasp, but he held tight.

"She's an Advisor now and that's a good thing, isn't it? She'll go far, won't she? Not like me. Not like Callie. She'll do better than us, won't she? You'll make sure, won't you?"

Tears streaked down her face, making her mascara run.

"Nora," I said, aware that she was getting looks again. "Come upstairs with me. We can wash your face and I'll show you my room. It's got a fireplace with gas logs. And the nicest quilt. I think it must be one you made, because I recognize the pattern."

Nora spent every winter night she could quilting. It was her hobby, her avocation, her passion. I always thought it was also a means to keep her hands and mind distracted from the fact she was trapped with an asshole like Jonathan for a bond mate, but then I was probably just a little bitter.

"I...I think it might be. I gave one to the Regional Council a long time ago." Her lower lip quivered.

Allerton let go of her hands and she turned to me and I helped her to her feet and put my arm around her bony shoulders.

While I told her all the colors in the quilt and the pattern I thought it was, I led her out of the room and up the stairs.

Jonathan's gaze was hot and resentful on our backs, but he didn't try to stop us. I'm not sure Kathy Manning would have let him anyway.

In my room, I showed Nora the gas log fireplace and got her to wash her face free of the tears and mascara smudges.

Then I showed her the quilt, somehow persuading her to lie down so I could spread it over her.

I sat on the edge of the bed with her, smoothing back her rough, lackluster hair as she babbled at me about the quilts she'd made in the past, begging me to remember the one she'd given me and Grey as a gift when we'd joined the pack.

"You still have it, don't you?" She asked feverishly, as if it were life and death that I still had that quilt and cherished it.

The last time I'd seen it, it had been in a dozen mangled pieces smeared with ketchup and mustard on my bedroom floor in New Britain. But of course I didn't tell her that.

I told her I had it at my condo in Boston and Murphy loved it, and insisted on covering himself with it every night or he couldn't sleep. I made him sound like something of selfish pig because he wouldn't even share it with me, but that made her laugh, pleased that someone like him would care so deeply for a quilt she'd made.

"You were so beautiful, Stanzie, in that party dress and those nice shoes. You always have the nicest shoes. I was always jealous of how much Grey loved you. You do believe I voted against you only so you'd get out, have a chance to...be...diff..." She fell asleep in the middle of a sentence.

# Chapter 7

Halfway down the stairs on my way back to the others, the doorbell gave its distinctive three-tone chime. Since I was right there, I opened the front door.

Cold air swirled in with two bundled figures, one male, one female.

He helped her off with her voluminous coat, and she was revealed as a tall, voluptuous black woman in a long, gold gown. Striking without being classically beautiful, she was a knockout.

He was no less appealing, with aristocratic features, tousled blond hair and keen blue eyes. Together they were arresting—her so dark, him light.

"Hello," she said. Her accent was British. "I'm Devon Talbot." She thrust out her hand and her fingers dazzled with flashy big rings of a doubtful provenance.

"Constance Newcastle." I shook her hand, noting her strong and confident grasp.

"Ah, you must be Liam's latest," he said. He had on a pair of dove-gray wool trousers and a dark blue blazer with a red-and-blue figured tie. He didn't precisely sneer at me, but there was a certain reserve. "Colin Hunter."

He shook my hand too, searching my face with his keen blue gaze as if he wanted to memorize it for some future, obscure use. "So was it you who fancy footed Liam's way back into Mac Tire or was it his pet Councilor then?" Although his features were upper crust, his accent was not.

"There wasn't any fancy footwork involved. They approached him, actually," I said, resisting the urge to punctuate my words with a haughty toss of my head. I had the feeling I was not going to like this guy.

"Oh, yeah?" Colin Hunter shrugged with a challenging sneer. "Imagine that one. Six impossible things before breakfast, I suppose."

Uneasily, I flashed back to the morning after Murphy and I had been bonded, when he revealed we didn't have a pack. I'd thought it was because of me and my reputation and he'd even confirmed that. Tracing it back, the one who made it sound like Murphy's former pack wanted him back and that's why he was attending the Great Gathering in the first place had been Murphy himself. However, even when I'd met the Alpha of Mac Tire, Padraic O'Reilly, there'd been something weird going on.

I'd supposed Allerton had persuaded O'Reilly not to take us back into Mac Tire just yet—so we could perform undercover work for him without pack affiliation. Right after we'd accomplished that, O'Reilly had contacted Murphy and offered us a place in Mac Tire. But maybe that was also due to Allerton's persuasion.

Colin Hunter read my confusion before I could school my features and a slow grin curled his lips.

"He hasn't told you a bloody thing about it, has he? Typical Liam Murphy, ignore the problem and it will just dry up and blow away."

"Colin," said Devon Talbot, as she laid one long-fingered hand on his coat sleeve, "why can't we let it go? It's been over for years. Let it go."

He shrugged his arm out from under her touch and gave her an amused smile. "I've let it go, Devon, but there's no harm in talking about things, is there?"

"There are enough difficult things happening tonight. We don't need any more of them," declared Devon with a sad smile. She turned to me, her eyes filled with compassion. "Constance, I know this can't be an easy night for you. I think you're handling it with great dignity." She gave me a slow, jolly smile. "Are we too late for cocktails and finger food? I'm starving." She patted her ample hips, laughing. Charmed, I laughed too.

"There's plenty left," I told her as she linked her arm with mine and let me lead them into the front room.

During my absence upstairs with Nora, Allerton had moved to sit with Kathy Manning and Jonathan.

Murphy and Peter sat with Callie and Vaughn. Everyone had a plate of canapes and when we walked in, voices hushed and eyes became watchful.

Smiling, Allerton was first on his feet approaching Devon, hand extended.

I took the opportunity to move to Murphy's side. He was on his feet too; his face shuttered tight preventing any of his true emotions to show.

Allerton brought Colin and Devon around the room to be introduced in turn.

I braced myself for the confrontation but apart from a coldly uttered, "Liam," and "Colin," the two didn't speak to each other.

With the adroitness of an Alpha, Peter managed to corral Colin and Devon in the farthest corner of the room from Murphy and engage them in small talk. Kathy Manning joined them while Allerton resumed his place beside Jonathan.

I sat next to Callie in Peter's vacated seat. After eating a plateful of canapes, some of the color had returned to her wasted cheeks.

"How's Nora?" she asked me.

"Sleeping on my bed," I said and Callie's and Vaughn's shoulders seemed to sag with relief.

"Thank you, Stanzie. She's really not herself lately. She probably shouldn't have come, but she wanted to see you."

Murphy wandered back to us with fresh drinks for me and Callie. He gave them to us and immediately went to mix more for himself and Vaughn. I thought maybe he was avoiding me but I wasn't sure.

"What's it like being an Advisor?" Callie wondered with a wistful smile. She'd curled her strawberry blond hair before piling it on top of her head and it made her look like a princess in a fairy tale. Callie's face had always conjured up the word ethereal for me. Not quite of this world. Now due to her recent miscarriage, she was all the more wispy and transparent, as if she were being slowly erased. I really didn't think she could withstand another miscarriage.

For the first time I thought about how I would feel if I found out she was dead. A lump rose in my throat and I struggled to contain my grief.

"You ought to let Colin and Devon be Alpha," I said. I always spoke before I thought—it was one of my curses.

Vaughn's face contorted. Callie's pale cheeks suffused with crimson.

"Who are you to tell me what I should do? Is that one of your Advisor duties? Telling people what they ought to do?" Her voice shook and tears made her blue eyes dark as indigo.

"She's just trying to help." Vaughn put an arm around her shoulders, but she shrugged him off. The scent of her fury made me bite my lip.

"I don't need her help," she spat.

Vaughn took a deep breath and the look he gave me could have blown a hole through a vault in Fort Knox.

"I'll give up being Alpha when I am damned good and ready," she snarled at me, her face glowing with her rage. I could smell how weak and unsteady she was and, for a moment, was sure she was going to pass out. It would be my fault because of my stupid, big mouth.

"I'm sorry," I said, horribly aware of the attention we were attracting. Peter was one second away from vaulting across the room to get to her. "I just I...I don't want to lose you, Callie. No matter what happened between us, I still think of you as my friend, I always have, and you just look so awful tonight, I'm scared."

I was sure I was making it worse but I had to say it. I was scared and I didn't want her to die, and everyone was tap dancing around her feelings and not actually doing anything constructive. If I'd been Vaughn or Peter, I'd have refused to have sex with her for one damn thing. I'd have refused to be Alpha anymore. She couldn't be Alpha if they wouldn't. Nobody wanted to crush her ego and, as a result, she was going to die right in front of them. Ego intact, body ruined. Bullshit.

Abruptly, Callie's rage died. Instead she laughed, almost condescendingly, but I understood she was simply denying everything.

"Silly Stanzie, I'm not going to die. You talk like I'm dying or something. I just had a miscarriage, but I'll be all right soon. I always am. Right, Vaughn?" She turned with a sweet smile that melted him like butter in a sauce pan.

At that moment he had a choice—to agree with her or to grow some balls and tell her the truth. She'd always been the leader in their triad. He and Peter had always danced to her tune.

"I...I'm really worried about you, Cal," he said. "You can't see what this shit is doing to you, but you don't actually bounce back after losing these babies. Each time takes more and more of a bite out of you."

Her smile faltered, but she regained it. "I'm just depressed. But I promise I'll snap out of it. I do feel sorry for myself, don't I? And I drag all of you down with me. I'll do better, you'll see." She patted his hand the same way she would a dog and turned back to me, missing the complete despair written all over Vaughn's face.

"Stanzie, that was awful of me. I'm sorry too, sweetie. Friends again?" She gave me one of her blinding smiles and, just like Vaughn, I melted. Everyone did when she smiled like that.

"We were always friends, like I told you," I said and she hugged me, burying her face in my neck, burrowing in for comfort I wasn't sure I could provide. I wanted to wave a magic wand and fix it so the next time she got pregnant—because she would, she was determined—it would stick and nine months later she'd have a beautiful baby who would be perfect and healthy and Callie's world would be complete. But it wasn't up to me.

"I've missed you," she whispered when she raised her head. We were both crying a little, but they were good tears. Vaughn handed us cocktail napkins which we used to wipe our eyes, carefully because cocktails napkins are stiff and tend to scrape the skin if pressed too hard.

Kathy Manning chose that moment to herd us all to the table for dinner. I'm certain she wanted us to get substantial food in our stomachs to counteract the alcohol we'd sucked down in self defense to get through the awkward reunion.

As we were a party of eleven and the Colonial dining room only seated six, the table in the small conference room had been covered with a fancy white tablecloth and pressed into service.

All offers of help disdained, Kathy had us sit around the table while she bustled back and forth from the kitchen with the food.

Allerton sat at the head of the table and she took the foot. The rest of us ranged out on either side of the table.

I sat between Peter and Devon. Murphy was between Devon and Allerton, and Colin was across from Peter, the farthest he could get from Murphy.

As predicted, the Brussels sprouts were delicious and so was the seafood casserole—a steaming hot combination of scallops, shrimp and flounder mixed with seasoned, buttered breadcrumbs. For appetizers we had lobster bisque and there were hot, homemade dinner rolls that seemed to be in endless supply no matter how heavy the demand.

The wine, a slightly chilled Chardonnay, was excellent and everyone concentrated more on their plates than on conversation.

Devon and I chatted amiably, but we were the exception to the rule. It was not one of the more convivial dinner parties I'd ever attended.

The fireplace crackled behind my back, casting off warmth that at times made me wish I could take off my bolero jacket. Beads of sweat popped out on Devon's face but she didn't complain. We both had seconds of the Brussels sprouts.

Nora's empty chair was a silent accusation and everybody tried to ignore it but we couldn't.

Once we heard the water pipes gurgle—a toilet upstairs had been flushed and I remembered with a gut-wrenching stab of dismay that Grandfather Tobias was locked upstairs in the bedroom closest to Councilor Allerton's master suite.

The sound did not help the atmosphere of the dinner.

A pall was upon us all and eventually even Devon and I gave up trying to liven things up.

She wiped her sweaty brow with her linen dinner napkin and I poured a generous amount of Chardonnay in my glass. I'd been going slowly on the wine until then, but there came a point in time where I didn't care anymore.

"I suppose we should discuss Tobias," declared Allerton, breaking the silence. He set his fork down in the middle of his Blue Willow patterned china plate and straightened even more in his chair.

"Afterward we'll have dessert and coffee," murmured Kathy Manning, as she dabbed her lips with her linen napkin and folded it with precision before placing it in the center of her empty plate.

The sound of cutlery against china was very loud as everyone stopped eating or pretending to eat.

Most of us grabbed our wine glasses. I was the leader of the pack.

Jonathan, who sat across the table from me, directed a spiteful look in my direction. "Does she have to be here? She's not a member of this pack."

"I'd be happy to leave the room." I threw down my napkin.

"Jonathan." Callie's voice rose above the swirling anger. "Of course she should be here. How could you even think of sending her away? Grey and Elena were her bond mates. She was falsely accused."

"But she's not a member of Riverglow. She has no vote, right?" Jonathan argued. "Let her sit here and listen, but she has no vote, am I right?"

"She has no vote," Callie agreed, making him smirk across at me. "However, she can say anything she likes."

"But we don't have to listen," muttered Jonathan.

"Not if we don't want to, no," said Callie.

Jonathan pushed back his chair, folded his arms across his chest in a classic gesture of defense and close mindedness, and feigned boredom with a yawn.

Next to him, Vaughn crumbled a piece of dinner roll between his agitated fingers. Peter's face was white and strained.

Colin and Devon looked keenly interested but they had no emotion invested in the subject. That made them the most impartial voters at the table, a fact that seemed lost on Jonathan but was appreciated by Callie.

"It is the Council's opinion, both Great and Regional, that Tobias Green did not willfully sabotage the car belonging to Constance Newcastle, but did, in fact, inadvertently sever the brake line which he subsequently concealed. We do not pass a sentence of death, but we do recommend exile from his pack." Allerton had prepared me for this verdict in advance but it was still a slap in the face.

Murphy didn't like it either by the swell of his jaw, but he said nothing. Neither did I.

"He's an old man, halfway senile," objected Jonathan. Tobias was his blood relation and that, in combination with his dislike of me, made him the absolute least objective person at the table. "We exile him, we might as well slit his throat. He'll be dead in six months. Old people need the support of their packs. His hands shake so much now he can't work as a mechanic any longer and he has no means to support himself. He'll end up homeless on the street. For a stupid mistake. Exile's too harsh."

"It could be said that Constance made a stupid mistake and for that you did recommend exile," pointed out Allerton in a neutral tone. Murphy glowered behind his wine glass. I couldn't move. I wished I were closer to him.

"It's a conscious decision to get behind the wheel of a car after drinking like a fish," argued Jonathan. He did have a point. "Shaking hands and getting senile, those aren't things you do out of choice. It's completely different. Besides Constance—" My full name was a sneer on his lips. "—was young and could start over. My grandfather won't last long. If we're going to kill the poor bastard, let's do it now and not drag it out. And if we're not going to kill him, let's just let him have his home and bring him groceries once a week and check on him and have a little compassion for the elderly. Just a little."

For such an asshole, he was a persuasive speaker when he wanted to be, although I sincerely doubted he'd be the one who'd bring over groceries and check up on the old man—blood relative or not.

"You volunteer for that? Making sure he's got food and he keeps his house? Out of your own money?" Peter wondered. He sounded extremely doubtful Jonathan would follow through.

"Yeah. Yeah, sure," said Jonathan.

Everyone at the table knew he was a goddamn lazy-ass liar. The duty would fall to Nora. It would be her money too, and she wasn't even at the table to agree to it.

"You can afford your house and his? And food?" Peter pressed.

"Between Nora and me, we'll figure it out," assured Jonathan. "I still get my pack subsidization toward my rent, don't I?"

"Of course." Peter looked like he wanted to roll his eyes, but he was good, he didn't.

"Then I can do it," said Jonathan rashly.

"It might be better if the old man moved in with you," suggested Peter and the whole pack nearly burst into derisive laughter.

"Yeah, right," said Jonathan with a sneer. "I haven't got room for him in my tiny little house. There's hardly enough room for me and Nora as it is. Be real. I said I can do it. Either you believe me or you don't."

"Do I understand correctly that the old man deliberately hid the fact that he accidentally severed the brake line?" Colin asked. "He knew he did it back then? He's confessed to it, right?"

"Yes," agreed Allerton.

"And he let Constance be blamed instead? Because he was too ashamed?" Incredulity spread across Colin's face.

Murphy's expression was sour. It apparently rankled that Colin defended me.

"Yes," Allerton said. He had his fingers steepled in front of him on the table and looked very authoritarian.

Colin did roll his eyes. "Well, then, what is the issue? Is he senile? Has that been established?"

"No," said Allerton.

Jonathan said, "The old man is losing his marbles. Just because we don't have some doctor's note confirming it doesn't mean you can't see him losing it for yourself. You don't know him, I do." He gave Colin a condescending smile which Colin returned with interest.

"Two years ago he was presumably more in control of his faculties than he is today," Colin said, making people shift uncomfortably in their seats at the logic of his words. "He knew he did it, he covered it up. There's no question what we should do. Just because he's old doesn't give him a pass to obliterate three people's lives—two of them dead, one made to suffer and go without a pack for something she didn't do. He needs to be put to death, and if the Council say we can't do that, we have to do what we can, which is exile. If he'd been thirty or fifty or eighty years old, we wouldn't even be arguing about this. The grandfather card cuts zero ice with me. I vote exile."

"Are we ready to put it to a vote?" Allerton addressed the table at large before Jonathan, his face red, could say something inflammatory. One by one everyone nodded.

"Where will he go?" Devon asked, in clear distress.

"You can abstain from voting, my dear," said Allerton. "He'll be taken from this state. That much we'll arrange. We can make sure it's a warm climate. Florida, perhaps? So if he does end up homeless, he won't be likely to freeze to death."

"No, just starve," sniped Jonathan.

Devon sighed—an unhappy, anguished sound. She looked pleadingly at her bond mate and he gave her an encouraging nod as if to tell her she could do it—it wouldn't be pleasant, but she could do it.

I thought about a fatal glass of warm milk. No matter which way they voted, Grandfather Tobias was not going to leave this safe house alive.

"Do we want to do this anonymously or out in the open?" Allerton looked at everyone around the table, skipping no one, not even me and Murphy.

"In the open," decided Callie for everyone. "There are too many secrets in this pack as it is."

Jonathan grimaced. "I know how you're going to vote anyway. And where the hell is Nora? Doesn't she get a vote or are we going cheat?"

"We'll get her in the event of a tie breaker, how's that?" Callie asked him, her mouth twisting with impatience.

Jonathan grumbled under his breath.

Allerton took that to mean he had no serious objections and said, "All right then. All in favor of exiling Tobias Green for his role in the tragic accident that took the lives of Grey Owens and Elena Demetrius, raise their hands."

Colin's hand shot into the air. Pale but determined, Callie raised hers. She looked directly at me and I knew she'd voted for exile in an attempt to right the wrongs she'd done to me personally. I wasn't sure how I felt about it, except that it stained my hands with the old man's blood just as much as it stained hers.

Vaughn raised his hand next. He kept his head down, eyes fixed to the table.

I knew Jonathan would vote against, I wasn't sure of Devon. I also knew Peter would vote against exile. His arms were folded across his chest and he made no move to raise his hand.

It wasn't surprising he'd be lenient. He'd suffered the most during my interrogation. He'd been very reluctant to accept the idea I'd been drunk and I knew it had killed him to turn against me. He was the kind of man who found spiders in the house and brought them out to the backyard to free them. He fed the stray cats in the neighborhood even though none of them would allow him near. His wolf never killed anything—not a squirrel, not a rabbit. Hell, not even a beetle.

Now for the first time, I wondered if he'd voted against kicking me out when my fate had been put to the vote.

My heart slammed against my ribs even though I knew Grandfather's Tobias's real future.

"Oh, Lord," cried Devon in an agony of indecision. But then suddenly, she put her hand up.

It was over then. Jonathan picked up his fork and threw it down on his plate.

Allerton still called for the nays and, rolling his eyes, Jonathan raised his hand. So did Peter. He wouldn't look anywhere near my direction.

"Exile it is," declared Allerton. "I'll arrange for him to be taken to Florida. As of the date of the next birthday of a member of this pack, Tobias Green is no longer a member of Riverglow or any other pack and he cannot petition for membership in an existing pack, form his own, or bond with another person of the Great Pack for a period of two years. So be it by order of the Great Council, in concurrence with the New England Regional Council and by vote of the Riverglow pack of Connecticut."

It wouldn't become official on paper until the next birthday a pack member celebrated, but it was in effect with Allerton's words. That's how it had been with me.

They'd voted to kick me out of the pack and the official date had been Jonathan's birthday, which fell in October. However, I left Connecticut three days after their vote. It hadn't even been September yet. I'd stayed only as long as it had taken me to arrange the journey and clear the bank account.

Allerton and Kathy Manning got up and left the room together.

A moment of profound silence was broken by Jonathan, who said, "What a crock of shit. Hope you're happy, Stanz, good going. You killed an old, senile man. What a coup."

"She didn't say a word." Peter defended me.

Jonathan threw him a contemptuous look. "She didn't have to. Just the fact she's sitting here was influence enough. She was planted here so you idiots would turn against Grandfather Tobias all according to plan. You were played and you don't even have the smarts to figure it out. Jesus. What a crock of shit." He pushed back his chair, his handsome face flushed with bad temper.

He got to his feet and pointed a finger at me. "Hey, Stanz, you owe me eight hundred bucks. I had to repaint half the walls and ceilings in your goddamn house and steam clean the hell out of the carpets after you just walked out and left everything a friggin' mess. As it was, I didn't even get the deposit back from the landlord because you broke the goddamn lease. You had a hell of a nerve leaving it like that and you know it."

That was typical. I was supposed to pay for the destruction of my own things. I'd cleaned up all the broken, destroyed belongings because I didn't want any of them touching Grey's things or Elena's, even if they were ruined. But I admit I did nothing to attempt to clean the ketchup and mustard stains off the walls, ceilings and carpets. And I'd broken the lease? Why? Because I'd been kicked out by him and the rest of the pack and forced to leave the state.

Before I could say all the scathing things I wanted, Murphy was on his feet and everyone, especially Jonathan, braced for violence.

All Murphy did was take his wallet out of his back pocket. He pulled out a sheaf of bills and began to count them out.

Although I argued against it, Murphy always had at least a thousand dollars in cash on hand. I don't know why he refused to use credit cards like normal people. Or at least get a debit card. Murphy insisted on cash.

So I wasn't surprised when he came up with eight hundred dollars, although the rest of them were a bit flabbergasted. It made Murphy look a little arrogant, but I'm sure he didn't give a shit.

"Eight hundred, you said?" Murphy walked to Jonathan's side of the table and extended the cash. Jonathan took it.

"Now you can shut the fuck up, you greedy bastard." Murphy's Irish brogue was very much in evidence and I knew that meant he was pissed off.

Jonathan flushed, his mouth open as if he were about to say something, but Colin Hunter spoke first. His voice was full of amused derision.

"Well, I see you're still the same old Liam Murphy, buying the affections of your bond mate because you can't get them any other way."

After a split second of appalled silence where nobody knew what to do or say, Murphy sprang into violent motion.

Colin Hunter's chair crashed to the floor and him with it, Murphy on top of him, fists flying.

Devon Talbot screamed. Her wine glass smashed on the floor. Wine splashed on my legs and little shards of glass nicked my skin. I sat there like an idiot with blood running down my legs while Murphy and Colin rolled around on the floor, their fists connecting with each other's bodies and faces making wet, meaty splats.

"What the hell is this shit?" Jonathan had an incredulous half grin as he watched the fight.

Cursing beneath his breath, Peter shoved back his chair and Vaughn reacted too, following his cue. The two of them waded into the middle of the fight, each choosing a combatant.

Peter ended up with Murphy, his muscles straining to keep Murphy's arms twisted behind his back with one hand while he wrapped his other arm around Murphy's chest and pushed one of his legs between Murphy's to keep him off balance.

Vaughn used his arms to pin Colin Hunter's against his side, and braced his legs so that even though Colin struggled to lunge at Murphy, he didn't get far. He murmured a steady stream of phrases like, "Take it easy," and "It's all over, Col," into Colin Hunter's ear. I wasn't sure Colin was listening. Instead he was smirking triumphantly in Murphy's direction, pleased as hell he'd provoked such a violent response. His nose was bleeding.

Murphy's lips were pulled back from his teeth in a vicious snarl. His dark eyes were wild with rage, and it took all of Peter's considerable strength to hold him back even though Peter outweighed Murphy by a good forty pounds.

He had a bloody abrasion high on his left cheek—the result of Colin Hunter's ring and his lower lip was split, also courtesy of the ring.

Blood ran down his chin and he wiped it away, his expression murderous.

"It's over." Allerton strode into the room trailed by Kathy Manning. His eyes were icy cold with anger and shock. Her face was pale.

Murphy spat a bloody wad of spittle in Colin Hunter's direction.

"We need to leave," said Callie in a high-pitched tone. Her dismayed gaze traveled around the room. "All of us. Right now."

Allerton stepped close to Murphy and Peter.

After a last shake, Peter let go and everyone waited to see if Murphy would lunge at Colin Hunter. He stood there, furious and deadly, chest heaving, but he didn't make a move.

Vaughn kept an arm around Colin Hunter's shoulders as he half-pushed, half-escorted him out into the hallway.

Someone went upstairs to get Nora. There were noises of people putting on coats and saying awkward goodbyes to Kathy Manning, who played hostess and saw them out.

I sat paralyzed in my chair, the fire burning my back. Allerton stayed with Murphy, who showed no signs of calming until the door had closed behind the last of the Riverglow pack and Kathy Manning returned to the room.

He relaxed slightly, the tension in his shoulders loosening, but his chest still heaved as if he couldn't take a deep enough breath to fill his lungs and his eyes were full of hectic murder.

He scared me. I knew I should go to him. Kathy Manning looked at me as if surprised to see me still sitting half a room away. Allerton was angry and disgusted—I could smell both those emotions from him and felt bad for Murphy but was also scared and very confused.

What had Colin Hunter meant by his words *buying the affections* of Murphy's bond mates? What did he know that I didn't? What was Murphy hiding?

"You know it was quite a step down for him to join Riverglow, Liam." Allerton gave a great sigh and paced to the bookcases on the far wall. He ran his finger along the spines of some hardcovers on a lower shelf and shook his head.

"Truth be told, he didn't really have much of a choice. His Alphas wanted him out of the pack, but Devon wouldn't bond with him unless he was a member of Mac Tire."

"So they let him stay in, big friggin' deal," said Murphy, his voice bitter. But it was a big deal.

"Only until the Great Gathering. Then he was told he needed to find a new pack. He joined Riverglow to have a shot at being Alpha. So he could keep Devon. Sound familiar?" Allerton swung around, eyes blazing. I'd never see him so angry and that scared the shit out of me even more than Murphy's rage. "Because it should!"

"You have a lot of influence within Mac Tire, Liam, and he has... Riverglow."

Murphy was unmoved.

Allerton watched him for moment. "You let him get to you. I'm disappointed."

"You didn't hear what he said," Murphy snarled, fists clenched at his sides. The knuckles of his right hand were bruised and bloody.

"I didn't need to, to understand that you let a man far beneath your status provoke you into violence in front of his entire pack. Pathetic, Liam."

Murphy looked like he wanted to spit again.

"He has no status because of your influence. Surely you can appreciate that and let that be your revenge. Do you really need to get into a fistfight over a remark, however inflammatory?"

"You have a hand in it?" Murphy demanded, his mouth tight. "In Riverglow, of all bloody packs for him to end up?"

Allerton glared at him. "I won't even dignify that with an answer."

Murphy gave a bark of contemptuous laughter. "You did, then. First you throw me and Stanzie together and then you put Colin Hunter in her old pack. You've got us all on strings, dancing to your tune, don'tcha?" He did not look at Allerton, instead he glared at the fireplace. Or maybe me.

"You try my patience tonight, Liam," Allerton ground out.

I couldn't breathe and little black spots began to whirl around my head in a maddening, sickening swirl.

Murphy did turn to him then, his face cold. "I've played along with it, Councilor, but I'm telling you right now I'm nobody's puppet. I'll be your Advisor, but I'll not be your puppet. Is that clear?"

"Crystal," said Allerton and I shivered because I'd never seen his eyes so steely and mercilessly remote.

He left the room and, after a moment, so did Kathy Manning.

To keep myself busy and distracted, I began to stack the plates. Murphy found his napkin, dipped it in his water glass and dabbed experimentally at his lower lip, wincing because it hurt. He was still glassy-eyed with rage, but was simmering down.

After a while he threw down his napkin with an Irish oath and helped me stack the dishes.

We brought them into the kitchen, loaded the dishwasher, started it, and because not all the dishes could fit, we left a sinkful of them soaking in soapy water.

Murphy followed me upstairs. A dim hall light burned. The door to the master suite was shut and a pencil thin line of light gleamed from beneath it. The doors to the bedrooms closest to the master suite were both closed. One, Grandfather Tobias's room, appeared dark. The other, where Kathy Manning presumably slept, had light beneath the crack in the door.

As I shrugged off my bolero jacket, I went into the room I shared with Murphy. He followed, shut the door behind him and locked it for good measure.

So far we hadn't said a word to each other.

The clock on the nightstand read 11:22 PM. I was exhausted and numb. I took my pajamas into the bathroom and put them on before scrubbing the makeup off my face.

When I came out, pulling the clips and bobby pins out of my hair, Murphy stood by the window in a pair of gray flannel drawstring pants and a white, long-sleeved thermal t-shirt. Both buttons at his throat were undone and I could see the gleam of the silver chain and pendant around his throat.

Blood was crusted on his lip and the abrasion on his cheek looked raw and painful.

As I crawled onto the bed, I moved the quilt I'd spread over Nora. Beneath it I discovered a small, red leather book.

With a frown, I picked it up and realized it was not a book, but a photo album.

I flipped it open at random and a photo of a laughing Elena standing in our old kitchen in New Britain confronted me. The breath hissed out of me as if I'd been punched. She had a beer in one hand. Her long white-blond hair spilled over one shoulder, leaving the other bare save for the spaghetti strap of the yellow-and-pink flowered sundress she wore.

Summer barbeque. I'd taken the picture. Grey had been out on the back deck with most of the rest of pack, grilling steaks. Elena had scooped the bottle of beer out of a red plastic cooler filled with ice that I'd dumped in there myself, an hour and half before everyone was supposed to arrive. One Saturday in July, five or six years ago.

"What's wrong?" Murphy asked.

I couldn't stop staring at Elena's laughing face. Her eyes were so blue, her smile so bright and sincere.

"I'd forgotten I'd given Nora copies," I whispered. "The originals got destroyed with everything else. I never thought I'd see her again except in dreams and my memory." I looked up at Murphy, who stared at me, clearly affected. "Look, it's Elena. Wasn't she beautiful?"

He came to sit on the edge of the mattress beside me so he could see the photo.

"Very." He watched me reverently trace the outlines of Elena's face beneath the protective plastic sleeve.

Bottom lip between my teeth, I turned the page and almost couldn't see for the burning tears in my eyes.

Grey and I, arms wrapped around each other, stood on a beach in Rhode Island. It was the same summer as the barbeque, maybe a month later. I had on a black string bikini I'd forgotten I'd ever owned and my hair was down to my waist in a messy, sun-streaked braid. Grey was in a bright blue pair of knee-length swim trunks and his hair was loose around his face. He was tanned dark by the sun and there was sand on the tops of his bare feet and clinging to the light dusting of hair on his legs. A smear of it on his elbow. He'd been playing volleyball with Peter, Vaughn, Elena and me, while Callie and Nora sunbathed on yellow towels spread out just above the surf line and Jonathan swam like a seal in the bay. We'd played guys against girls and even though there were three of them and only two of us, Elena and I had kicked their asses.

Grey stared at the camera—Elena had been behind it. I had my face turned to look at him and we both looked so damned happy it hurt to even try to remember. I didn't think it was even possible for me to be that happy anymore. That ability was lost, smashed to bits in blood and glass and twisted metal the night of my thirtieth birthday.

Beside me, Murphy smiled wistfully.

"You two look so happy together," he said and I could hear the little twist of jealousy in his voice.

"We had ten years," I mused, "and we were just as happy together at the end as we were at the beginning. It was almost like every day was the first day we'd ever met. Sounds stupid, doesn't it?"

"Not at all." He sighed. He kept his head down, staring at the quilt bunched up beside me on the bed. "I suppose you've figured out that Sorcha and I...we weren't like that."

I closed the photo album so I could think. I definitely couldn't do that when Grey's laughing face stared up at me. The minute I couldn't see him anymore, I felt bereft and alone, almost like it was that awful time just after the accident when I'd expected to see him around every corner, in every car that slowed near my house, in every face of every man with long dark hair I saw from a distance.

"Well," I began slowly, "Colin said you had to buy her affections and Allerton said you ought to be familiar with the idea of becoming Alpha to keep your bond mate from leaving you. So I guess I'm wondering if that's true or if I'm totally fucking it up."

"You're not fucking it up. It's true enough," he confirmed. Something died inside me at his words because I hadn't wanted to believe.

Still staring at the quilt instead of me, Murphy told me their story. "I met her down the pub when I was twenty-two and she was twenty-five. She was visiting from the Mac Tire branch in Northern Ireland. Her pack had sent her to mingle with us because she was getting on for not having a bond mate. I saw her sitting there by the fire, her red hair like a halo around her head, and I was gone on her, Stanzie. I knew right then and there she was the one. She didn't exactly see it that way herself, but I used all my charm and I convinced her to give me a shot. She was under pressure to bond as it was, and I wouldn't let anyone else near her and me. Da was on the Regional Council and so, you know, I was something of a coup, I suppose." Murphy's voice was full of self mockery, but when he talked about her, his eyes lit up with old remembered passion.

"So we bonded and I was over the moon. I convinced her she'd love me if she just gave me enough time. I can charm the birds out of the trees with me words when I want to and Jaysus, I wanted to charm that woman." His mouth twisted ruefully. "And I guess I did, for a few years anyway. But she never did fall in love with me. She tried, but it just never happened and one day she came to me and told me it was over. Her birthday was coming up and she was going to sever ties because she knew there had to be somebody out there she could love, only I wouldn't let her look for him because I was so demanding. Even then I didn't give up. I just asked her what it would take for her to stay with me. 'I'll never love you, Liam,' she kept telling me. But I didn't care. As long as she was with me, I didn't care if she loved me or not. I kept on and on at her, what would it take, what did I have to do and finally she said—"

"She wanted a baby," I finished for him and he nodded, his dark eyes bleak.

"The Alpha pair had been Alphas for nearly five years, so the time was ripe for another duo or triad to take over. I made damn sure that duo was us. I never lack confidence, Stanzie. I have that much going for me. I never doubted for a second we'd be voted in and I was right. There we were, Alpha pair, and she got pregnant and I thought everything was fixed."

"Where does he come in? Colin Hunter?" I asked, but thought I knew.

From the look he gave me, it was plain he thought I knew too. "That's easy. He's the one she actually did love."

His cheeks flushed with shame. I knew he was thinking about the fight. I could picture what had happened between Sorcha and Colin. They'd probably fallen in love between one breath and next. Easy. Uncomplicated. Meanwhile Murphy'd been knocking himself out for years trying and failing to attain what Colin Hunter had accomplished without effort.

Murphy took a deep breath and continued the story, his face and voice bitter. "He'd just lost his bond mate. They'd split up amicably enough and his branch of Mac Tire sent him to Dublin to drown his sorrows a bit. Although the bastard wasn't precisely suffering. Even less after he met Sorcha."

"Whose baby was it?" I demanded, although it was none of my business.

Murphy shrugged. He seemed to brace himself before answering. "I don't know for sure. I think it was mine, but I don't know and I'll never know now."

"Why is he in disgrace? That part I don't really understand," I confessed. The rules of sexual relationships in packs were fairly lenient. People could and did sleep with anybody they wanted, even the Alphas. An Alpha could have any man's baby she wanted, it didn't have to be her bond mate's but ninety-nine times out of a hundred it was. An Alpha male whose bond mate had someone else's child was not openly laughed at, but his authority was definitely undermined. We could and did sleep with anyone we liked within our packs, but there were fine lines we took care not to cross and egos we avoided bruising.

I wondered then how carefully Sorcha and Colin had treaded with regard to Murphy. I wondered if he'd become the laughing stock of his pack or the object of their pity.

He hated Colin Hunter and harbored a lot of resentment. I suspected it wasn't entirely due to the fact that Sorcha had fallen in love with him. No doubt Hunter had rubbed Murphy's face in the whole situation as well. He didn't seem the subtle type to me.

I felt a swell of anger on Murphy's behalf. We never made our Alphas look bad, no matter how much we secretly hated them. It wasn't easy leading the pack. It was a heavy responsibility and pack mates were supposed to support each other.

Murphy took another deep breath and held it for a moment. His lip was bleeding again and he touched his tongue to the blood, tasting it, as though reminding himself of the fight.

"She wanted to leave me for him but we were Alpha and we still had three and a half years to go. So, the three of us were in negotiations to form a triad when she had the accident. I would have gone through with the bastard thing to keep even one part of her. If I had to share her with fucking Satan himself, I would have made a triad with him too. Colin accused me of murdering her so I didn't have to share her. And that's why there was an investigation not only of her death, but of me too. The friggin' Alpha male of the bloody pack."

There it was—the reason behind Murphy's animosity. I didn't blame him one bit. What a bastard Colin Hunter was. Belatedly, I tumbled to something that ought to have been fucking apparent from day one of knowing Murphy. "Allerton was the Councilor. That's how you know him. He investigated you too." I'd figured he'd investigated Sorcha's death, but it had never even ghosted across my mind that Murphy would have been suspected of her murder.

Murphy nodded. "Allerton no more believed I would've harmed Sorcha than the rest of my pack. They were all behind me. They knew how I felt about her. So I was cleared, there was no tribunal, and Colin Hunter was disgraced. I wasn't exiled by my pack, Stanzie. I left voluntarily. I didn't want to be around anybody. I just wanted to be left bloody alone. I was never going to come back to the Great Pack, let alone Mac Tire, but Paddy would not let me be. I agreed to go the Great Gathering and now here I am. I'm fucked if I know a damn thing about anything anymore."

He waited for me to say something, but I could only stare at his lowered head, at the shame and grief all over his face. He'd been afraid to tell me the truth about Sorcha. He'd kept us away from Dublin for as long as he could so I wouldn't know. I don't know if he thought I'd be ashamed of him or what.

When he'd first started to speak, my head and heart had reeled in disbelief because everything I thought about how it was with him and Sorcha shifted and was destroyed. I'd thought they'd had what I'd had with Grey and Elena but it couldn't have been more different. How hard had it been to love when he knew he wasn't loved back? How had he not gone fucking insane? Had just the thought of her being there with him been enough? Or had he brainwashed himself to believe it was enough?

Murphy deserved to be loved. He was a good man. A kind one. No one had ever taken better care of me than him or looked out for me as he had. Not even Grey. With him, I'd been the caretaker. I made sure the bills were paid and there was food in the cupboard and the laundry was done. Grey was always there to pick me up and whirl me around in a giddy circle and knock me down on the bed to make passionate love to me at two o'clock in the afternoon when I had to be downtown at four for a gig. But I was the one who'd nursed him through sicknesses and made sure he'd eaten vegetables at least twice a week and arranged all his doctor and dental visits, his hair appointments and cashed his paycheck.

I fit together with Murphy and, for the first time since we'd met and I'd heard Sorcha's name, I allowed myself to think we had a chance to be happy together. As a real couple. To fall in love. Because Murphy deserved to be loved back and I wanted to be the one to show him what it felt like.

I leaned toward him and brushed my lips ever so gently across the abrasion on his cheek. His eyes were closed and he was nearly in tears. I kissed one eyelid and then the other, marveling that he let me touch him first and so intimately. I never even kissed him like this when we were in bed together. I had never dared.

Something inside me soared, a brief, shining moment of hope and a glimpse of the kind of happiness I thought I'd lost forever.

And that's when he shoved me. I went flying and smashed into the wall so hard all the breath was knocked out of my body and, for a moment, I could see myself lying crumpled on the floor, my head lolling on my neck, eyes glazed and unfocused, while most of me floated near the ceiling looking down in suspended disbelief.

"Fuck you, Constance. Don't you dare ever feel sorry for me, you hear me?" He was on his feet now, the terrible rage back in his eyes, and I saw myself staring up at him, my face full of shock then fear.

I slammed back down into my body and curled up into a fetal ball to protect myself because I thought he was going to hit me and I wanted to protect my head and make myself as small a target as I could.

I waited, tense and breathless, for him to strike me, but he never did.

Instead I heard him weeping, great, racking sobs, above me.

I cautiously lifted my head and saw him face down on the bed crying like baby, clutching the pillow as if he were drowning.

I had to use the wall for support to get to my feet because my head was swimming from the blow it had absorbed hitting the wall.

It kept replaying.. Me reaching out to him, him shoving me away. I was an idiot. A romantic fool. And the worst part is that I didn't know who he was anymore. The past two months—what had they meant? What had they been? Two lonely people trying not to be so lonely anymore. But that's all.

I wondered then, at Murphy's terrible rage. I wondered if Colin Hunter had maybe had a point after all, no matter what the rest of Mac Tire thought. What must it have been like for him to have to face the fact that the woman he loved, the woman who wouldn't love him, had likely gotten pregnant with some other man's baby and, worst of all, rubbed that guy in his face and the fact that she loved him and not Murphy?

I turned my back on him, and walked out into the hall into the bedroom across from the one I was supposed to share with Murphy. I locked the door and fell onto the bed but my head hurt so much I couldn't sleep. I couldn't cry either. I wished I had the guts to leave the safe house and go back to Boston on my own. Sometimes there was such an edge to life, and tonight I felt as if my balance was so precarious any little thing could knock me off into oblivion.

Every time I closed my eyes I saw Murphy's face. I waited for the anger to hit me so it wouldn't hurt so goddamn much. He was going to walk away, I just knew it, and I would be alone again. How could I miss someone who was still there? How could I hate someone and still love him more?

Jesus. I *loved* him. I really did. Now I'd ruined everything with my clumsy attempt to show him. But what else could I expect? The night the car crashed, all my good luck died with Grey and Elena. I wished I knew how to fix it, but I couldn't even get up the courage to get out of the goddamn bed.

I clutched at my bond pendant and just when I'd given up hope, the empty void of sleep wiped everything away. At least for a few hours.

# Chapter 8

*The moon is gone from the sky but the sun is not here yet. I am in the dark but I am not alone. The chase makes me tired. My head hurts but I can't stop. I am afraid of who is chasing me. I don't want to know, so I run. But I can't run much farther. My head hurts, so I shake it, to try to make the hurt fly out and my heart beats so fast. I am wet with sweat and something else. Blood? But it is cold. Wet. I hear it hurting the leaves in the trees. I don't know the word but if I think, it would come to me. But I have to run, I can't stop running. My head hurts and I can't stop. The wet stuff falls down like rain but not rain. My fur protects me but now the leaves are slippery and I can't think because of the pain in my head. I hear it hurting the leaves—what is it? What is that sound? I want to know the word for the sound. I have to think and then...*

\* \* \* \*

Sleet striking the windows of the bedroom roused me from my dream. For a hazy moment I didn't know what form I was in because in my dream I'd thought almost like me in  human form, but I'd been wolf. Using a vocabulary and a grasp of cause and effect that was in real life just beyond me.

In dreams, some margins are narrowed, some impossible things are possible, and the senseless makes perfect, horrible sense.

I sat up in bed, stifling a groan when I shifted my head and a wave of pain bounced through my skull. I wondered which had woken me—the sleet against the window or the pain in my head.

I had to pee but I knew the bathroom door to this room was locked. It was Grandfather Tobias's bathroom and I couldn't go in there.

I lay in bed, trying not to move, trying not to jar my head or my bladder as the sound of the sleet intensified against the glass of the windows.

I thought about Murphy and wondered if he were awake or asleep. Was he still mad at me? Shouldn't I be mad at him? A part of me had desperately wanted to feel his arms around me as I had for the past two months, but, of course, I was alone. Again, I reached inside for anger but found only hopelessness.

Ten minutes of torture passed, twelve. At the eighteen-minute mark, I couldn't stand it any longer and forced myself out of the bed. Maybe if I stood under a hot shower the pain would wash away.

Outside the bedroom window was a sheet of ice where the world used to be. I had to breathe on the window pane and rub at it to melt the frosted condensation and then I could see the telephone and electric wires sagging beneath the weight of a thick accumulation of ice. I looked at the clock on my nightstand, the numbers still glowed red but I wondered for how long. If those wires snapped, goodbye electricity, goodbye heat, hello dark and bitter cold.

As I rushed for the bathroom, I glanced furtively down the hall, hoping I would not run into anyone.

Allerton's door was open and so was Kathy Manning's, but they were not walking down the hall so I supposed they were already downstairs.

Grandfather Tobias's door was shut, of course, and so was Murphy's. There was a light on, I could tell that much, and I tried the bathroom doorknob wondering if he were in there. It opened under my touch and I was able to lock myself in from both the hall and his room so I could pee in peace.

After peeling off my pajamas, I got into the shower. I washed my hair, but wished I hadn't when my fingers inadvertently pressed the back of my head and an explosion of sick pain and nausea nearly caused me to puke. There was a lump the size of a robin's egg right where the back of my skull had slammed into the wall last night.

I couldn't help the half scream, half groan of pain that escaped me when I touched it, nor the string of obscenities that followed. It was either swear or vomit, and I didn't want to puke on my bare feet.

The water was a tease. It helped when I was underneath it, but once I was toweled dry and wrapped in one of the waffle knit bathrobes, my head still throbbed.

Teeth gritted, I unlocked the bedroom side door. I could not possibly go downstairs in a bathrobe or even my damn pajamas. I had to get dressed and all my clothes were on Murphy's side of the door.

He'd known for half an hour that I was in the bathroom. He could hardly have failed to hear the water or my muffled curses, so I wasn't surprised to find him slumped on the edge of the bed, facing the bathroom door. He was fully dressed, but he looked as if he hadn't slept at all. His eyes were puffy and dark circles underscored them, giving him an oddly appealing appearance, more fragile and vulnerable than I'd ever seen him.

I'd always considered him strong and confident, even during moments of grief when he thought about Sorcha. This morning he looked beaten down and weak.

His split lip was a little swollen. It would have been fine if he'd thought to put ice on it the night before but he obviously hadn't. The abrasion on his cheek had spread into a subtle bruise the color of dusk—gray-black and almost invisible. Blood crusted along the cut edges. He should have put peroxide on it last night or at least washed it with antibiotic soap, but he hadn't done that either.

His dark eyes held a sort of mute apologetic agony as he looked at me. In his hands he held the small red leather photo album. It was open to the page where Grey and I laughed on the beach in Rhode Island.

At last anger swelled inside me and spilled into my veins, igniting a protective fury.

"That's mine," I snarled at him. "I want that back."

He saw where I was looking and without a word, his eyes huge, he held it out to me.

I snatched it away and a photograph fluttered to the floor and landed face up on the Oriental rug.

As I bent to snatch it up, I realized two things—it had not been a good idea to move so quickly, and the photograph was not from my album.

I saw vivid red hair and lots of green grass and it hit me that it was Sorcha's picture.

I didn't want to see her, didn't want to confront her beauty and perfection and understand graphically why I didn't now, nor ever would, measure up.

My outstretched hand froze and Murphy said, "Go ahead. You can look at it. It's only fair. It's Sorcha."

Trapped, I picked up the photograph and, bracing myself, looked down at it.

Sorcha's flame-red hair stood out like cloud around her decidedly plain face. Her chin was too pointy, her hazel eyes too close together and her cheeks were obscured by a battalion of freckles. Not a light dusting, but freckles upon freckles, a freckle free-for-all jostling for space and dominance.

I couldn't believe it. She didn't even have a nice figure. Too skinny and flat-chested. I honestly could not understand what a gorgeous handsome man like Murphy would see in her. Or why someone so plain wouldn't go crazy with joy at having a man like him madly in love with her. Not just for his looks either, but for him, for the kind of man he was. It did not make sense, but then nothing did anymore. Nothing had for so long. What was one more inexplicable thing?

Her hair was gorgeous, that much was true. Auburn, the color of autumn leaves, thick and wavy.

Murphy waited for me to say something but I couldn't find any words. I hoped my expression did not give away my incredulity.

"She wasn't beautiful like you are, Stanzie, but she had something. Some sort of wild mystery to her. Men went crazy about her. Mad to solve the mystery. I wasn't the first one, but I had enough to charm to get her to bond with me, I guess. She never got serious about anybody until...Colin Hunter." Murphy managed to get the name out without hitting something.

I still didn't say anything. I could not come up with anything.

He waited a moment, watching me stare intently at the photograph of that plain, freckle-faced, flat-chested woman and eventually said, "What are you thinking?"

I blurted the first nice thing I could think of and it was a damned good thing I'd had at least two minutes to reflect. "Her hair's pretty."

Murphy laughed. It was subdued, but a laugh nonetheless. He probably was insulted. "I told you she wasn't beautiful like you." He made my so-called beauty sound about as appealing as moldy bread in comparison to her goddamn wild mystery.

Now I was more jealous of this dead woman than ever. Plain as hell and still I couldn't compete. I was about as wildly mysterious as yesterday's newspaper.

I handed Murphy the photograph and went to the dresser and picked up my brush. I completely forgot about the knot at the back of my skull and ended up dropping the brush on the floor and having to cling to the edges of the dresser to keep from collapsing into a puking ball of nausea.

"Stanzie, are you all right?" Murphy was beside me in an instant, his voice full of concern and fear.

When he tried to touch me, probably to help hold me upright, I flailed away from his touch. He was such a liar. Such a two-faced bastard. What did he care if I was all right? Who was the one who'd frigging shoved me headfirst into the wall to begin with?

Reproachful and guilty, he retreated a few steps, but still hovered as if he were afraid I would fall down.

"Are you all right?" He sounded scared.

I rode out the last of the wave of nausea and took a deep breath. "I'm fine." It wasn't precisely a lie so much as a wish.

"When can we get out of here?" he asked, his voice rough as if he'd smoked a pack of cigarettes the night before.

I shook my head then, and when another wave of nausea enveloped my skull, I wished I hadn't.

"Have you looked outside?"

I heard him move to the window, part the curtains then swear in Irish.

"Besides, we came here so I could talk to Grandfather Tobias and I haven't talked to him."

For the very first time, I wanted to talk to that man. Everything was so fucked up between Murphy and me because we'd come here, so now I was damned if I wouldn't talk to that old man.

I took out the first things that came to hand from my suitcase—the jeans from the day before, an eggplant purple v-necked wool sweater and a new pair of panties.

"Stanzie, I'm sorry," Murphy whispered as I limped back toward the bathroom with my clothes. There was no way I was dressing in front of him even though he knew my body intimately.

I didn't answer him. I just closed the door.

\* \* \* \*

Pain must have showed in my expression when I came into the bedroom because I couldn't even get to the dresser to find my brush before Murphy said, "You need your head looked at. You hit the wall pretty hard. I'm scared."

"I'm not going outside in this ice storm to find some emergency clinic and I'm sure as hell not going to wait hours at an ER. I'll be fine," I argued even though sick flashes of nausea kept stabbing at me and the back of my head felt exquisitely *there* as if I'd never known I'd had a back part of my skull except intellectually.

"You don't need to," he countered. "Allerton's a doctor."

That idea was too much. I turned around with a careful slowness that was not lost at all on Murphy and said, "He'll want to know how I happened to hit a wall with my head, Murphy. What am I supposed to say? I don't want him knowing what happened."

Murphy was in enough deep shit with Allerton as it was, thanks to last night's brawl with Colin Hunter. He surely didn't need to add to it with me bleating about how he shoved me against a wall later in the evening.

Murphy's face got very white and his eyes darkened. "I don't need your protection, Constance! Not now, not ever!"

I stood there feeling like the world's biggest fool for a moment. Waves of hot and cold washed over me and I felt so small and so stupid.

I put down the brush and started for the door.

"That came out too harsh," Murphy said.

"I understand," I half whispered. "You don't need anything from me. I get it." I turned around again and I could see the shame in his expression.

I looked at the floor, unable to face him, and fixed my gaze on his boots.

"It's funny, Murphy," I told him as I stifled bitter laughter, "you've given me and my wolf so much the past two months and I've given you... shoes." I did laugh then, but it was more of a sob. "Kinda lopsided, isn't it?"

"I love it when you give me shoes." His voice was full of warmth, but also shaky, as if he were having trouble finding the words. "I pretend not to notice the new pairs, but I always do. It's one of our rituals, Stanzie."

Yeah, right. It was just me trying to indulge my shoe fetish vicariously through somebody else. It was me being selfish. Take, take, take, that's what I did best.

"Let's go find Allerton," Murphy suggested as the silence stretched unbearably between us.

"No," I said. "I can do things on my own. I've been leaning too much on you."

"Stanzie," he whispered, but he let me leave the room alone.

\* \* \* \*

"Mild concussion," diagnosed Allerton. We were in the small conference room with the door shut. I sat on one of the chairs facing away from the table while he peered into my eyes with a penlight and probed the back of my skull with surprisingly gentle fingers.

"You haven't been sick?" he asked for the second time and again I shook my head.

He drew one of the other chairs away from the table so it faced mine and sat.

Even though he wore a pair of sharply creased jeans and a brown v-neck sweater, he still looked polished and intimidating, as if he'd stepped out of a higher-end clothing advertisement in a men's magazine.

"Care to elaborate on how you came to suffer this mild concussion?" His dark blue gaze bored into mine and I was powerless. I'd never met anyone with half his presence.

Still, I tried to resist. I maintained a stubborn silence for about thirty seconds before he said, "Does he hit you often? Liam?" There was such anger and steel in his voice, I shuddered.

"He didn't hit me. He's never hit me. You don't understand."

"Try me. Tell me what happened? For instance, how did you do this?" He reached out a finger to gently touch my cheek, and at first I didn't understand but then I remembered the scratch.

"My wolf," I said, hating the fact that I sounded like every woman everywhere who'd ever been in denial about her abusive partner. "She gets angry sometimes when she can't think of words for things and she believes her head is full of her anger and doesn't have room for the words, so she—"

"Scratches at her head," finished Allerton. He looked like he actually might believe me. "Liam told me that. I remember now. But your concussion, Constance, was not caused by your wolf, was it?"

"I hit my head against the wall. Murphy pushed me away from him, but he didn't mean to hurt me." My explanation sounded lame but it was the truth, damning as it might sound. "He was upset last night, Councilor."

"Jason." He sounded almost impatient with me. "Don't you think it's time you called me by my first name? You are my Advisor, after all. That affords us a certain familiarity."

I took a deep breath. "Jason, it sounds like I'm defending him, but I'm not. It was a stupid accident. I knew better than to touch him when he was feeling vulnerable. He thought I pitied him."

"I'm not pleased with him," Allerton stated, his mouth grim. "I know it wasn't easy for him to confront Colin Hunter, but it's been over three years and he has you now."

"Me?" I couldn't help but laugh a little. "I'm not anything to him like she was. You can't compare us."

"I'm not comparing you, I'm merely pointing out that he is not alone anymore and he has to let go of a past that is as dead as she is."

I shuddered again and wrapped my arms around myself. He frightened me with his intensity and I was very glad he wasn't angry at me.

He got to his feet and moved toward the door. He paused and said, "If you weren't offering him pity, what were you offering him?"

"Love, actually," I admitted because the man saw right through me anyway.

"He really can be an incredible idiot," murmured Allerton before he opened the door.

# Chapter 9

I must have fallen asleep. I'd gone upstairs after Allerton left the room and lain down on the bed because my head hurt. I could smell Murphy's cologne in the pillow case where I buried my head and it was oddly soothing.

The next thing I knew Murphy stood there next to the bed and the shadows had shifted in the room because the sun had moved in the sky. I'd been asleep for hours and, from what I could hazily tell, it was nearly nightfall.

"Councilor Manning is going to have a fit if you don't come down and eat dinner with us, you know," Murphy told me the minute he was aware I was awake. "She's been baking bread all afternoon and a cake too, I think. Plus she made some sort of gourmet dinner the spare three seconds between. You hungry?"

My stomach growled at the thought of bread and cake and a smile twitched the corner of Murphy's mouth.

At some point during the day he must have showered and shaved, and he was dressed in a different pair of jeans and one of the cashmere sweaters I'd given him for Christmas—the beige one with the navy blue accents at the collar and cuffs.

I slid off the bed and went to the mirror above the dresser to peer at myself, careful to avoid brushing against Murphy. I looked like hell.

With a sigh, I picked up the brush and tried to calm my wild blond hair. On the plus side, the knot on the back of my head no longer seemed so exquisitely *there*. On the minus side, Murphy wouldn't stop staring at me and his expression was somewhere bad between frustration and shame.

"I'm on everybody's shit list today," he remarked without a trace of a smile.

"I told Jason the truth about what happened." I sounded defensive, and sighed.

"Jason?" Murphy cocked a sardonic grin at me as his eyebrows raised halfway up his forehead.

I flushed unaccountably. "He asked me to call him Jason." The brush trembled in my hands as if I'd done something wrong, perhaps betrayed Murphy somehow.

"Well, he sure as hell hasn't asked me to do that," drawled Murphy. "But then I'm not in line to be his next mistress either, am I? Kathy Manning look out, Constance Newcastle is up and coming." His voice dipped derisively on the last word of the sentence and I could feel the hot blood of shame burning my face. How could I have been so dumb, to have missed the truth? I'd never felt as though I were a real Advisor and if Murphy was right, I wasn't.

"Kathy Manning is Allerton's mistress?" My mind boggled for a moment, but then I was frequently slow on the uptake. Now I started playing back moments that had passed between them and I could see it. I could definitely see it. And, if that part were true, then, of course, the other part was too—the part where I was next.

"But Allerton has a bond mate," I protested, even though I knew, and what's worse, Murphy knew, that meant next to nothing.

Murphy's lips drew back into one of his sardonic sneers. I hadn't seen one of them directed at me in months, not since we'd bonded. One night could change everything, though. "A lunatic bond mate, sure. You don't know that? He hasn't tried that line out on you yet? About how his bond mate went insane after the death of their stillborn son and since she's got all the money in their relationship, he considerately didn't sever the ties but instead has climbed to practically the top of the Great Council, taking understanding mistresses along the way to ease his suffering and loneliness? And now you're the next one in a long line." Murphy still smiled, but it was the kind that was cold and sharp as a knife in the ribs.

"No, that's not true. That's not the truth!" I struggled to breathe but it felt as if there were a twenty pound weight on my chest slowly crushing me to death.

"Why don't you ask Kathy Manning? She knows she's on her way out. You can see it all over her face when she looks at you." Murphy grinned at me and, for a moment I allowed myself to believe I was having a nightmare but I knew damn well I wasn't.

Every second I'd ever spent alone with Allerton flashed before my eyes. Where I'd once seen fatherly concern, now all I could see was patient lust, going as far back as the investigation into Grey and Elena's deaths when he'd singlehandedly saved me. Not just because he'd thought something strange was going on in the Pack, but because he'd wanted me and he'd set me up so I'd owe him and be obligated to him.

The money in my bank account he'd said I'd earned as an Advisor was really just payment for services yet to be rendered. I somehow doubted Murphy's bank account had swelled as much as mine, and I had been too stupid to see it for what it really was.

I bowed my head as both shame and self-loathing swept over me.

Now it was clear why Colin Hunter had been so arrogant to Murphy. He'd been laughing at him and so had the rest of my former pack. No wonder Murphy had been so humiliated.

I chewed at my lower lip and turned back to the mirror. I had to do something with my hands so I started brushing my hair again. I couldn't even see myself in the mirror because of the goddamn tears.

A terrible thought tore a devastating hole inside me. I felt panicked and trapped and wanted to run away but I couldn't even move.

"Will I have to shift with him too? I will, won't I? Sleep with him and shift with him, and I don't want to do either. I'm scared to shift with other people. He'll make me, won't he, and my wolf doesn't know his and I don't know what she'll do. She'll want the words for things and maybe his wolf will want to do other things. I don't even know how to ask him not to make me. Oh God, how could I be so stupid as to not even think I'd have to pay for the things he's done for me? He sat there with me yesterday and told me how much money he's putting in my bank account and I thought it was because I was his Advisor, but we were having two different conversations, weren't we? I don't understand how I could have missed it, but it's all there when you point it out to me."

Tears of shame and humiliation poured down my cheeks and I couldn't breathe. Through the watery prisms of my tears, I saw Murphy's expression change and all the sarcastic anger was gone and, for a moment, he was the man I thought I'd known.

I dodged past him and locked myself in the bathroom. I had to get a grip and to think, and what I didn't need was any more confusion and false friendship.

"Please, Stanzie," he called through the door. "I'm the idiot, not you. I'm frustrated and pissed off at myself and I used you as target practice. Please come out and let me talk to you face to face. I can't stand this. I don't know what broke between us but I want to fix it."

"Why? Because Allerton told you to?" I whispered through the crack in the door. I was pressed against it, my palms splayed out on the wood, my cheek mashed to it and I thought he might be in the exact same position, our hands and bodies reaching out to each other through the barrier of the door, but I was damned if I'd open it. Damned.

"No," he said with a groan.

"Is Kathy Manning his mistress? Don't lie to me, Murphy."

Murphy swore under his breath. "Yes, she is, but that doesn't mean you're next on his list. I'm just...I'm jealous, Stanzie, don't you get it?"

"Jealous. Fuck you, Liam. You fucking liar."

"Liam," he whispered. "Since when do you call me Liam?"

"Since I don't know who the fuck you are."

I heard him leave the room and waited a few moments before I went to the sink and splashed cold water on my face. The tears had stopped, burned away by fury, but now I was numb.

I put on makeup and jewelry, avoiding the necklaces and rings Murphy had put in my Christmas stocking, and went downstairs.

* * * *

The three of them were in the Colonial dining room. A gleaming oval table of mahogany was set with off-white place mats and the Blue Willow dishware from the night before. Taper candles flickered, casting circular shadows on the ceiling above. A small crystal chandelier was set on the dimmest setting, barely illuminated.

Councilor Allerton got to his feet when I entered and gallantly pulled out the chair next to his for me.

I sat, acutely aware of his hands hovering near my body as he pushed the chair in, then he sat and poured me a glass of red wine. The wine goblets were thick pebbled glass, cobalt blue and expensive.

"I hope you're feeling better, Stanzie." Kathy Manning beamed at me as she passed me a platter of roast beef. All the pieces were perfectly sliced, pink and juicy. I took one and passed the platter to Allerton, who took three before passing the platter to Murphy. Their eyes did not meet. Allerton was solicitous to me, but for Murphy he had nothing but cold contempt.

Bowls of mashed potatoes, French runner beans and gravy traveled around the table. Homemade bread was piled in silver baskets lined with white cloth napkins.

I took some of everything but couldn't eat. My throat felt about as narrow as the eye of a needle. I wanted to drink the wine but thought that would choke me too.

I played with my food instead of eating it and nobody said anything. We sat there in silence broken only by the sounds of silverware striking china.

"When can I see Grandfather Tobias?" I asked after I'd given up all pretense of playing with my food and pushed my plate away.

Allerton eyed it and then raised his gaze to mine. "You're not hungry, Constance? Does your head hurt?"

*No, just my fucking heart*, I wanted to say, but I didn't.

"My head's much better," I said instead.

"Then why don't you eat?"

"If you don't like roast beef, there's some seafood casserole left from last night. I could heat it up for you?" Kathy Manning gave me a sympathetic smile.

I looked at her and pictured her naked in bed with Allerton. I thought of Allerton's insane bond mate and how I would never be able to look at the man himself and think of him being charitable and good, only empty and driven, filling his hours with Council business and an ever-expanding parade of mistresses.

"I'm sorry. I'm not hungry," I whispered.

Murphy had managed to eat maybe half a slice of roast beef and three or four mouthfuls of mashed potatoes. He'd crumbled a piece of bread onto his plate and he was on his fourth glass of wine.

His pale cheeks had taken on a low, alcoholic flush but his eyes were clear and miserable, not clouded by wine at all. He looked at me then looked away.

"Can I see him tonight? I'd like to go back to Boston. I'm not comfortable here in Connecticut anymore. It's not my home."

"You can see him tonight," Allerton told me, "but I'm not sure you'll be able to leave tomorrow. It's snowing now and the roads are unsafe. I'd prefer it if you and Liam would stay here for a few more days." His blue eyes bored into mine. "There's also the matter of settling Tobias Green. Have you made a decision regarding your role in that yet?"

Murphy stopped reaching for the wine bottle, his hand arrested in midair. Kathy Manning smiled at me again and I couldn't tell if she meant to offer empathy and encouragement or was some sort of fucking ghoul.

"I want to talk to him first," I said carefully.

"What do you mean settle him?" Murphy sounded pretty convinced he knew damn well what it meant.

"Exactly what you're thinking, Liam," said Allerton in a glacially smooth tone. "You surely didn't think he was going to Florida, did you?"

"No, I figured he'd be going to hell, but not that she'd be the one sending him there." Murphy's eyes narrowed. "How can you even ask her to do such a thing, Councilor? Can you not see how all of this is affecting her and now you want her to kill the old man on top of it? How are you going to have her do it?"

"In a civilized cup of hot chocolate," I said before Allerton could say anything. "Grandfather Tobias and I always drank hot chocolate together on winter afternoons when I visited him. It's tradition." I flashed him what I hoped was an empty, soulless smile.

"You're in no shape to be doing anything of the sort." I knew he was upset because his Irish accent was more apparent than it generally was.

"You're in no position to tell me what to do," I pointed out and Kathy Manning's smile faltered for a second before recovering.

Allerton went very still beside me while all the blood seeped from Murphy's cheeks.

He threw himself backward in his chair and slumped. "Yeah, I guess that's the truth, isn't it," he muttered. Abruptly, he reached out for his glass and filled it to the brim with more wine. He shoved back his chair and stalked out of the dining room.

"After you talk to Tobias, we'll have cake and coffee." Kathy Manning got to her feet to begin clearing the table.

I almost started to laugh at the absurdity of her statement, but instead looked at Allerton. He reached into his pocket and drew out a key.

"Last door on the left. Please lock it again when you leave." He gave me a measuring look. "Do you want me to come with you, Constance?"

"No thank you, Councilor." I made sure not to use his first name and I was aware he knew it was deliberate. The last goddamn thing in the world I wanted was for him to accompany me. "I can do this on my own."

As I left the room, I could feel the both of them staring at me and I was certain they were wondering if I actually could. As a matter of fact, so was I.

* * * *

Grandfather Tobias sat in front of the gas fireplace in a blue armchair with a high back and rolled arms. He had the fire on the highest setting and a blast of heat brought a light coating of sweat to my face when I walked into the room.

The first thing I thought when he turned his head toward me was that he'd aged horribly during the past two years. His dark gray hair had thinned and turned a ghostly white. His brown eyes were faded to the color of weak tea and the lines and seams in his face had deepened and become underscored.

He'd lost weight too and his clothes bagged on his wiry frame. I'd always thought he'd looked a lot like Jonathan but now I could no longer even pretend I saw a familial resemblance. He was an old, old man.

When he saw me he smiled and I remembered his smile. Slanted and slow, it gradually took over his whole face and emphasized the laugh lines and crow's feet around his gentle eyes.

"Dear one, I knew you were here. I could smell you. Four parts Dior perfume, six parts unique Stanzie. Sit down." He gestured toward the matching blue chair opposite his, as if this were just another one of our weekly visits and he was playing host.

The heat from the fireplace combined with his smile was making me sick. Was he senile? Did he not even remember he'd murdered my bond mates? How could he smile at me as if we were still friends?

I stood by the door and made no move to sit. I couldn't talk, I could only stare.

"They aren't with you anymore," he said after a moment. His brown eyes were both sad and strangely relieved. "The last time I saw you when you came to my door and I wouldn't answer it, they were with you, one on either side, their arms around you as if they were holding you up and supporting you. Maybe you don't need them anymore. You've moved on and left them free to move on as well. Good for you, dear one."

"What," I blurted, my stomach roiling, "the hell are you talking about?"

But I thought I knew and if he said it, I would probably puke all over the floor.

"Grey and Elena of course," he said matter-of-factly. "Or, rather, their ghosts I'd suppose. Their spirits. I can see them sometimes. I always could. I suspect Jonathan can too but he's too damned afraid to admit it. It's in our blood."

"You're a senile old man." I clutched at my stomach. I was grateful for not having eaten anything but then I wondered if I had, maybe I would feel less nauseous.

"I'm an old man, but I'm not senile," he told me.

"They were with me?" I couldn't help but ask. I was fascinated, repulsed, grief stricken and appalled they'd tried to comfort me and I hadn't even known they were there.

"They were," he affirmed. "I'm sure if you think hard, dear one, you can remember when they moved on. Wasn't there a time when you felt like they weren't there anymore?"

"They were never there because they died," I choked out. But I did remember a moment lying in a bed in a Paris hotel listening to Murphy take a shower and trying to bring Grey and Elena to mind and realizing I was missing whole pieces of them. Had they really been there with me until that time? Had they really?

Grandfather Tobias watched my face. "It's a good thing they moved on. It means you moved on too. I knew you would. We all do. We have to."

"I don't want to listen to you. I wouldn't have had to move on if you hadn't killed them. Why? What for? I don't understand how you could do it to them. They were your pack and so was I!"

"Of all of the people in Riverglow, Stanzie, I thought you were the most respectful of the old ways. It isn't just wanton destruction we do, we recruit as well. We have to or the whole thing would die out, wouldn't it?"

"Recruit?" I gasped in outraged shock. "But I'm not a grandmother!"

He shook his head pityingly. "Did you really think it was only us?"

I reeled backward against the door as if a cannonball had propelled me. I turned away from the old man who sat placidly in the chair in front of the fire and pressed my forehead against the cold unyielding wood of the door and pounded one of my fists against it weakly. "Never would I have ever joined in something that meant murdering innocent people!" I hit the door again then a third time. If Grandfather Tobias had seen something in me that made him think I was a candidate, maybe he was right and it was a part of myself I had to acknowledge.

"It's not murder," he said. "It's an unfortunate thing, but these people who die, dear one, they choose their path. We all choose a path to walk down and we all pay the consequences those paths demand."

I let out a soft wail of despairing protest. "Grey and Elena did not choose to die. You made that decision for them. They were helping the pack. They were doing things they loved and were good at doing. Just because you don't understand or like the technology doesn't mean the entire Pack should avoid it."

"There are ways to embrace the present, Stanzie," he said in a patient tone. "You embraced it with your music. You entertained at modern weddings and board meetings and company parties and yet you remained true to the Pack. The only thing that ever held you back was your wolf. You kept her innocent and pure and childish, and that blinded you in this form to things you needed to face. I said I wished I could recruit you not that I ever would have, not with your wolf the way she is."

"Was!" I swung around, fists clenched. "My wolf is changing and evolving and learning the words for things and she would be disgusted by this conversation the same way I am. You are trying to twist everything but the truth is that you and everyone who choose your path are cowards and murderers and blind. Why do you need to kill? Why can't you talk and use reason? It's because you're talking shit, that's why, and you know it. On some level you must know it!"

"I knew there was a change in you that wasn't due just to losing Grey and Elena and the subsequent grief." The old man smiled at me and I longed to bash his face in with my fists. Then, appalled, I shrank against the door and shuddered.

Had I really wanted to use my fists on a helpless old man? Even if he was a murderer? Was using violence against violence ever the right answer?

"Nothing is black and white anymore!" I was incensed at the way my world was changing and crumbling. The shreds that were left were all turning to dust beneath my clutching fingers. "Nothing is easy to figure out. Nothing!"

"I know, dear one, I know," said Grandfather Tobias. He got out of his chair and walked on his unsteady old man's legs toward me. He was so weak, so powerless, so old and frail. I remembered a vital man. Yes, he'd been old, but he'd worked on cars and kept up a huge backyard garden and had been strong enough to lift spare tires and car parts and big bushel baskets of tomatoes and corn. Now he looked as though he might fall down taking seven steps across a perfectly level floor.

He meant to take me in his arms and hug me, and if he touched me I might disintegrate. I might do anything. I might hurt him or worse, hug him back.

"Please stay away from me. Please don't touch me!"

He had one hand stretched toward me and it would have been so easy to reach back. The path down the road to destruction could be a simple touch away. Or maybe it was the opposite. If I didn't reach back, maybe that would condemn me.

He let his arm drop to his side and gave me a sad smile. "I'm not alone on this path. Not in the Great Pack, not even in Riverglow. And you, dear one, you ought not to trust everyone at face value the way you always have. You bring out the best in people because you're so open and honest, but you make it easy for them to exploit you. You don't know the first thing, for instance, about the Councilor you've tied yourself to or your new bond mate. You believe what they've told you about themselves, but most people hide things. They have secrets and those secrets could hurt

*Amy Lee Burgess*

you. I had hoped, Stanzie, that you'd stay away from the Great Pack. That you'd be safe on your own, but that was not to be.

"We are a social breed and we need our own. You've never had Others for friends and companions and you probably never will so I'm sure the past two years have been torture for you and not release the way I wished them to be for you. So be it, you're back. I just wanted you to know that this is not Riverglow with Grey and Elena buffering you from reality anymore. You've put yourself on the edge of a precipice and it's a long way down. Be careful, dear one. I was always proud of you and I couldn't love you more than if you were my own flesh-and-blood granddaughter. I won't be here for very much longer and you need to choose your protectors wisely. You also need to fend for yourself. I'm glad to hear you've woken your wolf. Just be aware that it gets much worse and darker the more she wakes up. And she can never, ever, go back to sleep again."

He did touch me then—a light touch on the shoulder but it was electric and burned as though his fingers were made of fire.

I felt galvanized as if he were passing something within himself and putting it into me. I felt it sink beneath my skin, into my blood and bones, my very sinews and I knew he was right. My wolf would never sleep again. She would forever be on the prowl.

I keened softly beneath my breath as I fumbled open the door and slammed it shut behind me. Somehow I remembered to lock it.

# Chapter 10

I found the others in the front room. At some point during the day the Christmas tree had been dismantled and the poinsettia plants taken away. Now the bay window stood revealed and a series of green houseplants in colorful pots decorated the shelved expanse beneath it.

Two cream fabric chairs with gilt-edged woodwork had been placed where the tree had been, with an expensive antique end table between them. A lamp with a Tiffany shade stood on the end table.

Aware they were all staring at me, I crossed the room to one of the chairs and sat.

Allerton and Manning were on the sectional sofa beneath the lighted cityscape portrait. They were drinking rye and soda on the rocks.

Murphy had graduated from wine to cognac and stood by the drinks cart as if guarding the bottle from anybody else who might want some of what he'd clearly staked as his own.

His dark brown eyes were wide as he stared at me. His fingers clutching the glass full of cognac were white and bloodless.

I must have reeked of anger and defensive grief. They all exchanged glances in a tacit, wordless understanding that if I went ballistic, they'd act in unison to subdue me.

That pissed me off. I was not so wildly out of control that I'd lose it and start wrecking the priceless furniture. I didn't even want to drown myself in drink like Murphy.

I shifted restlessly in the chair because I was unsure of what I wanted to do. Maybe that's the part they were worried about. Not that they thought I would go crazy, but that they couldn't tell what I might do which could be anything.

For a minute, nobody moved and everything hung in the balance. Then I did do something. I laughed.

Murphy nearly dropped his cognac, his eyes widening even more, and both Allerton and Manning tensed and stared. This reaction, they had clearly not anticipated.

I admit I hadn't either. The laughter that poured out of my mouth was both wicked and dark, not the way I'd ever laughed before. There was a black hilarity about it that was just short of murder.

"Tell me the truth." I demanded. "I'm the only person sitting here that, up until five minutes ago, actually believed it was only the grandmothers and grandfathers who were involved." I laughed again. "You all knew it couldn't be just them, am I right? I'm the idiot, the one who trusted everybody, especially the Great Pack. Fuck."

"It did seem indicated," Allerton said, his tone low and placating. "The logistics for one thing."

"Yeah," I agreed with a snort. "Grandmothers and grandfathers have no real power. Not like Alphas or former Alphas with friends in high places." I cast a malevolent look at Murphy, who seemed to hold his breath. "Or Regional Councilors?" My gaze swept insolently over Kathy Manning who, for once, was not fucking smiling. "Or even the Great Council. A Councilor on the Great Council. What a coup that would be, wouldn't it?"

I locked gazes with Jason Allerton and refused to look away.

Allerton said, "I think it is safe for you to trust the three of us in this room with you."

"Ha. Forgive me, Councilor, if I prefer to make up my own mind about that."

"Of course you should, I'm merely stating my position. You are free to accept my words or reject them. Of course, though, I can't have an Advisor who doesn't trust me, can I?"

"I wouldn't think so, no," I agreed. We stared at each other, neither one backing down.

"You can't seriously believe I would have had anything to do with Sorcha's death, can you, Stanzie?" Murphy sounded as if someone had stuck a knife into his guts and twisted hard. Someone like me.

"Yesterday morning I wouldn't have," I said, still staring at Allerton. "But then the whole fucking world turned upside down like a ship hit by a tidal wave. I'm not sure, but I think I might have drowned. Nobody's who they say they are. That old man upstairs, for instance, says he's my protector. But he killed the two people I loved more than anything or anybody in the whole world. And now he's got me thinking that maybe even they weren't who I thought they were. Maybe they had secrets they kept from me, the way you all have secrets you've kept from me. And you have them, Murphy, you know you do. Why shouldn't it be that you're a part of this whole fucking conspiracy?"

"Because I'm not!" he yelled. "Yes, I have secrets, but not that kind. Christ, Constance, no! You know me!"

"I don't!" I shouted back, turning away from Allerton to glare at my bond mate. A part of me needed to go to him, to turn back time and start over again, but another, bigger part of me wanted to spit at him.

"I don't know what secrets you think I'm hiding from you, but my cards have always been on the table," said Allerton and I swung back to him.

"Except for the ones up your sleeve," I retorted. "For instance, does the whole world know Kathy Manning's your mistress or just Murphy?"

For once I'd taken the man completely by surprise. Whatever he'd been expecting me to say, I don't think it was that. I also saw by the flicker of his eyelids that I was right on target. She was his mistress and he didn't advertise it.

"No, the whole world does not know it. I would appreciate it if you'd keep it to yourself as well," he said. "It's not a secret. It's simply none of your business."

I nearly choked to death on my laughter. "One of those not a secret but nobody knows anyway secrets. Yeah," I said.

"I would appreciate it, Constance, if you'd leave the room now. I don't wish to continue this conversation. It's irrelevant and insulting and I won't tolerate it." Allerton's voice had turned to pure steel and, despite my fury, I found myself on my feet. His power was immense and now I'd crossed him.

Poised at the edge of a very steep precipice, that was me.

# Chapter 11

Twenty minutes later someone knocked on the bedroom door. I'd retreated to the room I was supposed to be sharing with Murphy because I couldn't bear to be in the room next to Grandfather Tobias. It was bad enough he was just down the hall.

I doubted like hell Murphy would knock, and I was right. Allerton, impeccable and implacable as ever, stood outside in the hallway.

"I would like a word with you. Downstairs in the small conference room." He turned on his heel and, confident I would follow, started for the stairs.

When we passed the front room, I glanced in out of the corner of my eye and saw Murphy sitting in the chair I'd vacated, head down, full glass of cognac cradled in his hands. Kathy Manning was nowhere to be seen. He didn't look up although I knew damned well he was aware of us as we walked past.

Allerton shut the door behind me and gestured to the chairs surrounding the conference table.

He adjusted the lights so the room was bathed in a soft, non-threatening light and, instead of sitting himself, walked to the built in bookshelves and pretended to peruse the titles on the spines.

In my inferior seated position, I waited for him to tell me I was no longer his Advisor and he wanted nothing further to do with me. I waited for him to tell me I was a disgrace and weak and could not handle difficult things and that he was disappointed in me.

The twenty minutes I'd spent in my room alone had sobered me like a slap of cold water in the face. I wasn't angry anymore, I was lost. On the whole, I preferred the treacherous warmth of anger to the cold, slick sweat of being lost.

"I don't know if you'll believe me or not, Constance," Allerton said, turning away from the books to gaze at me with a deceptive gentleness, "but I never for one minute intended on making you my next mistress."

I tried to make myself even smaller in the chair. This was hell. Murphy, the bastard. He had to go and say something.

"Forgive me for this, but you're not in my league, frankly. You have no power and no social standing compared to mine. I choose my mistresses from my equals or my near equals. Enough so that it would never be something that could be construed as coercive. I want my mistresses to want to be my mistresses, not feel as though as they have no choice or that they somehow owe me. And I would never take one of my Advisors as a mistress, no matter what her social standing or power. That's much too incestuous and not fair, because, you see, I select my Advisors carefully. I want them to become powerful, but not through sexual services rendered. I've never taken a former Advisor as a mistress either and I never will. Whatever power and success they aspire to, it can never be said that it was because she slept with me. So you see, Constance, I think you have the wrong impression of things as they stand between us. I apologize if I've ever given you any indication I intended otherwise."

I hadn't thought it was possible to feel so ashamed. Or so huge when I wanted to be so small. I felt as if I took up every molecule in the room not taken up by him or the furniture. It was horrible.

"Can we agree to let this go now? We don't need to refer to it again."

As if I'd ever voluntarily go near the subject again. Unable to speak, I jerked my head in agreement.

"Now can you trust me enough to stay my Advisor? Can you do that?"

I nodded again although there was a part of me that wanted to run away, tail between my legs, and never, ever face this man again.

He smiled at me then and I was pretty sure I'd surprised him. I was almost positive he thought I would have taken the opportunity to run and liked me all the better for not doing it.

"Because of his lamentable experiences, Liam is going to be insecure with you as his bond mate. You'll have to bear with him, work with him. It won't be easy and, as much as he wants desperately to turn to you, he'll fight you. You've worked enough of this out on your own and I think you've been doing a wonderful job with it. I'd hate to think that man upstairs could poison you so much you'd turn against someone like Liam, who needs you."

"All he said was I shouldn't trust people at face value the way I used to. He said I've put myself in danger being your Advisor, being against the conspiracy, and I should choose my protectors wisely. He said people aren't always who they claim to be. He didn't specifically say Murphy was corrupt or you were. Just that I didn't know."

"I am one of your protectors now," Allerton said.

"I need to fend for myself." I jutted my chin and he smiled again and this time the smile was mostly pity.

"You need allies. Don't let that man make you believe you're alone, because you're not."

I stared at him, trying to find the words to describe things but I couldn't. Both of them were trying to twist me. Everybody tries to twist everybody else, that's all Grandfather Tobias had said to me. I was supposed to figure out how not to be twisted, or at least how to understand *why* I was being twisted. For reasons benign or selfish, for good or bad.

Allerton wanted me on his side of things. I was in a position to help him, to root out some of the conspiracy because of my ties to it, however destructive they'd been. Grey and Elena had been killed by the conspiracy and that gave me a connection to it. I was closer to it than Allerton, and so was Murphy, and that's one of the reasons he wanted us.

"Grandfather Tobias said he's not alone in Riverglow. Somebody else in the pack is also involved. Maybe more than one. Maybe the whole damn pack, for all I know," I whispered. I felt as if I were stabbing my friends in the back but I had to say it. I had to. "I can't tell you who because he didn't tell me and obviously I'm not the best judge of character so I couldn't begin to even guess."

He said nothing and something clicked into place.

"Is that why you have Colin Hunter here? Is he working for you too? Like Murphy thought last night?"

Allerton smiled at me again. "I do tend to put people into places where they might be useful."

"But that man accused Murphy of being involved in Sorcha's death!" I cried then realized I was defending Murphy and shut my mouth.

"And did himself no favor by doing it," Allerton reminded me.

"Desperate to redeem himself, he's trying to figure out if anyone in Riverglow is involved in the conspiracy." I stared at the empty fireplace and marveled at how Allerton's mind worked. "And why am I here? To try to confirm it and figure it out through Grandfather Tobias?"

"Maybe," said Allerton. "I'm not keeping secrets. I'm merely on fishing expeditions. That's all. I may catch nothing. There may be nothing to catch."

"Grandfather Tobias said there was someone else in Riverglow," I protested.

"Did he? Or did he insinuate it? He knows what I'm after, and he's covering his tracks and doing a good job of it. He told you what? That you couldn't trust anyone and no one was as they appeared. He cast doubt in your mind about me, about Liam, about all of Riverglow, but did he come out and speak actual names?"

Reluctantly, I shook my head.

"This is how it's going to work, how we're going to be forced to uncover people's involvement. It's not fun. It's dangerous and dirty and demeaning and everything you've ever believed will be called into question and doubt. You have to be strong enough to remain true to yourself and your convictions. And strong enough to believe in people and not lose faith in everything or you will be lost. You will drown just the way you talked about it earlier. I think it might be too late to walk away, but you can still try if you want."

I shook my head because he was right. It was too late. "Grandfather Tobias said if my wolf was awake, and she is, she can't ever go back to sleep again. So I'm in, Jason. For however long it takes and whatever it costs me, I'm in."

The use of his first name was not lost on him and the smile he gave me was warm and approving. I felt a small glow of gratitude and pride. The man was a master at motivation. Maybe someday I would be half as good, but I sincerely doubted it.

\* \* \* \*

*Amy Lee Burgess*

Murphy was sprawled on the bed when I returned to our room. The glass of cognac, mostly empty, was on the nightstand with the bottle. That was mostly empty too, but there was enough to half fill the water glass I retrieved from the bathroom.

The lights were blazing and Murphy was wide awake and not a bit drunk even given the amount of alcohol he'd consumed. He lay in the same position he'd been in the night before—one arm curled around his head, the other at his side. He'd taken off his shoes but was still dressed and his face was full of bitter self-condemnation. He watched me gulp at the cognac but didn't say a word.

When I reached over to put the bottle on the nightstand, I saw a scrap of paper, a piece of something that been torn to shreds.

I picked it up, curious, and saw the auburn blaze of Sorcha's hair on the other side of the scrap. He'd ripped her photograph to pieces. My heart hurt when I thought about him doing it.

Where were the other pieces? Had he thrown them away? I could never bear to throw a photo of Grey or Elena away, even if I were drunk.

"Grandfather Tobias said he could see their ghosts." I stared at the tiny piece of Sorcha's photograph as it lay like an accusation in my palm. "Grey's and Elena's," I clarified even though I was relatively sure he was following me. "The day I went to his house after they died, wanting him to tell me it was just an accident, he said he saw them with me. They had their arms around me, supporting me. I didn't feel a thing. He said some people can see ghosts. He says it's in his blood. You ever heard anything like that before?"

"Yeah," he answered after a moment when I doubted he would say anything. "There's a few people in Mac Tire who swear they can see the spirits of the dead. Until they move on. I don't see a damned thing, me. And I doubt like hell Sorcha ever put her arms around me from beyond the grave." His voice dipped derisively and his chest heaved as if he fought to keep from crying.

"You said you saw her in the hotel room in Houston," I reminded him.

He grimaced at me. "Bullshit hallucinations. I was pumped through with narcotics. I saw a lot of shit that wasn't really there." He gave me an accusatory look as if I were one of those things.

"He says they're not there anymore. Grey and Elena have moved on," I said. I very carefully put the piece of the photograph on the nightstand and took another sip of the cognac. It was warm and pulsated through my veins like an electric current.

"Is this some sort of subtle hint that I ought to do the same bloody thing?" He sneered at me. He half sat up and I realized he was a little drunk. Maybe a lot drunk. "I ripped up her picture. What do you want from me next? A rewrite of history deleting her out? Believe me, I wish I fucking could."

"I never asked you to rip up her picture," I pointed out, but there was no reasoning with Murphy half drunk on wine and cognac.

"I'll betcha you wouldn't rip up one of your precious pictures of Grey and Elena!" He stabbed a belligerent finger in my direction. I pretended I needed something from the dresser, so I could put some distance between us.

"And now you think I'm gonna hit you, don'tcha?" His Irish accent was very thick and I had to concentrate to understand him. "Why don'tcha just fuck off, Constance. Go sleep across the hall the way you did last night. What in the hell are you here for anyway? Rubbing it in that I was wrong about Allerton maybe? Well, fuck, I admit it. I was wrong. The man never had designs on your body. Only the fuck he didn't! He may not have intended to act upon it, but he sure as hell has thought about what it'd be like to screw you."

I didn't know what to say to that.

"Go on," he yelled at me. "Get the fuck out. Can't you tell I want to be alone? Always crowding me when I want to be alone!"

"You're such an asshole." I snatched up my pajamas.

He twisted his body so he was face down on the bed and covered his head with his arms, blocking me out.

After I retreated across the hall, I climbed into the bed alone and resigned myself to another sleepless night.

# Chapter 12

Murphy was pulling a navy blue sweater over his head when I walked into the bedroom the next morning at just past eight. Beneath it was a t-shirt and it had ridden up a little to reveal a slice of his flat stomach and, despite myself, I felt a little lick of lust ignite in my belly. He had a pair of dark jeans that hugged him like a second skin and a black belt—one I'd given him. It looked damn good around his waist.

His face appeared, cheeks stubbled with a night's growth of beard he apparently wasn't going to bother to shave, his hair tousled. His lip was not swollen at all and the bruise on his face had faded, leaving just a trace of the abrasion caused by Colin Hunter's fist.

He saw me looking at him and gave me a rueful grin. "Jesus Christ, I was drunk last night."

"I know." I turned to the mirror and picked up my brush. I was still in my pajamas. My feet were bare and I was cold. One look out the bedroom window had revealed a winter wonderland with snow still sifting down from the sky.

Our eyes met in the mirror.

"You ripped up a picture of Sorcha," I reminded him and his grin turned sheepish.

"I've got others."

"I'll bet," I said, none too charitably. He was driving me crazy standing there in his sexy sweater with his erotic beard and bedroom hair.

Sometimes in the mornings when our eyes met in the mirror like this, he'd come over to me, wrap his arms around my waist and rub his bearded cheek against mine. It always drove me crazy and nine times out of ten we ended up back in bed, but I had a feeling today was not going to be one of those days.

Another thing we'd discovered along our road trip—we were great in bed together. We'd started off tentatively because we were both scared and unused to each other—hell, we'd barely known each other. But as time wore on and we had become friends, things in the bedroom had heated way the fuck up. Astronomically. I felt a little guilty, but I could barely even remember how it had been with Grey anymore. And Vaughn and Peter and Rudi, the only other male partners I'd ever had could not even come close. By a long shot.

He watched me get dressed but made no move to come near me and together we went downstairs.

\* \* \* \*

Allerton was just finishing what appeared to be his second cup of coffee when Murphy and I walked into the dining room. Kathy Manning saw us, hopped cheerfully to her feet and asked us how we wanted our eggs.

"Scrambled," said Murphy without consulting me. "And I hope for all our sake's there's ketchup in the house or we're in for a bad few moments."

I extended my middle finger, making him laugh. Allerton hid a smile behind the rim of his coffee cup.

I began to think that maybe today might be better than yesterday.

However, I had barely had a chance to sit and grab my glass of orange juice before Allerton remarked with all the finesse of a true killjoy, "I believe today should be the day we deal with Tobias Green, don't you, Constance?"

I set my glass down before I took a sip and choked to death on it.

Murphy's smile vanished as if he'd never before smiled in his life. He pulled out the chair nearest mine with barely restrained violence and all but threw himself into it.

"I was half hoping he died in his sleep last night. He doesn't look good," I said in a subdued tone.

Murphy picked up my orange juice and made me take it. He watched me drink some, keeping one eye on Allerton as if he could possibly keep Allerton from speaking.

"The weight of his actions have taken a steep toll on his physical health," said Allerton when my glass was empty.

Murphy pulled the milk and sugar closer to me so I could fix myself coffee. His mouth was pulled tight but so far he hadn't blown up. He was close though.

"Regret? Remorse?" I said doubtfully. The Tobias Green I'd spoken to last night had not seemed in the least regretful or remorseful.

"Responsible," said Allerton succinctly. "He may feel no regret or remorse on behalf of the Great Pack and the ideals he espouses, but he does keenly feel the weight of the responsibility of taking two lives in their prime. And for sending you into a personal hell. He's very fond of you. He made that clear over and over again when we were questioning him."

I grimaced because I didn't want to hear that. Murphy scowled and I knew he was thinking something colorful and derogatory in Irish even if he didn't dare say it aloud.

"Oh, fuck it," he said all at once, making me a liar. "If he's that bloody fond of her, why should she be the one to administer the fatal dose of whatever hell brew Councilor Manning is no doubt whipping up on the kitchen counter?"

"At the moment I'm making breakfast. Yours," said Kathy Manning as she walked into the room with two plates of eggs and link sausage. "And when I do make something poisonous I won't do it in the kitchen. That makes absolutely no sense, Liam, does it?"

Murphy looked like he wanted to argue the point of any of it making sense, but I gave him a kick in the shin beneath the table and he kept quiet.

Kathy set the plates between us. I had way more sausage than Murphy and when she went back into the kitchen to get toast, I picked up three links and put them on Murphy's plate. He promptly snatched them up and two more on top of that and deposited them all on mine.

"Eat them. You ate fuck all yesterday and if you don't put something into your stomach you're going to faint. You might break a heel or scratch the leather of your damn shoe if you do, so listen to me."

I stared at him. "Even I cannot eat six, seven, nine links of sausage, Murphy. If I eat all this I won't faint but I won't be able to move out of this chair either. And I might even throw up."

"Oh, Jesus," he said. "Just eat what you can."

Under his watchful eye, I consumed five links of sausage and all the scrambled eggs—liberally doused with ketchup, of course. He ate only after he was sure I was not going to stop.

We took cups of coffee into the front room, where I sat on the sectional sofa and watched the snow whirl in a white blur across the panes of the bay window.

Kathy Manning took our cups away when we were finished. Before she left the room, she and Allerton exchanged a glance. Murphy's face hardened.

When she came back in bearing a tray with a pot of hot chocolate and two mugs, he made a sound of protest. "I'll do it," he said, trying to take the tray away from Kathy Manning, who dexterously evaded him.

Allerton cleared his throat. That was all he did, but Murphy retreated to his seat with a muffled oath and Kathy Manning held the tray out to me.

When I took it, she reached into her pocket and pulled a small vial full of a clear liquid.

"Put the whole dram in just to be sure." She placed the vial on the tray. "It's painless. He'll become gradually paralyzed and he won't be able to breathe."

"Coniine," I said and a flicker of respect dawned in her eyes.

A wordless exchange passed between us and I saw us both as the grandmothers we would one day become. Maybe someday I would teach an herbal class at some distant Great Gathering.

Socrates died by coniine poisoning. Grandfather Tobias was no Socrates.

"It might take hours, Stanzie. There's no need to stay there the entire time," Kathy Manning told me.

I shook my head. "No. If I'm doing this, I'm doing it all the way. I'm not going to sneak out and leave him to die alone."

"He doesn't deserve his death to be witnessed. He didn't witness Grey's and Elena's." Kathy was, for once, not smiling. She looked almost angry.

What was it Allerton saw in her—that drew him to her? What did they say to each other in bed? Did she love her bond mate? Did he know about how it was with Allerton? Did Allerton take care of his insane bond mate or did he pay other people to do it for him?

"I witnessed their deaths. I'll witness his too. Full circle," I said as Allerton placed the key to Grandfather Tobias's room on the tray.

He put his free hand on my shoulder and gave it a gentle squeeze. "He's expecting you. I talked to him this morning. He won't give you any trouble."

"I want to come with you, Stanzie." Murphy moved to my side and his face was full of determination. "I don't want you to do this alone."

"This has nothing to do with you, Murphy," I said as gently as I could. Still, I saw his hurt expression and I wanted to touch him but my hands were full.

"You could do your own dirty work, Councilors." Murphy said.

"Liam, if this were Mick Shaunessy wouldn't you be the first person to assert your rights of Pack vengeance?" Allerton wondered in a deceptively mild voice.

"Stanzie's not a vengeful person," Murphy pleaded. "I know her, Councilor. She's not prepared for this."

"Who is, really?" Allerton's hand was still on my shoulder and he gave it another squeeze.

"You don't have to do this, Stanzie," he said but I could tell by his expression he knew I wouldn't change my mind.

"I am too vengeful," I said, walking for the door. I tried to conjure up images of Grey and Elena and, while I could see bodies, where the faces went was blurred and indistinct. I wished myself back in my Boston condo but all that happened was that I came to the staircase and climbed it, the fatal tray clutched firmly in my fingers.

\* \* \* \*

Grandfather Tobias sat in the chair in front of the fireplace. It was on high again and the room was swelteringly hot but he was bundled in an ancient blue sweater with patched elbows. Beneath it was a blue-and-white shirt I remembered giving him for his birthday one year.

I realized then he was dressed in his favorite outfit. I could see the glint of the silver chain around his throat but could not see the pendant hanging from it. I knew the pendant held a tiny sapphire chip—his birthstone. There was a small wooden box on the table between the chairs. Dark wood. It looked old. It was open and inside were two bond pendants—his and hers. His had only a diamond chip in it. Hers had both diamond and sapphire. His bond mate's. She'd died in childbirth long before I'd been born. His daughter—Jonathan's grandmother—had survived and he'd brought her up. He'd joined a duo, but only so he could stay in the pack. Even they'd died before him, but by the time the female of the triad had died, he'd been close enough to a hundred. There was no need for him to take another bond mate because he could stay in the pack and be taken care of. He'd earned it.

When Jonathan had bonded with Nora and formed Riverglow with Callie, Peter and Vaughn, he'd taken Grandfather Tobias with him. Both Jonathan's grandmother and his mother had died few years before that and Jonathan was Grandfather Tobias's only remaining living relative.

Now, unless Jonathan severed ties with Nora or formed a triad with a fertile woman who bore a live child, his line was over.

"Hello, dear one." Grandfather Tobias rose creakily to his feet. He moved the small wooden box away so I could put down the tray of hot chocolate. If he saw the poison bottle he gave no sign. He acted, for all the world, as if I were visiting him the way I once had. For hot chocolate and conversation.

"Sit down. You can stay a bit and talk, can't you?" He looked anxious, as if I would poison him and rush off. I admit that's what I wanted to do, but I couldn't. If I were brave enough to give him the poison, I was damn well going to be brave enough to watch its effects.

I sat and he sank back into his chair, still clutching the small wooden box.

"Carol used to come sometimes and watch us. When Tracy was a little girl. Tracy saw her. Tracy's daughter, Alison, could see too. All of us in the family could see spirits. Tracy was almost ten before she figured out that Carol was her mother. Until then she was 'that pretty lady I can see through'."

"How come you never told me about that before?" I asked. I could smell the hot chocolate as well as the fabric softener Grandfather Tobias had used the last time he'd laundered his sweater.

My throat felt dry, my eyes scratchy. It was the heat of the gas fireplace and my guilt. Not a very good combination.

"Some people don't like to hear about spirits," he said gently. "Death had never touched you before, Stanzie."

"That's not true," I said. "You don't know what I went through in my birth pack. I saw a woman die once."

"Did you?" His voice was mild and only a little curious. He looked old and I struggled to keep from feeling compassion for him.

He killed Grey and Elena, I kept telling myself. But all I saw was an old man who looked tired and alone.

"I was only little." I didn't want to talk about it and I wasn't sure why I'd even brought it up.

"Shall we drink our hot chocolate?" His wrinkled fingers tightened around the wooden box.

"Will you see them again? Carol? Grey and Elena?" Saying their names aloud in front of their murderer hurt me inside. I bit my lip and reached out for the white china teapot that held the hot chocolate. Knowing Kathy Manning, it was going to be the most delicious hot chocolate I'd ever tasted. That seemed blasphemous almost.

"They've all moved on," he said, his light brown eyes infinitely sorrowful. "I don't think I'll move on right away. Not with all the blood on my hands. Even if it is righteous blood."

"It's just blood, Grandfather Tobias. There's nothing righteous about what you did to them." My hand shook only a little bit as I poured thick, rich hot chocolate into the bone-white china cups. Chocolate-scented steam wafted into the air and I tried not to choke.

"You persist in thinking in such black-and-white finality, Stanzie. It's not the way of the world, you know. It never was and never has been."

Grandfather Tobias watched me set the teapot down. I made no move to pick up the poison. My heart beat sickly in my chest and silver spots danced up and down before my eyes. Blood thudded in my eardrums and I wanted to throw up. I knew I would never, ever drink hot chocolate again after this cup. Never.

"There's a cancer in our Great Pack, dear one," he said, his eyes fixed on the poison bottle.

"You should know. You're one of the cancerous cells." I squeezed my hands into fists, nails digging into my palms. The pain was bright white and dazzling, like the silver spots dancing in front of my eyes.

"Is it Jonathan? Did he help you kill Grey and Elena?" My voice sounded high and shrill and I struggled to control it.

Grandfather Tobias was too canny to look at me and let me read the yes or the no in his eyes. He was too smart to even move. He just sat there, head bowed, gaze fixed on the bottle of coniine as I went through all their names—an accusing litany, an impossible song, an agonized plea.

He went somewhere else inside of himself and gave me nothing. Not one thing. Not that I'd thought he would.

Picking up the glass bottle, I recklessly yanked out the cork stopper and was lucky I didn't spill the whole damn thing all over myself. Not a drop escaped.

Grandfather Tobias watched me empty the contents into his steaming cup of hot chocolate. He waited for me to stopper the bottle and put it on the tray. His gaze remained fixed on me as I picked up my cup and took the first sip.

I was right. Kathy Manning had outdone herself. It was the best cup of hot chocolate I'd ever tasted. Would the coniine make his taste bitter? I decided it would. A shame, really, because it was damn good hot chocolate.

Grandfather Tobias reached out a remarkably steady hand and picked up his cup.

I let him raise it to his lips, fighting myself against knocking it away.

*What are you doing? What are you doing, Stanzie? What are you doing? You're not going to let him do it, are you? You aren't!* I argued with myself as I sat stiff as a statue watching the cup get closer and closer to his mouth.

*There's still time. He hasn't taken a sip. There's time to stop him. Stop him, Stanzie! Stop him!*

I bit my lip to keep from crying out. My fingernails dug crescent moons into the flesh of my palms. I smelled blood. My blood. But I felt nothing. No pain because I was a statue.

"I'm glad it was you to give me this," said Grandfather Tobias. Then, before I could stop him because time which had been going so slow abruptly sped up faster than I could follow, he swallowed every last drop of the hot chocolate in two, steady swallows.

He couldn't help but grimace at the bitterness. He put the cup down, and snatched up the wooden box so he could clutch it tightly. It was obvious he wanted it in his hands when he closed his eyes for the last time.

"I wouldn't have liked to have had one of those Councilors watch me die, dear one. They aren't family like you."

*I'm nothing to you*, I wanted to protest, but I couldn't speak.

It was strange—coniine paralyzes the central nervous system and death occurs because the victim literally can't draw a breath—muscles won't work—yet he was the one talking and moving and I was the one who was paralyzed.

I watched him for a long time. He stared back at me. Neither of us said a word, we just waited.

"The sooner you forgive me, the sooner I can move on," he told me, smiling as if he knew I would never let him down.

He leaned back in his chair, the wooden box cradled in his hands, and his eyelids flickered a little. His movements were stiff and jerky. Something was wrong with his smell. It wasn't just fabric softener and his own scent now. It was the subtle smell of death just before it pounced.

"I don't know how to forgive you, Grandfather Tobias," I whispered. "You killed them. I miss them every single day. I was supposed to grow old with them and you took that away from me. I can't forgive that."

"Then you condemn me to walk." He struggled to form the words. "I did what I thought was right and good for the Pack. I'm not an evil man, Stanzie."

"Don't do this to me," I whimpered. "I would have taken care of you always. I loved you, Grandfather Tobias."

"I still love you. I never stopped loving you," he said.

A low groan burst out between my clenched lips. My paralysis broke and I was out of the chair in one fluid motion. I ran for the door, intending escape, but just as my hand closed around the knob I heard him plead.

"Don't make me die alone, Stanzie. I'm alone enough as it is. And so are you. Let me at least have your face as the last thing I see. Please."

I groaned again, but I returned to the chair and sank down into it. My legs felt rubbery and detached—limp and useless.

Grandfather Tobias tried to smile for me but one side of his face wouldn't cooperate. He slumped in his chair, his muscles locked and rigid, which was the only reason he didn't slide to the floor.

The smell of death intensified. Beneath it was fear—bright blue and shot through with snaking, flashing tendrils of red and putrid green. I could smell myself too. Sweat and perfume. Shampoo mixed with guilt and horror. I wanted to forgive him. I wished I could turn back the clock and take the poison away. I wanted to go back two and a half years and give him a chance not to sabotage the car. If only I could go back to the night of my birthday and try to do it over again and somehow get a different outcome. I wished I'd never met Liam Murphy or Jason Allerton. I wished I'd never gone to Paris, never met Rudi in the first place, never even been fucking born.

"I can smell you," he said, uncannily. "Four parts Dior, six parts u... nique...Stuh..."

"Stanzie," I finished for him as once again I watched the light leave someone's eyes and the body become a shell that housed nothing in particular.

His fingers remained rigid around the little wooden box and his mouth still formed my name but no sound emerged and never would again.

Grandfather Tobias was dead. By my hand. Forever and ever no turning back.

# Chapter 13

The fucking lock on the front door wouldn't budge. Somehow I'd left the room and gotten down the stairs, but damned if I could remember any of it.

Something heavy and woolen settled down over my shoulders. My coat.

"If you want to go outside, you need to wear a coat," said Murphy. He stood two feet behind me and had his coat on. "It's cold, Stanzie."

Another damn thing I had to fight. I fumbled with the sleeves and he helped me, his expression grave.

Behind him Allerton and Manning hovered. Their faces were somber.

"Gloves and a scarf too," said Murphy as if it fucking mattered a damn what I wore or if I stayed warm. Who frigging cared?

I made an impatient sound of protest. Murphy wound the scarf around my neck. For a moment, I fantasized that he wouldn't stop winding. Instead, he wound tighter and tighter and tighter until I couldn't breathe, until I strangled, and the black and silver spots in front of my eyes went dead dark as my body spasmed for the last time before it gave up.

But he didn't do that. He wound it around my throat loosely and stood back waiting for me to put on my gloves and when I did, he reached around me and casually manipulated the lock.

I flung open the door and a gust of frigid cold wind blasted in. Beneath the ten inches of snow that coated the stairs and sidewalk was a slick layer of ice and when my sneakered soles hit it, my feet went out from under me like I was a baby who didn't know how to walk.

Murphy grabbed my arm before I hit the stairs, snagged the iron railing with his free hand and somehow we both managed to keep our balance.

"You'd better get boots," he said to me, as the wind tried to tear the words away.

Fuck that. I had my balance again and a good sense of the ice and I was down the stairs in an instant. Once on the sidewalk, I bent my head against the blasting wind, and trudged forward. My Chucks slipped a little on the ice beneath the snow, but I didn't fall.

Murphy followed me. The Timberland boots I'd given him had soles that gripped much better than my Chucks. They were also waterproof. My Chucks, of course, were not.

Fucking piled-up snow made it impossible to push the wrought-iron gate open more than three or four inches. It was certainly not enough to let me out. Murphy tried to help but I was impatient. The ornamental fence was low enough to climb over. Murphy held his breath, clearly expecting me to skewer myself on the sharp spikes.

I didn't. I fell on my ass but was up before Murphy could make it over the fence to help me. He fell too. I didn't help him. I walked away.

It was frigging cold. Every breath seared my lungs and particles of ice formed on my eyelashes, while the wind scoured my cheeks.

I pulled my scarf over the lower part of my face. It smelled like wet wool with a faint undertaste of J'adore perfume.

"Four parts Dior, six parts unique Stanzie," I whispered. I couldn't even begin to count how many times Grandfather Tobias had said that to me. A hundred maybe? Five hundred? Never again though.

In the far distance snowplows ground their gears as they scraped the snow from the street. Flashing yellow lights pierced the gray afternoon darkness. The snow swirled down and I could hear it hitting my shoulders. I pulled up my hood and bulled through drifts up to my knees. Nothing as ephemeral as snow would beat me.

Murphy was my shadow, a second skin, doggedly trailing me, breath pluming white as he struggled to breathe the frigid air.

A siren wailed a few streets to the south. Ambulance? Police? For a terrible moment I thought the whole world knew I was a murderer and the police were out to arrest me. Put me behind bars where I would surely die. I didn't want to be confined. I didn't want to be trapped or muzzled or chained. I wanted to be free.

I wrapped my arms around my head and tried to block out the sound of the siren. Idiotically I thought if I couldn't hear it, they couldn't find me.

"Stanzie." Murphy's gloved fingers touched my arm. He didn't grab or restrain me, but still I whipped my arm away from him.

"Where are we going?" he asked me, letting his hand drop to his side. His black pea coat was dusted with snow and the ends of his gray scarf fluttered grimly in the winter wind.

He'd worn that same scarf the day we'd gone to the Eiffel Tower. We'd sat together on one of the wooden benches, shoulders brushing, as we read file after file filled with deaths and accidents that had befallen young members of the Great Pack. This was before we'd known about the conspiracy.

Snow sifted down into his eyes and he wiped it away with his gloved hand.

I took that opportunity to start walking again without answering him because I didn't know where we were going. If he'd asked me two weeks ago I would have thought I'd known but today, right now, in the middle of a snowstorm, I had no fucking clue.

A bus shelter loomed ahead out of the snowflakes. The buses weren't running of course, so there was nobody there.

The bench inside was scratched full of graffiti. The remains of someone's lunch lurked beneath it along with hard lumps of frozen gum.

Graffiti and scratches made by bored kids with nothing to do while they waited gouged the plastic windows.

An empty condom wrapper was stuck to a piece of gum and pressed to the back window. It was an odd statement but a deliberate one. Who in the hell would try to have sex in these temperatures? But then again, an empty condom wrapper did not prove there'd been sex.

Why did I have to think such stupid nonsense anyway? Maybe my guilt was destroying my goddamn sanity.

My feet were blocks of ice attached to my ankles. I sat on the bench before I fell. Beneath my wet jeans, my skin crawled with clammy goose bumps. My cheeks burned and a dull ache made my head throb. Even my goddamn earlobes hurt.

Murphy sat next to me, his hands jammed into his pockets. He shuddered against the wind, which tried its damndest to get inside the shelter, and partially succeeded too.

"If you want to take the bus, I think we've got a long wait," he predicted and I ignored him. I wondered if Grey and I had ever waited for the bus at this particular stop and concluded we had not. There were more places in the world where we hadn't been than where we had. This was just one of them.

We sat there in icy silence.

A snowplow scraped past, lights flashing yellow and white, muted through the plastic but enough to make me shut my eyes until it was past.

I stole a look at Murphy, at the way he sat so patient and still.

"Thank you," I said, making him startle upright on the bench. I grimaced. "I know I'm being terrible. I can't seem to help it, and I know that's no excuse, is it?"

His eyes were very dark as he turned his face to stare at me. For a moment I thought he wasn't going to say anything but then he did. "Stanzie, I swear to you on the Great Pack, on my ancestors, on everything that I hold most dear and sacred, I had nothing to do with Sorcha's death. Nothing. And the only involvement I have with the conspiracy is trying to end it."

I could smell his sincerity and beneath that, his fear. Fear of what? That I wouldn't believe him or that I'd sniff beneath the sincerity and find the rot that might exist?

"You didn't tell me the truth about Sorcha," I accused, my throat aching with the pain of such betrayal that I could barely breathe. It wasn't just his betrayal, it was everyone's.

"I never lied. I told you the truth about how I felt about her. The only thing I didn't exactly say is that she didn't feel the same way back. That wasn't lying." His mouth twisted and he took a deep breath, as if preparing himself to face something brutal. "Don't you understand? I was ashamed to tell you. I knew how much Grey and Elena loved you and I was ashamed to tell you that it wasn't like that for me. All I ever hear from you is Grey and Elena, Grey and Elena. I was jealous and ashamed and I don't know, Stanzie, I don't think it has to ruin everything between us, does it?"

"Grey and Elena probably hid secrets from me too," I said bitterly and he sighed. "They're not who I thought they were either. They can't be." I gave a ragged little laugh and saw him clench his gloved fists.

"You're going to let that old man poison what you had with them, aren't you? You're going to let that old bastard win."

"It's not a question of winning or losing, it's a question of reality. Of perspective, Murphy. Nobody is who I thought they were. Not you, not Allerton, not Grandfather Tobias, not anybody. Why should Grey and Elena be exempt just because they're dead?"

"If I'd had anything half as special as you had, I'd fight for it. I'd never let anyone tear it down with their bullshit scare tactics and propaganda. Jesus Christ, they loved you. Do you know how lucky you were to have had that? I've never had that. I'd give anything to have that."

He was such an impossible liar. If that's what he really wanted, why did he push me away every time I tried to get close enough to give it to him? He didn't want it. At least not from me.

At that sobering thought, I jumped to my feet and plunged out into the snow storm. No sense in freezing to fucking death just because the world was full of liars.

Murphy followed me probably because he had nowhere else to go either.

* * * *

The warmth of the foyer was like a wet kiss when I staggered through the front door of the safe house. I gasped aloud and tore off my snowy outer garments. My Chucks were ruined, and I kicked them aside, curling my lip in disgust.

Murphy stamped snowy footprints onto the welcome mat and I followed his gaze to see Allerton and Kathy Manning emerge from the front room. They both had wine glasses in hand.

"Stanzie, you look frozen. Come upstairs and I'll run you a bath," ordered Kathy. Damn. The last place I wanted to go was upstairs where Grandfather Tobias's dead body presumably remained, but she was a Councilor and I was weak, tired and very cold, so I did what she said and left Murphy behind without a backward glance.

While she fussed with the tub, I shed my clothes, kicking them into a corner of the bathroom by the shower stall. The second the tub was full I sank beneath the concealing vanilla-scented bubbles. The hot water stung my cold skin and I welcomed the pain because it drove away some of the fogginess that clogged my head.

I thought she'd leave me in peace, but instead she picked up my discarded clothing and deposited it neatly into a wicker hamper.

"I've got some chicken soup in the freezer. I thought I'd heat that up with some of the bread I just baked and we'd have that for dinner along with a salad. Will you eat that, Stanzie?"

I made a rude face at her. "Why the hell are you so hung up on food? You're skinny as a rail but all you do is cook."

She merely smiled at me.

"And does anything make you stop smiling? Jesus, it's like living with the Cheshire fucking Cat, I swear."

"I know you're grumpy, dear. Would you like some brandy? And maybe some chocolate? I always like brandy and dark chocolate when I take a bubble bath. It's so decadent somehow."

"Chocolate?" A shudder of revulsion twisted my spine. "I am never going to eat, drink, or hopefully, smell chocolate ever again."

"How about a cookie then? I have some sugar cookies left." The bitch was unfazed. I nodded. Anything to get her the hell out of the bathroom so I could bathe in peace.

Smiling, she drifted out of the room and I scooped up a fistful of bubbles and water and threw it after her, timing it so she didn't see. It landed nowhere near the door or her body and didn't do the slightest bit of good at dispelling my foul mood. If anything, it intensified it.

She was back all too goddamn soon with brandy and a plateful of cookies. She handed me the glass of brandy and waited for me take it and a cookie before she retired to the sink, where she perched on the counter and nibbled hers. So much for being left in peace.

"Does your bond mate know you're sleeping with Allerton?" I asked in my nastiest voice, hoping to drive her away. All she did was smile at me as if I were a petulant child who needed a nap and continued to nibble at her cookie.

I took a huge swallow of brandy and it burned like hell on the way down. Had the coniine burned when Grandfather Tobias swallowed it?

I set the glass on the side of the tub and squeezed my eyes shut so I wouldn't cry. I was damned if I would cry in front of Kathy Manning.

"He knows," she answered me when she finished nibbling her cookie. She was like a goddamn mouse, nibble, nibble, nibble. She couldn't even take a proper big bite. I'd finished my cookie in three bites. I never nibbled at anything.

"He's got his own mistress," she continued as she contemplated the cookies left on the plate before selecting a Christmas tree-shaped one. Again with the nibbling. I could feel my blood pressure skyrocketing so I averted my eyes in the vain attempt to distract myself. I could still hear her, though. Her little sharp mouse teeth nibble, nibble, nibbling away.

"Sounds like a great relationship," I remarked and she laughed to herself.

"We've been bonded nearly thirty years, Stanzie," she answered. "Things get a little..."

"Boring?" I finished for her. My tone was belligerent because I was secretly terrified. Would Grey eventually have gotten bored with me after thirty years? Was Murphy already bored after only two months? It wasn't fair. It was not fucking fair. I hated the world at that moment. Everything on earth could go fuck itself.

"I was going to say predictable, but boring will do, I suppose," she mused. "So you do things to liven it up. Matt and I compare notes and that usually turns us on and we're all over each other. I thank my lucky stars for meeting Jason. He's brought me back to being close to Matt again. I didn't realize how much I'd missed him until after I started sleeping with Jason."

"Do I want to hear this?" I was relatively certain I so fucking did not.

"You asked." She extended the plate of cookies and, despite myself, I took another one. Treacherously sweet. Just like the woman who'd baked them.

"When did you start sleeping with Councilor Allerton?" I stuffed the whole cookie in my mouth to shut me the fuck up but it was too late.

"Oh, about a month after we met. Here at the safe house two and a half years ago."

I flushed. They'd met during my interrogation.

"Well, I'm sure you gave my dilemma your full attention and weren't too distracted with carnal thoughts while you were supposed to be listening to my story," I muttered and she smiled at me brightly.

"It was strictly business between us, Stanzie. I did give your dilemma my fullest attention. And I've already apologized for coming to the wrong conclusion."

"Well, that's makes everything all right then, fine," I snarled.

"I wish you would forgive me." She set aside her half-nibbled cookie and regarded me fondly. "You're so passionate about everything. I admire that about you. Everything's life or death to you, isn't it? Me, I've always been somewhere in the middle. I don't experience the highs you do. Or the lows, thankfully. I try not to feel sorry for you."

"Oh, well, thank you very much, Councilor Manning." I pulled the plug on the tub because it was obvious she wasn't going to leave me alone. I needed to run away from her. This was pure hell.

"I've insulted you when I was trying to express how much I admire you. I wish you would listen to what I'm saying instead of feeling sorry for yourself. You're not the first person who's had to act as executioner in this Great Pack of ours, you know. We have our laws. You know them, presumably."

"He was supposed to go to Florida. His pack voted to exile him, not put him to death," I snapped as I reached for a towel.

Kathy Manning ran her slanted elfish gaze across my nude body and I felt unaccountably self-conscious. I was a huge stork in comparison with her. Why did she have to be so petite and perfect, damn her?

"The Great Council and the Regional Council of New England outrank the local pack. There was a secret vote, as you well know, and he was condemned to death. You broke no laws doing what you did. You performed a service to the Great Pack. It was also your right, considering the fact that he caused the death of your bond mates."

"I thought you said you knew I know our laws." I gave her a dirty look as I wrapped the towel around my body. "Why do you have to lecture me about them if you know I know them?"

"Because you're acting like you don't," she said with another patented Manning smile.

I briskly toweled myself dry while she watched me.

"So I didn't break any goddamn laws," I all but shouted at her. She was impossible to ignore. "It doesn't make what I did any easier to take. Maybe for you! Maybe for someone who doesn't experience any highs or lows, maybe you're the ones who ought to be the fucking executioners in this Great Pack of ours. Maybe people like me make sucky executioners."

"I would think for someone who sees only black and white, up or down, right or wrong, this would have been a piece of cake for you." Kathy Manning regarded me as if I were a bug squirming on the end of a pin just before expiring.

"Yeah, you'd think," I said bitterly. I stomped into the bedroom to find clothes to wear.

# Chapter 14

Murphy and Allerton sat in the front room when I clattered down the stairs. Allerton was drinking wine as he read a book on the sofa. Murphy stared out the bay window at the snowy darkness. He had a glass of wine too, but it was full and I half suspected he'd forgotten he even held it.

The wine bottle was on the glass-topped coffee table with an empty glass and a plate of cheese sticks that did not come out of a box but had been twisted together by Kathy Manning. The woman was relentless.

That didn't stop me from scooping up a handful of the damn things. They were light and crunchy and melted in my mouth. Cheddar cheese and herbs—simple things but she managed to make them taste like magic.

I poured myself wine and ignored Allerton's blue eyes as he stared at me above his book. Murphy didn't turn around from his contemplation of the snow.

"I want to go back to Boston," I said to Allerton then took a huge gulp of the wine.

"There's the funeral to attend first," he replied.

My jaw dropped. "I'm supposed to go the funeral of a man I murdered?"

"You didn't murder him," Murphy snarled from behind me.

"I suppose he was just the slightest bit complicit in his own death. He watched me pour the poison into his cup and he drank it anyway, but he still died by my hand. That makes me a murderer." I helped myself to another handful of cheese sticks and took them to the farthest corner of the room where I could get away from Murphy and Allerton.

"You were acting as the Hand of the Great Council," Allerton explained to me.

"I heard all this upstairs from Councilor Manning. You can make it sound as flowery and noble as you like, but it doesn't change the fact I killed him."

"It's our law. It's our way." Allerton sighed and set aside his book. He picked up his wine glass and walked toward me. I had nowhere to go— my back was literally against the wall.

"You accepted the task, Constance." His handsome face loomed closer and closer until I felt trapped and wanted to hit out and scream, but instead I took another big sip of wine.

"He said he was grateful that he got to die with someone he loved. Can you believe that shit?" I muttered, swiping my free hand across my eyes. They burned with tears but I did not want to cry. I so did not want to cry.

"You were compassionate, Stanzie," said Allerton and that did it. I had not been compassionate, I'd been awful and paralyzed and accusatory and bitter and mean and, shit, the man had killed Grey and Elena. He'd been lucky I hadn't torn him apart with my fingernails.

I burst into ugly tears. Allerton took my wine glass away and put it somewhere. The next thing I knew he was holding me, his arms strong and supportive around me while I wailed into his shoulder.

The second Allerton knew I had control again, he let me go and stepped back. His expression was grave and full of empathy and I felt ashamed of myself.

"I can't do anything right," I complained and he took hold of my chin so I was forced to look him in the face.

"You did fine. You did exceptionally well."

I almost started crying again, only that's when I realized Murphy had left the room.

* * * *

Murphy didn't come to dinner. It was just Kathy Manning, Allerton and me seated in the Colonial dining room. They made small talk between them while I silently devoured two bowls of chicken soup and five pieces of bread. I drank water instead of wine because I didn't want to get drunk. I'd fall apart for sure even worse than I already had if I got drunk.

There was hot apple cobbler for dessert with a scoop of real vanilla bean ice cream on top. When I tasted it I knew Murphy would have loved it. He had a sweet tooth, Murphy did. I loved to watch his face when he tasted something especially sweet and delicious because the most incredible smile of contentment drifted across his mouth as he chewed and swallowed.

Halfway through, I put my spoon down and excused myself from the table.

Allerton and Kathy Manning watched me leave the room but didn't say anything.

Murphy sprawled across the bed upstairs—one arm curled around his head, the other straight to his side. He stared at the ceiling and didn't look at me when I walked in.

I was incredibly tired. All the adrenaline in my blood had deserted me and left me weak and disjointed. All I wanted to do was crawl onto the bed beside him and curl up against him so I could sleep the rest of my life away.

But then I remembered that a dead man lay across the hall and I gulped back dismayed tears. If I hadn't been so goddamn tired, I would have punched something.

"I can't sleep here in this house," I whined to Murphy, who had yet to even acknowledge me. "I can't do it, Murphy. Give me the car keys. I'll sleep in the car."

"You'll freeze in the car," he said, still staring at the ceiling. "Stanzie, it's about twelve degrees out there. Be serious."

"I am serious. I can't sleep here." My voice wobbled and grew very high pitched. "I'm so tired and I can't sleep here!"

"I'm tired too. I think I've gotten about four hours of sleep the past two nights. If that." He cast me a bitter look. "It's stupid, but I can't sleep without you in the bed with me. That's so goddamn dumb."

"It is nice to have someone to sleep with again," I allowed. "I'd forgotten how much better I sleep with somebody else in the bed with me. It's the same for you too, huh?"

Another bitter look followed, this one tinged with something almost akin to hate. "I've never slept in the same bed with anybody else before you. I guess that's another lie I've let you believe, isn't it? That Sorcha actually deigned to sleep in the same bed with me? Oh, we had sex, Stanzie. But always in my bed and she always left afterward. Said she didn't like sharing, getting too hot, being crowded."

I stared at him, aghast. "That woman was so cold. How the hell did you fall for somebody so cold? You're not cold, Murphy."

"Yeah? I'm intellectual. I analyze everything. I don't feel. Those are words you've said to me, remember?"

"I said the only time you let yourself feel was for her. And now I understand even better why you're so closed off now. But you're not cold."

"Closed off is better than cold?" He gave me a sardonic look then returned his gaze to the ceiling. "Good night, see you in the morning."

Jesus. I did not want to sleep alone. I was so tired I couldn't think and I didn't want to sleep alone. I stared at him for a moment, but, of course, he didn't say anything, so I left the room and went across the hall to the bedroom next to Grandfather Tobias's. My hand closed around the doorknob but I couldn't make myself twist it open.

The door was cold against my back as I slowly sank to the floor and drew my knees up to my chest. I covered my face with my hands and sobbed as quietly as I could so the whole goddamn world wouldn't hear me. Would this fucking day never end?

Murphy's door opened a few minutes later and I smelled his cologne mixed with his remorse and frustration.

"Stanzie, come back in here. You don't have to sleep alone. I'm sorry. I'm so goddamn tired, I'm being an asshole, I know."

I lifted my tearstained face. He reached out a hand.

His fingers were warm against mine as he helped me to my feet.

"Will anything ever be the same again?" I asked him and he gave me a sad smile as he shook his head. He didn't know either.

In the bedroom, he shut off all the lights and turned the gas fire down. I stripped off to my underwear and crawled beneath the covers, shivering a little even though it was not cold. I curled up on my side and shut my eyes.

The mattress sank beneath his weight and he was beneath the covers too. His arm stole across my waist and I wriggled backward until my body fitted against his.

We both sighed then everything, for me at least, went dark.

# Chapter 15

Ten hours later I woke to the pleasurable sensation of Murphy's lips against the back of my neck. I wriggled against him so I could fit the hard length of his erection against my ass. I bit my lip when he moved his hand between my legs. He slipped a finger beneath my panties and stroked me until a rush of desire made me wet.

With practiced ease he removed my panties and slid into me from behind. We both groaned aloud as he penetrated deeper and deeper until he was all the way inside me. I couldn't see his face, and not being able to see his expression was erotic somehow. One of his hands was tangled in my hair to hold me still while he kept the other between my legs so he could tease me with his fingers.

At first he moved slowly, very slowly as I braced myself on my knees and reached out for the headboard to stabilize myself. When he knew I was steady, he moved faster, harder and I could hear him panting, his breath hot in my ear. He bit my earlobe and I moaned because that always drove me crazy.

He skimmed his hand up my body, gliding his fingers across my belly and then he undid the fastening to my bra and tossed it away. He let go of my hair so he could cup my breasts with both his hands as he moved his mouth to my neck.

Murphy talked in Irish to me as he fucked me. I had no idea what he said, but it was sexy as hell. I was so goddamned in love with him.

"Talk to me," I begged when he fell silent. I needed to hear his voice. I couldn't see his face, but if I could hear his voice, I knew I'd come so hard I'd scream.

He murmured my name, bit my earlobe again and moved faster. He was so hot inside me, so hard. I cried out and all but crushed the headboard between my fingers.

Normally, at this point, he grabbed me by the hair and jerked my head back, but this time he didn't do that and I knew it was because he was worried about the bump on the back of my skull. He didn't want to hurt me.

As my orgasm built inside me, I could feel *her* too, my wolf, waking, somehow coming alive through the sweat and saliva and the heat between our bodies.

"Stanzie," he said urgently. "Stanzie."

He bit my neck hard, and the pain and pleasure of it sent me hurtling over the edge. Waves of bliss rolled over me and I bucked wildly beneath him, catching him up, and he cried out too. Hot semen jetted into me and I came again. This orgasm was not as intense as the first, but somehow sweeter and more sublime because I was with him at the same time and we were together.

I collapsed to the mattress, soaked with perspiration, and felt the weight of his body as he allowed himself to come down on top of me, his face buried between my shoulder and neck. His skin was hot. We were slippery with each other's sweat and scent.

"Jaysus God, that was good." He rolled off me onto his back.

I lay unmoving on my stomach, my blood hot in my face, hands and toes. Love made me so giddy I had to shut my eyes.

A moment later he moved the sweaty hair away from my cheek.

"Are you all right? I didn't hurt your head did I?" His voice was soft and so concerned.

I was right. He had been worried about hurting my head.

Smiling into my pillow I murmured, "I can't even feel my head. I can feel my toes though. Why is it I can only really feel my toes after an orgasm, Liam?"

"Damned if I know." His fingers were gentle against my face as he tucked my hair behind my ear.

He got up first to take a shower and I followed a few minutes later. The shower stall was large and, judging by the dual showerheads, built for two.

Murphy obligingly moved over to let me in, but he didn't touch me. He concentrated on washing his hair and, before I'd even lathered mine, he was out on the bathmat, toweling dry.

Beneath the steady thrum of the water, I heard his electric razor and I hummed to myself as I rinsed the shampoo from my hair.

\* \* \* \*

Allerton stood at the bottom of the staircase, cellphone pressed to his ear as he paced the parquet flooring. "I'm very sorry to have to tell you this, Jonathan. Your grandfather passed away last night." My euphoric mood evaporated as if it had never existed.

To my credit, I only faltered for a second between one step and the next. Murphy noticed because he noticed every damn thing. He reached out to steady me in case I fell, but I evaded his hand because I was not going to tumble down the damn stairs. Sometimes his protectiveness irked the shit out of me.

Kathy Manning presided over the breakfast table in the dining room. Belgian waffles with four different kinds of topping: strawberries, maple syrup, blueberries and Nutella.

The smell of the chocolate in the Nutella made my stomach clench and I shot her a dirty look which only made her smile at me.

"Hot chocolate?" she asked Murphy. She held a white china teapot in her hands and I'm damned if it wasn't the very one I'd used the day before in Grandfather Tobias's room.

Any appetite I had left vanished, but I sat anyway because I wanted coffee.

Murphy forked two huge waffles onto his plate and went straight for the Nutella like I knew he would. He watched me go into the kitchen with my coffee mug but he didn't say anything.

When I came back with a full mug, half of one of his waffles was gone and the other half didn't look long for this world.

"Aren't you going to eat?" He raised an eyebrow at me when he noticed that all I was doing was gulping coffee. I shook my head.

His brow knotted and he looked as if he didn't want to ask but he forced himself to anyway. "You don't want ketchup on the damn waffles, do you? Even you wouldn't do that, would you now?"

My face must have reflected complete revulsion because he looked relieved and amused. "Want some of mine?" He generously tried to give me his second waffle but I hastily moved my plate away.

"Stanzie has decided to put a moratorium in place against chocolate and all chocolate-related products," Kathy Manning declared with a feisty smile that made me want to get up and belt her right in the mouth.

Of course Allerton walked in at that exact second and his startled expression was almost as priceless as Murphy's.

"You make me sound like such an idiot," I complained. She smiled serenely and poured hot chocolate in Allerton's mug as he sat at the head of the table.

"You're really not eating anything chocolate?" Murphy gaped at me and stared at his Nutella-smeared waffle with both longing and guilt. I couldn't stand it.

"Oh, for Christ's sake," I snarled and snagged a forkful of his damn waffle and stuffed it into my mouth before I could change my mind.

The chocolate coated my tongue and, for a moment, I saw Grandfather Tobias lifting the poison cup to his mouth. But then he was gone and I became aware that I was starving.

Both men pretended to be very invested in their own plates as I speared my own Belgian waffle and liberally coated it with maple syrup. Kathy Manning made no such pretense and instead watched me with a knowing smile. I gave her a deadly sarcastic grin back then drained my coffee and held out the empty mug so she could fill it with hot chocolate.

Allerton hid what I suspected was a smile behind his napkin, while Murphy kept his head down as he demolished the rest of his plate.

"Women," I heard him mutter. "I'll never get the hang of them."

\* \* \* \*

"The funeral has been set for tomorrow morning at ten," Allerton informed us when we'd finished eating and were relaxing with coffee.

"Murphy, how about you and I leave for Boston at nine?" I suggested and he grinned at me from over the rim of his coffee mug.

"Aren't you going to attend? I thought we went over this yesterday," said Allerton.

"You want me to go to the funeral so I can possibly smoke out whoever else in Riverglow was involved in Grey and Elena's deaths, right?" I knew I sounded surly but I couldn't help it. Or maybe I could but didn't want to.

"Do I get any input into this at all?" Murphy wondered, all the amusement gone from his expression. He set down his empty mug and gave the whole table a belligerent smile.

"I'm always ready to hear what you have to say," Allerton said, which made Murphy snort. "Within reason, Liam."

"Is it within reason to say that I don't want Stanzie staked out like some sacrificial goat in your game of flushing the predator, Councilor?" Murphy's eyes were very dark and intense and I was glad he wasn't looking at me.

"What would you have me do?" Allerton asked him. "I don't know this pack, Liam, she does. She's in a unique position to ferret out the truth, and isn't that what I've asked the both of you to do as my Advisors? Ferret out the truth, however unpalatable it may prove?"

"I thought putting our necks on the line ended after I had my goddamn stomach pumped in Houston," snapped Murphy. "Why is it that I reckon none of your previous Advisors routinely risked their lives as a part of their job description? Why is it just us?"

"I would have thought it was obvious that these are different times and desperate circumstances." Allerton's blue eyes were steady and grim as he and Murphy glared at each other across the table—two Alpha males scrabbling for dominance.

"I've lost one bond mate to these different times and desperate circumstances, Councilor. I don't intend to lose another one. Just so we're clear."

"Sorcha had no goddamn idea what was going on. Give me a little credit, Murphy. I'm not helpless and you don't own me," I said.

All the blood slammed into Murphy's face for a moment. Then it all ebbed out, leaving him pale and furious, his jaw rock hard.

The look he gave me was full of betrayal. "Fine. What I want matters fuck all, as usual. You do what you want. You will anyway, damn you." He shoved back his chair, threw his napkin down on the table and stalked out of the room.

The resulting appalled silence made my ears ring.

"He makes it sound like I constantly get my way and he never gets a goddamn thing." My mouth trembled and I pressed it shut. Now both Councilors were staring at me, which was precisely what I didn't want.

The front door slammed resoundingly and I cringed in my seat wondering where in the hell he was going and, worse, whether he would ever bother to come back.

"I tried to get Grandfather Tobias to tell me who was involved but he wouldn't." My napkin was coming to pieces between my fingers as I twisted and shredded it. "And maybe he was lying. Maybe nobody's involved. Only it's true that it's not just the grandmothers and grandfathers, so it's probably true that somebody else was in on it from Riverglow. I don't know what the fuck he wants from me. He's the one who wanted to be an Advisor. I wanted to go to Dublin and just be in a pack. He's the one who wanted this, not me. But now I'm in it and I'm not quitting. He can't ask me to quit just because this time it's me who's in the most danger. And anyway, who says that I am? Jesus, he's so paranoid. So goddamn paranoid. I'm not dumb. I'm not going to do anything stupid."

I jumped to my feet, ignoring Allerton when he tried to call me back. Instead I ran down the hall and out the front door. I had no idea what the hell I thought I could do, but the last thing I expected to see was Murphy shoveling snow off the front steps.

"What the hell are you doing?" I blurted, grabbing onto the stair rail to keep from plunging headlong into him.

He stopped and stared at me. "What the hell does it look like I'm doing? I'm shoveling snow. I'm pretending the snow is Councilor Jason Allerton's smug face and I figure it's going to take me less than an hour to clear this whole goddamn lot because that's how friggin' pissed off I am. You want to make something of it? And what the hell are you doing out here without a coat? You want to die of pneumonia before someone in that fucking ex-pack of yours kills you first?"

I gaped at him for a moment, trying to catch my breath. My heart thudded sickly in my chest. "Are all Irish bastards as melodramatic as you, or are you just being an asshole?" I wondered and for a moment it hung in the balance whether he would throw the shovel at me or burst out laughing.

I relaxed just a little bit when I saw his mouth twitch and the next thing I knew we were both almost hysterical.

Sometimes that's the way it was with us.

# Chapter 16

The sky was so vitally blue it seared my eyes. I shaded them with my hand and wished I had sunglasses.

Murphy and I were in the Honda, following Allerton and Kathy Manning in her sporty, bright-green Jaguar.

Sunlight bounced off the still-white snow covering the sidewalks and yards of the houses and office buildings in Hartford as we made our way to the funeral home in East Haddam where Grandfather Tobias's body had been cremated.

Murphy wore the same suit he'd worn to the dinner. He had exchanged the tie for a more sober gray one and he looked remote and unhappy as he concentrated on the road.

I had on a basic black wool dress with silver buttons down the front all the way to the hem, which reached mid calf. Black stockings and black boots completed my ensemble. My bond pendant and a pair of silver stud earrings were my only jewelry.

It was a hard struggle not to feel like a complete hypocrite for attending this funeral. I wasn't doing a very good job and, as we merged onto the highway and the snow on the side of the road turned slushy and dirty, I wished we could keep going and head back to Boston.

Murphy was thinking the same thing, judging by his grim expression. I knew better than to talk to him when he was in this mood, although I wished he would talk to me.

Anything was better than the oppressive silence that wrapped the car in an invisible web as sticky and deadly as a spider's.

I could see the back of Jason Allerton's dark head in the car in front of us. I thought about the conversation we'd had after breakfast. My stomach knotted.

Although it was Kathy Manning's car, Allerton drove. She perched beside him, her head tilted toward the window as if she were tired but maybe she was just resting, bracing herself for the hell to come. She'd prepared the fatal dose of poison. She should be feeling some sort of reaction to her role in this whole damn nightmare.

The Pack did not own the funeral home. However, there would be no Others there today. One of the New Hampshire pack's members was a mortician, and he'd arranged to take over the crematorium. He'd been there for Grey's and Elena's funerals too.

Pack were nearly always cremated. We took the ashes of our dead and scattered them in the woods where we'd all run together as wolves.

It had been summer when I'd scattered Grey's and Elena's ashes in the woods of the Devil's Hopyard, a state park in the same small town as the funeral home. Riverglow had loved to run there at night together. We knew every square inch of the eight-mile stretch of woods and fields, brooks and bridges. We'd be scattering Grandfather Tobias's ashes there too.

I stole a glance at Murphy and wondered if he were thinking about scattering Sorcha's ashes somewhere in the green hills of Ireland. He probably was. It was a natural association.

He had the faintest ghost of a bruise on his cheek and a little split in his lower lip that was only noticeable if I was close to him—the only outward signs of the after dinner fiasco of the other night. The inward signs and scars were legion though, and not so easily healed, I suspected.

Silence crackled between us. I kept my head down and my hands clenched together in my lap.

Sometimes we hadn't talked, Murphy and I, when we'd been on the road visiting cities between Houston and Boston. But the silence then had been restful and easy. He'd concentrated on driving or the song on the CD and I'd watched the trees and fields blur past as the road unspooled beneath us. Everything had been magical because most of our lives were on hold and we were free.

Well, we weren't free now and our lives were most definitely not on hold. It occurred to me that maybe Murphy and I existed best in the spaces between time, between responsibility and day to day living. Maybe we would never figure out how to relate when time mattered and life was not one big road trip and instead little bites of reality and pain.

The car slowed as Murphy took the exit for East Haddam. We flashed down a road crowded by a rocky hillside, across a shining silver bridge that spanned the Connecticut River, past the Goodspeed Opera House with its gables and widow's walk and into the heart of the town.

There wasn't as much snow piled up in the yards and sidewalks here because we were close to the shore, but there was still quite a bit of accumulation.

The Rosewood Funeral Home was also gabled and had a widow's walk, just like the opera house. It was on the riverbank and had tall, forbidding dark windows and a shiny black front door with an imperious lion's head knocker.

Three cars were already in the small parking lot. Murphy parked between Kathy Manning's Jaguar and a gold Toyota Camry. I was out onto the carefully sanded asphalt before he could take the keys out of the ignition and hurried to stand with Allerton and Kathy Manning, squinting against the sun reflected off the snow.

We waited for Murphy to join us then Allerton strode to the imposing black door and opened it.

The scent of flowers, chemicals and death wafted out and I wanted to gag. I squeezed my eyes shut and kept moving.

Murphy struggled against the smell too. Allerton and Kathy Manning seemed impervious to it. Or maybe they were just older and better equipped to block out strong scents.

It was cold as ice inside the front foyer, which wasn't surprising since the floor was Italian tile and the fireplace was ornamental only.

Several occasional tables were crowned with huge arrangements of funeral flowers and beneath the bow window was a long sea foam green sofa. Callie, Vaughn, Peter and Nora sat on it, all dressed in black, with their coats on, huddled against the cold.

Jonathan stood beneath a portrait of one of the founding fathers of the funeral home—a dour gentleman with improbable side whiskers and a paunch. Jonathan studied the man's belly as if it were a personal affront and when he heard our footsteps on the Italian tile, he turned around.

The instant he saw me, his face turned black with wrath. His eyes were red rimmed and very dark. An unwanted surge of sympathy washed over me but before I could say anything, he stabbed a finger in my direction. "You!" he screamed, choleric with rage. His voice was so loud it hurt my ears and the Italian tiles gave it an acoustic boost it did not need. I was sure the whole state of Connecticut heard him. "What the fuck are you doing here? Get out of here, you little hypocritical bitch!"

He swung around to face his pack mates, nearly dancing with fury.

"What the fuck is this? You knew she was coming and you didn't bother to tell me? Fuck you. I may not be Alpha anymore but I damn sure count more than that bitch over there. I deserve a little bit of respect. He was my grandfather, for Christ's sake, and this is how you treat me? Fuck you. Fuck all of you!"

"Jonathan, calm down," said Callie in a very soft voice.

Nora, beside her, looked like she might burst into terrified tears. Her eyes were glazed, and once again, from several feet away, I could smell the booze on her breath and soaking through her skin. Being drunk at your bond mate's grandfather's funeral was not good. I felt another horrible surge of pity for Jonathan and wondered why they all sat together and he stood alone and isolated.

"Don't tell me to calm down, Callie, goddamn you!" Jonathan shouted. "She's a hypocrite for coming here, can't you see that? He's not even a pack mate of hers. What's she doing here?"

"We're not pack mates of his either," Vaughn pointed out grimly and that only made Jonathan more furious.

"Technically we are. It's not your birthday yet, it wouldn't have been official until your birthday!" Little flecks of saliva dotted Jonathan's mouth and he swiped at his eyes with his coat sleeve.

To my horror I realized he was crying, he was so upset.

"He killed her bond mates. She has no reason to be here!"

"He killed our pack mates and we're still here," said Vaughn, his eyes dark and hard. "Sit down, Jonathan, and stop being such an asshole. You barely spoke to the old man when he was alive. All this melodramatic pseudo grief now that he's dead is the real hypocrisy, if you ask me."

Stunned, Jonathan stared at him. He looked like a little puppy who'd been kicked into a corner. More tears leaked out of the corners of his eyes.

"He's feeling guilty he didn't pay the old man more attention," Vaughn said to us all. Angry and disgusted, he drove a hand through his hair. "We don't have to put up with his crap, today of all days. Sit down, Stanzie. Alfred's down in the crematorium getting the ashes and we're all going to go to the Devil's Hopyard and scatter them together. And there's not going to be any bullshit scenes, Jonathan, you understand? Or I will kick your ass."

Jonathan swallowed so hard, his throat clicked audibly.

He looked around the room for allies and found none. Abruptly, he lunged for the door and was gone.

"Motherfucker," muttered Vaughn, getting to his feet. "I warned him."

"No," I spoke up. He froze. "Tobias was his blood relation and his pack mate, Vaughn."

"You know firsthand how he ignored the old man, Stanzie," Vaughn argued with me, his mouth tight. "You were more of a grandchild to that man than Jonathan ever was. This is a joke, this parade of grief. It's guilt, just like I said."

"So it's guilt more than grief," I said. "At least he's feeling something."

"I'll go get him." Peter started to get up, but I stopped him too.

"Let me try," I said and they all gaped at me.

"He might take a swing at you, Stanzie, better bring your bond mate. Maybe he can take the first shot," Vaughn suggested and both Murphy and I paled at the insult.

"I can take care of myself," I snapped.

Vaughn snorted. "Against Jonathan? I'm sure you can. Be my guest, but if he does manage to actually hit you, don't come crying to me."

"Nobody will come crying to you, you cold unfeeling bastard," Nora snarled at him. Then she took a silver flask from her black purse and guzzled from it.

"Jesus," said Vaughn half under his breath. "Welcome to our dysfunctional little pack, Councilors." He gave Allerton and Kathy Manning a sarcastic grin but I didn't wait to hear if either of them replied.

Outside in the cold parking lot, Jonathan was hunched over the hood of the Camry, sobbing. I didn't know what to do.

Murphy, who was dogging my footsteps, nearly barreled into me when I stopped dead halfway across the lot.

Car doors slammed nearby and a moment later Colin Hunter, with Devon Talbot beside him, approached us.

"Need some help?" He looked between us and the sobbing Jonathan and sounded sincere. He and Murphy were careful not to make eye contact but Devon and I did and we both held our breaths.

"I think we've got it," Murphy said. His gaze flicked in Hunter's direction.

I looked at Colin Hunter too and saw that he had a faded black eye courtesy of Murphy's fist. Otherwise he was perfect, from his crisply curling hair to his Kenneth Cole boots.

Devon Talbot had very long hair. She'd worn it coiled at the back of her neck the first night I'd met her, but today her hair was long and loosely waved, obviously straightened. Her almond-shaped eyes were full of compassion as she looked toward Jonathan.

"Good to see you again, Stanzie. I'm only sorry it has to be under these circumstances." She gave me a subdued smile, squeezed my shoulder and nudged Colin in the direction of the front door.

He moved forward, gaze still locked with Murphy's. Devon nudged him again and he reluctantly turned around. Murphy continued to watch him go, his expression unreadable.

I waited until I was sure he wasn't going to do anything stupid, and walked over to Jonathan.

"You saw him, didn't you?" I guessed when I'd drawn close enough to touch him, only I didn't. "That's why you yelled at me, isn't it? Because you saw Grandfather Tobias standing there with me."

A fresh gust of tears wracked his body even as he violently shook his head.

"I don't know what the fuck you're talking about, Stanzie."

"Yes, you do. Grandfather Tobias told me you can see spirits. He could too. So could your mother."

"Bullshit." Jonathan's voice held no conviction.

"If you saw him, it's because of me. Because he can't rest until I forgive him. He told me he was going to walk until I did."

"Then he's gonna fucking walk a hell of a long time, isn't he?" Jonathan choked out. "He only killed your bond mates. Why the fuck would you forgive him?" He swung around then, his face streaked with tears, chest heaving. "He's not going to leave me alone, is he? I paid no attention to him when he was alive and now I won't be able to escape, will I?"

"I don't know," I said. Typical, selfish Jonathan. Some of my sympathy began to evaporate. He never saw anything but himself. He'd always been his own best friend and worst enemy.

"I did love him, you know." He swiped at his eyes again. I reached into my coat pocket and found a clean tissue. When I handed it to him, he took it. "I brought him with me to Riverglow. I didn't have to. They didn't even ask me to. I asked." He drew himself up to his full height and braced himself as if he thought I would argue with him or disbelieve him. "He just...he always lectured me about the old ways and it got boring, Stanzie, you know? Or maybe you don't because you always listened to him. You probably even liked listening to him, knowing you."

I smiled a little. "I did. Don't you agree with the old ways, Jonathan?"

Behind me, Murphy came to attention, very interested in the answer, in Jonathan's very reaction to the question.

"Oh, I don't fucking give a shit," said Jonathan with a petulant sigh. He wiped at his eyes with the tissue and grimaced. "Look at me. I work a dead-end retail job because I never went to college, never mixed with Others unless I had to. And what did it get me? This fucking stupid pack in the ass end of nowhere. But then Elena went to college and had a great job and she ended up here too. So old ways, new ways, what the fuck difference does any of it make? We're Pack. We go nowhere." He grimaced again, and I gave him an impulsive hug. He froze in my embrace for a moment, but then hugged me back. He buried his face in my neck and nearly choked on his tears.

"It fucking kills me you're the only one who understands." His eyes were bloodshot and full of baffled grief when he pulled away from me.

"He was your blood relative. Your only connection," I said and he nodded.

"You see," he said over my shoulder to Murphy. "She does get it."

"I know," said Murphy. "It's because she lost her connections. She knows how it feels."

"Nora may still be bonded with me, but I lost her the second our son died," said Jonathan, and shook his head. "I took her for granted the same way I took Grandfather Tobias. And now I've got shit and it's just what I probably deserve. Bet you think so, huh?" He gave me a belligerent grin, but there were tears in his eyes.

I almost told him then, that I'd killed his grandfather. I wanted to comfort him but I didn't want him to accept my comfort because I was guilty, so guilty. Somehow I kept my damn mouth shut, but it wasn't easy.

"If you could get Nora to stop drinking and feeling sorry for herself, you'd get her back," I predicted and Jonathan made a scoffing sound.

"I have tried to keep her away from the booze, Stanz. I've dumped more bottles of whiskey down the goddamn drain than I want to think about. She just buys more. And hides them. Every night when she passes out, I go all over the damn house to find her secret stashes but there's always one I seem to miss. I swear people are going behind my back to give her the shit. I'm paranoid, I know, but I think I've found it all and they come over to visit and the next thing I know she's shitfaced and locked in the bathroom with a bottle of Wild Turkey."

"They? All of them?" I wondered. "Or someone specific?"

Murphy took my elbow and gave it a warning squeeze, I'm sure to tell me not to press so hard.

"Ah, they come over in pairs mostly, but sometimes all of them. I don't know if anybody's giving her stuff. I just said that because I'm paranoid, because I can't make her stop and right now it's a toss-up which one dies first, Callie hemorrhaging to death from some miscarriage or Nora choking on her own vomit, drunk and passed out. It's coming. You hear me? It's coming." He stabbed a finger at me as if I doubted him, but I didn't. He was right on target.

All at once he stiffened and fixed his attention on something over my shoulder.

I turned around to see the rest of the pack, the Councilors and a small, balding man with a pointed chin emerge from the front door. Pointy Chin held a small black urn under his arm and when I saw it, I gulped.

"Can I come to the Devil's Hopyard, or do you want me to stay away?" I asked Jonathan, turning back to him. "I'll do what you want, Jonathan, don't worry about Vaughn."

*Amy Lee Burgess*

A muscle in Jonathan's cheek twitched. After Vaughn's threats inside, he knew he'd be in for trouble if he objected to my attendance at the funeral.

"You can come," he allowed. "Do you think you could give me and Nora a ride? I don't feel like driving and she's fucking drunk."

"Come on." Murphy took the keys out of his pocket and unlocked the doors to the Prelude.

Nora stumbled over to us and most of Riverglow watched in absolute shock as she and Jonathan got into the Prelude with me and Murphy and waited for them to get into their cars so we could all go scatter Grandfather Tobias's ashes.

# Chapter 17

The interior of the car reeked of gin but it was too cold to put down the window. Murphy cracked his anyway, forcing me to huddle in my coat.

"Can we make a packy run?" Nora begged. She hiccupped then giggled at herself, while Jonathan silently fumed beside her in the back seat.

"What in the hell is a packy run?" Murphy had never heard the term before and was curious. He was also suspicious.

"She means booze. She wants more booze," snapped Jonathan. He shot Nora a dirty look which she ignored, no doubt from lots of practice. Flask uncapped, she made a big show of upending it to prove there was nothing inside but a few drops. They dripped onto her black skirt but she didn't seem to notice. Jonathan did, judging by the tightening of his mouth.

Nora's hair needed a good brushing. It crackled around her head full of static electricity. She'd put eye makeup on but forgotten eyeliner on the left while overdoing it on the right. Her lipstick was uneven and her skin was an unhealthy bluish white. Her cheekbones jutted aggressively and I thought if a good wind blew up while we were standing in the state park, she was likely to blow away.

"You know, Nora," I remarked, half turning in my bucket seat so I could look at her. "There are much easier ways to kill yourself than drinking yourself to death."

"Jesus, Stanz," objected Jonathan wretchedly. Murphy's eyebrows shot up, but he didn't say anything, so I went on.

"I thought of at least six different ways when I was in Boston after Grey and Elena died and you guys kicked me out of Riverglow."

Jonathan winced, but Nora leaned forward, fascinated.

"You were all alone there, weren't you, Stanzie?" she whispered, licking her cracked lips. Most of her lipstick disappeared, which was a good thing.

"You had family in the area. Your birth pack came from around Boston," Jonathan declared with an argumentative sneer.

"I was in exile, Jonathan," I reminded him sweetly. "You and the rest of Riverglow put me there, remember?"

"Not for real. The Council voted in your favor. It was a bullshit pack thing."

"Yeah, but I took it to heart. You made me feel like shit about myself. After you threw me out, I didn't have anyone left to turn to." My voice was too bitter, and I struggled to control it.

"You had your family. Your mother and father—" Jonathan began and I cut him off with a ruthless smile.

"—told me to fuck off, basically."

Murphy's fingers clenched around the steering wheel. I hadn't shared any of this with him. Or anyone. There hadn't been anyone to share it with.

"You called them, didn't you?" Nora wondered.

"More than once," I agreed. "After the third time they stopped taking my calls. After that I left messages every couple of months. For the first year. So I felt like somebody was out there even though I knew there wasn't. The whole of last year I didn't bother and it actually was better. Those messages were hell. What did I have to say? 'Hi, Lauren, hi, Paul, it's Stanzie. Nothing much to report, really. I got a new plant for my kitchen window sill. I made spaghetti for dinner last week. Still have a job. Talk to you soon, bye.'" My tone was mocking and I laughed a little.

"We thought you were drunk, and that's why they died. If that had been the truth, you'd have deserved everything you got," Jonathan muttered.

There was nothing to say to that, so I didn't bother.

"So you thought of all those ways to kill yourself, why didn't you?" Nora brought us back on track and I gave her a grateful smile. For a moment I had been back in time, exiled and terribly lonely and I remembered those phone calls from hell and the two days afterward when I told myself there might be a chance, a slim one that they'd call back. They never had.

"Well, what's suicide but a big fuck you to everybody?" I asked her. "Nobody gave a shit about me so who was I going to tell to fuck off? I thought people might actually be glad I'd done it and I said to hell with that. I'm not sure I believe in reuniting with your loved ones in the otherworld after you die so I didn't really think I'd see Grey and Elena, and yet a part of me was a little afraid I might. And they'd blame me too. I mean, I was driving the car. I wasn't drunk, but I was driving. And even now that I know Grandfather Tobias did something to the brake line, it doesn't make much difference. I'm the one who brought the car to him in the first place. There's some guilt you just can't escape, I guess. Anyway, Nora, who are you trying to tell to fuck off? Jonathan?"

Nora snorted. "As if he'd care. Probably can't wait to find me dead one morning. Can you?" She turned to him and dared him to deny it.

"I don't want to find you dead," he half-whispered. "Why do you think I go around pouring out all the goddamn booze you hide? If I wanted you dead, why would I bother?"

Nora tossed her head and gave him a disbelieving smile. "You know what he said to me after our baby died? Stanzie, you know what he said?" Twins spots of color blotched her pale cheeks and her fists were clenched so tightly I could smell blood from where her nails cut the skin.

A look of bewilderment crossed Jonathan's features, and I knew he hadn't expected her to say this. He also clearly didn't know what it was he'd said. Either he didn't remember or didn't believe she was referring to what he remembered.

"What?" I prompted.

"The egotistical bastard said, 'At least you've still got me, Nora.' Can you freaking believe that shit?" The look she gave him was scorching hot with contempt. Jonathan sank in his seat, shoulders hunched until he looked like a little boy swamped in his father's clothing. "Men think everything revolves around them, don't they? Or is it just Jonathan?"

Jonathan's long black lashes swept his ashen cheeks. He said nothing in his defense. I still didn't think he understood what he'd done wrong.

"You know the last time he told me he loved me, Stanz?" Nora was on a roll and there was no stopping her now. I almost wished we'd found a package store and bought her a boatload of gin so we didn't have to hear this.

"No," I said because I had to say something.

"Neither do I. It's been that friggin' long." Nora gave him another blistering look.

"You just went to the Great Gathering, Nora. If you're this unhappy with him, why didn't you sever ties and look for somebody else?" I wondered.

Jonathan's chest heaved and his dark eyes accused me silently of betraying him.

Now Nora's scorching contempt was directed at me. Her mouth curled in absolute derision. "Who the hell would want me, Stanzie? A barren drunk, that's what I am. I have nothing to offer anybody. Who'd want me?"

"You're beautiful. Lots of guys would want you," Jonathan whispered, head down.

"Oh, sure, right. The best I could have done was to be the spare to the pair in some triad. Bullshit. No way."

"Jonathan, you could have found somebody else," I reminded him.

"I don't want anybody else." He lifted anguished and ashamed eyes to stare at me. "And anyway, who'd want me? Listen to her, listen to what she says. I'm an egotistical bastard. Clueless, and I never say 'I love you'. She's right, I don't. But just because I don't say it doesn't mean I don't feel it. She always knew that before, or maybe I was just being egotistical. And I don't understand why what I said was wrong. Callie came out of the room after...after the baby was born dead and she said, 'I'm sorry, Jonathan,' and it seemed so damn stupid and inadequate. Anybody can say 'I'm sorry'. I'm sorry doesn't mean shit. You say it if you accidentally bump into somebody or if you reach for the same piece of bread. It's not what you say to somebody who's just lost a baby. All I meant was that she wasn't alone. That she had somebody who loved her and wanted to take care of her. That's all."

A potent silence filled the car. My throat closed over and my eyes burned with tears. I stole a glance at Murphy. He was subdued and his gaze was fixed desperately to the road.

Nora was very still, her expression blank, but her eyes were feverishly bright as Jonathan's words seemed to sink in and penetrate her fog of drunken self-pity.

For a moment the Nora I remembered, fuller of face and figure, Jonathan's constant shadow and devoted companion, floated over the person she'd become—bitter, emaciated, drunk.

"Why didn't you say that? Say it the way you just said it?" She asked and Jonathan grimaced.

"I could barely squeeze the words out that I said. You looked so fucking destroyed and I felt so tiny and scared because I knew anything I said wouldn't be enough. I don't know, Nora, you wanted that baby so much. You say I never say I love you, you never say it anymore either and you used to say it a lot. I felt replaced. You were so different after Grey and Elena died, and Stanzie left Riverglow. Somehow you lost respect for me. I know you did."

"We did a piss-poor thing to Stanzie and you know it," Nora said, her eyes hard. "You were the ringleader, Jonathan. You turned most of us against her. We weren't against you at first, Stanzie. Peter was talking about Vaughn bonding with you and everything."

"Vaughn." I shook my head.

"Everyone knew Jonathan wouldn't take you into a triad with us. Even if you'd be the spare to the pair. But Peter thought Vaughn should bond with you, only Vaughn was dead against it."

I looked at her and she looked at me. I knew she knew then.

"Elena." We said in unison.

"What?" Jonathan was lost again.

"Vaughn was in love with Elena," Nora explained to him. "He wanted to bond with her. Did he ever ask her, Stanz?"

"Yeah," I confessed, feeling dirty for doing it.

"Poor bastard," sighed Nora. "Is it a man thing again? Callie certainly understood. I did. Grey must have, but that's because he was part of your triad."

"Understood what?" Jonathan looked between us, face creased in confusion.

Nora and I exchanged another look of silent understanding.

"Elena was in love with Stanzie. The only way she'd ever have bonded with Vaughn is if Stanzie came too. Stanzie loved Grey and would never have severed ties with him."

Jonathan stared at Nora as if she were talking a different language.

"Elena was a dyke?" he blurted and Murphy choked a little bit and pretended to clear his throat.

"That's elegant, Jonathan." Nora rolled her eyes. "She was Pack, she was bisexual, the same as most of the rest of us. But she did prefer women to men. Only, if she ever wanted to shift, she needed a man, didn't she?"

"You prefer women too, Stanzie?" Jonathan looked fascinated and slightly turned on. Murphy choked again.

"I liked being with Elena," I told him. "But now that she's gone I'm not really interested in being in a triad. She was special. We fit somehow. Me, her and Grey."

"All the best triads are like that." Nora smiled.

"You mean one of them prefers the opposite sex more?" Jonathan looked shocked to even contemplate it.

"You. You think every triad you see made up of one guy and two women means the women are all over the man and only with each other to please him, don't you?" Nora rolled her eyes again.

"There are triads with two guys and one girl," Jonathan pointed out. Then he narrowed his eyes as he obviously started wondering about Vaughn and Peter's triad with Callie. "That's how all triads are? No way."

"No, not all of them. Some of them though," Nora explained. "You've got such a thick skull sometimes, Jonathan." She turned to face me again. "It was Vaughn who trashed your house, wasn't it, Stanz? You figured that out too, right? Because of Elena."

Murphy shot me a look to see whether I'd agree.

"Vaughn?" Jonathan gaped. "Nora, Stanzie did it herself. To get back at us for kicking her out."

"That's crap," declared Nora so forcefully Jonathan's eyebrows raised nearly to the top of his skull. He opened his mouth to argue and Nora said, "Crap," again very loudly. He shut his mouth.

"I guess I owe you eight hundred bucks, Liam," said Jonathan. He seemed contrite. "I thought it was Stanzie."

"Keep it." Murphy cast a look in the rearview mirror. "Take Nora on a trip somewhere with it. Get away together somewhere different."

Jonathan didn't look like he thought Nora would go for that, but Nora's eyes lit up.

"We could go to New York, couldn't we? I've always wanted to go to New York. We could stay in a nice hotel and have room service. I've never had room service. I know we just went to Paris, Jonathan, but wouldn't New York be nice?"

"Yeah, sure," Jonathan agreed, sounding a little stunned.

"Could we see a play? On Broadway?" Nora was tentative, as if expecting him to scoff and shoot her down. I couldn't imagine Jonathan sitting still for an entire play, or even following it if it was complicated, but he agreed with alacrity.

"And go to the museum? There's a natural history museum, Jonathan. With dinosaurs."

"I like dinosaurs," Jonathan said. Initially the word *museum* had brought near panic into his eyes.

"Oh, it sounds like fun, doesn't it?" Nora's whole face was shining and she leaned into Jonathan, snuggling against him companionably.

By Jonathan's expression, she hadn't voluntarily touched him in ages. Boldly he put an arm around her and she put her head on his shoulder.

When I looked out the window, I saw a small plaza with a drug store, a dry cleaner's, an antique shop and a small package store.

"There's a package store, you want to stop?" I wondered. Murphy shot me another look, which I ignored.

"No," said Nora with zero interest. "I can have a drink at the restaurant if I want one."

I looked at Jonathan and he mouthed the words *thank you* to me and, for one moment, we were actually okay with each other. For the first time since we'd been teens and had kissed in the back of the room at the Great Gathering in Louisiana.

# Chapter 18

A cold, biting wind tore at our hair and scoured our faces as we walked single file down a snowy path that led into the Devil's Hopyard state park.

My wolf, already awake, nearly went crazy inside me, clawing to get out. She smelled the pine needles and the frozen brook just as keenly as I did. No, more. She did not understand why I wouldn't let her loose. This was her space, her time.

Behind me, Murphy put a gloved hand on my shoulder as if to steady me, although my steps were even. I was next to last in the line and the path was being broken by the others. I had only to keep in their footsteps.

I wanted to shake free of his touch because it confused me and made me resentful that he could touch me first, but I never could take the initiative with him. However, my wolf was comforted inside me, settled. She trusted him and his wolf. She would never understand the nuances that ran between me and him in human form. I didn't want her to, but I suspected some day she might.

I pulled my scarf over most of my face and breathed in the scent of wool and my perfume. That also settled my wolf. They were not her smells.

A part of me wanted to let her free so I wouldn't have to bear witness to the final dispersion of Grandfather Tobias's ashes. Often at Pack funerals, people shifted into their wolves to honor the dead. But there was no honor in today's funeral. Anyway, I couldn't let my wolf out at a funeral because the concept was beyond her. Still, she clamored within me. Was Murphy struggling with his wolf too? Somehow, I doubted it.

Up ahead, Jonathan carried the urn because he was a blood relative. The Councilors followed behind Jonathan and Nora then Colin Hunter and Devon Talbot. Behind them, Vaughn, Callie and Peter, then me and Murphy.

Callie moved more slowly than the rest of us. Her face was white and pinched and I suspected she was in pain. The wind blew her scent back to me and my suspicions were confirmed. Not only was she in pain, she was bleeding. The after-effects of her recent miscarriage were still manifesting themselves.

Peter had a guiding hand on her frail shoulder and Vaughn made sure to clear the way for her so she wouldn't stumble.

I slowed my steps in response and Murphy squeezed my shoulder. I could have looked back at him, one reassuring glance, but I kept my face forward and my gaze fixed on the ground so I could see where I was going.

A crow cawed from the top of a pine tree as we filed beneath. It was a macabre sound—a lonely one. There was a rush and flap of wings and he was gone, soaring away to another tree where he wouldn't see predators such as us.

I smelled deer and squirrels and lots of birds, too many to individually identify by species although I could have if I'd wanted to concentrate hard enough.

As we got farther beneath the canopy of the trees, the snow cover thinned and eventually we were walking on crushed pine needles and leaves—leftovers from autumns past.

The wind died down too, blocked by the branches.

It got darker and miserably cold, and I tried not to let memories rush over me because I knew where we were going. I knew the clearing well. We'd always shifted there before scattering into the woods. Grey and Elena had blocked my wolf from going toward the parking lot and the road, but she had never wanted to go that way. She'd wanted to go deep into the woods, to the heart of the forest. The second I'd finished shifting, she was off, leaping into the pine-scented woods, certain that her mates were behind her, but only wanting to be free to run and run and run some more.

Grey and Elena had walked here. Lived here. Spoken here. Laughed here. Again, I tried to bring up their faces and they were blurred the way they always were since sometime in Paris. More and more I began to believe the old man that they'd been with me in spirit until that night in the Paris hotel room when I could no longer distinctly bring up their features in my memory. I would always need a photograph now.

Up ahead, the others stopped and ranged around into a loose circle. Murphy and I fell into our places, closing it.

From where I stood I could see the frozen brook, iced over white in the dark gloom of the forest. The wind was gone and it became eerily still and silent, as if the trees mourned with us.

All the birds and wildlife fled the way they always did from us. We were isolate and alone, thirteen of us. Twelve alive and standing in a circle, one dead and in ashes in an urn.

Jonathan moved to the center of the circle, his handsome face white and grim. His eyes were red rimmed and bloodshot but he was not quite as broken as he'd been at the funeral home. He looked to Nora as if for support and she gave him a sad, sweet smile which he returned.

He held the urn above his head and turned in a slow circle so we could all see it clearly.

I pressed my scarf to my face and watched the tops of the pine trees, looking for movement, for air, but they were still.

Jonathan started to speak, but I didn't listen. I put myself in a different space away from the clearing. The old man was ashes because I'd put coniine in his hot chocolate. He'd begged me to watch him die, stay with him so he wouldn't be alone. But where was he now? Nothing? Or a spirit condemned to walk—more alone than he'd ever been when he'd breathed?

In the middle of the circle, Jonathan carefully pried the top off the urn and with his gloved hand reached in and took a handful of the ashes.

He said something—I saw his lips move but I was beyond hearing. He scattered the ashes in a circle around himself and I didn't hear them patter against the leaves and needles but I knew they made a sound.

Nora stepped up and took the urn. Jonathan took her place in the outer circle and Nora repeated the process. She said something too, but I don't know what.

There was no set order to who went into the inner circle, but there were no lulls or awkward transitions.

Jason Allerton looked particularly striking in his gray cashmere blend dress coat, his black hair perfectly in place, his piercing blue eyes meeting everyone's in the circle before he scattered a handful of the ashes of the man he'd condemned to death.

Kathy Manning moved like a ballerina elf, tiny and precise. Her short brown hair, tousled by the wind, gave her a gamine look, almost feral.

Callie almost fell when it was her turn. Peter and Vaughn were tense, ready to go to her if she needed them.

She held the urn as if it weighed a hundred pounds and her hand shook as she scattered ashes.

When she returned to the outer circle, Peter was there to take her into his arms and she leaned against him gratefully, not seeing his anguish as he buried his face in her strawberry blond hair.

Murphy said something in Irish when it was his turn in the inner circle. I'm sure it was one of the traditional sayings. There were phrases we used at funerals when we didn't know what to say from the heart. Things like, "May your wolf run free in the otherworld" and "Although your time here with us is at an end, you are just beginning somewhere else and that thought will give us much comfort in the days to come."

He looked so handsome and familiar as he stood in the inner circle and held the urn. I came back from the space I'd hidden, drawn by the realization of just how much I loved him. He was my anchor, my beloved one. And the love I had for him was different from the way I'd loved Grey. Grey was springtime and Murphy was Indian summer—complex, deceptively warm, a season within a season, the last of the warmth before autumn's breath frosted over the land.

I was the last one to scatter the ashes. Somehow there were just enough for a gritty, grayish-white handful. Bits of bone and dust, all that remained of the old man I'd loved and trusted.

I stood there with the urn in my hands and I knew what I had to do even though a part of me didn't want to do it. I wished I could be like Murphy and resort to one of the traditional phrases, but this was too good an opportunity not to plant a seed which might bear fruit in our search for Grandfather Tobias's accomplice within the pack.

I looked around the circle and saw all of Riverglow except I didn't see Grey and Elena, who should have been there, and would have, if not for him. It became easier then to do what I needed. Because I wanted to. Badly.

"You had a hundred and thirty years, old man," I said. "Grey and Elena had thirty. You asked me to forgive you but here's my answer. Never. Not ever. So walk, pull your guilty chains behind you and never, ever rest. That's my answer to you."

Callie went three shades paler and started to cry. Jonathan couldn't look at me. Peter's face filled with pity. For me. The Councilors remained impassive. Colin Hunter and Devon Talbot looked uncomfortable. Vaughn stared at his boots.

Murphy was the only one who met my gaze, and even as I knew he understood, I also saw the suspicion dawn in his face. He quickly hid it.

I let the ashes trickle through my gloved fingers then I walked over to Jonathan and gave him the urn.

He still wouldn't look at me although I stared at him hard enough and when he wouldn't, I turned around and walked back to Murphy.

* * * *

We ate lunch in a private room in a small restaurant near the river. It had once been a farmhouse which had been converted. The room had a fieldstone fireplace piled with sweet-smelling birch logs that crackled and snapped behind a fine mesh screen.

The table was a long refectory style with mismatched farmhouse chairs set around it.

The Councilors sat one at each end of the long table and the rest of us ranged around it. Murphy and I sat together facing the fireplace. By tacit agreement, everyone kept him and Colin Hunter as far away from each other as the table would allow. Neither of them took much notice of the other, though.

When the waiter took our drink orders, just about everyone fell out of their chairs when Nora ordered sparkling water. Across the table, Jonathan shot me another grateful look and ordered the same thing himself.

"So you talked to Grandfather Tobias, Stanzie?" Callie tried to sound casual but fell rather short. She wore a cowl-necked black knit dress that bagged on her even with a tightly cinched belt. She'd French-braided her hair and the style suited her, made her look young and innocent, but she was too pale and all the makeup in the world couldn't fix it.

Around the table people became inordinately interested in their appetizers.

"I did," I said with a shrug. I took a sip of red wine and savored the taste. There was a hint of blackberries with the grape and I couldn't decide if I liked it.

"So he told you it was an accident. He made a mistake. He asked for your forgiveness, obviously. Why can't you forgive an old man? You never used to be so hard."

"I never used to be, but two years of exile with nothing to talk to but a fucking house plant can change a person. So can losing your bond mates. What if it had been Vaughn and Peter in the car that night? Would you be rushing to forgive that old man and his mistake?"

"He was senile, Stanz," muttered Jonathan. He didn't want to argue with me but he couldn't keep silent. He put his spoon down, clam chowder not even half gone, but he was done.

"Like hell, Jonathan. For some reason you want to spread that lie around, but I talked to him and he was as sane and as lucid as anybody at this table, so don't give me that senile crap, please."

He winced and shook his head. "You know he suffered too. He was never the same man after you left the pack."

"My heart fucking bleeds." I snarled. Murphy quietly fumed beside me but he hadn't said a word yet. He wanted to, I knew him well enough to know that.

The Councilors continued to spoon clam chowder as if they weren't aware of the seething animosity spreading around the table like a virus.

"What do we have to do to make it up to you?" Callie asked.

I laughed. "You can't," I explained as if to a four year old. "Unless you can figure out a way to bring Grey and Elena back to life you can never make it up to me. Fuck this pack, I'm glad I'm out of it, but only because you didn't stick by me. I'm supposed to forgive that old man for a mistake but you couldn't forgive me for a mistake."

"Not the same thing. We thought you were drunk." Callie's face was tight and pinched.

"I wasn't. And let me tell you, Callie, he said something else to me when he asked for my forgiveness. He said someone else in this goddamn pack knew the truth all along too. The whole time. And that person said nothing, just sat back and let me take the fall."

"No!" Bright color surged into Callie's cheeks. "Stanzie, we wouldn't have done that!"

"Maybe you wouldn't have, but somebody did."

"Who?" It sounded like a chorus of owls as the question flew at me from all directions.

Vaughn had tried to ignore the whole conversation, doggedly consuming his soup, but now even he threw down his spoon.

"I don't know," I confessed, my body sagging a little. I straightened up tall in my chair and looked around the table at each of them in turn. "But I'm going to find out, and I'm going to find out why whoever it was didn't say anything at the time. The old man had a secret and I want to find out what it was. At least one of you around this table knows it. I want to know it too."

"What the hell will that change? That won't bring back Grey and Elena either, goddamn it." Peter tossed his napkin down on the table and shoved back his chair. "You were right, Jonathan, we shouldn't have let her come today." He gave me a long look before stomping out the door.

Callie jumped up and followed him.

"Well, so much for lunch." Vaughn cast me a disgusted glare before he followed Peter and Callie out.

"I want to go too but I don't have my fucking car here. This sucks," declared Jonathan.

"Come on, mate." Colin Hunter pushed back his chair.

Jonathan surged to his feet and stomped around the table. He stopped by me and stuck his finger in my face as he all but shouted. "You're insane, Stanz. You couldn't let it lie there, could you? What in the hell is the matter with you?"

"My bond mates are dead, you stupid bastard, that's what's the matter with me," I snarled at him.

"Funny. I thought your bond mate was sitting right next to you. Guess he doesn't count then? Jesus."

"Stop shaking your finger in her face or you'll only ever be able to count to four on that hand," Murphy warned in a deceptively calm tone.

"You don't think it's me or Jonathan, do you? That knew the truth?" Nora moved around the table to stand beside Jonathan. "That's why you were so good to us in the car. You don't think it's us."

"I don't know who it is. It could be either of you," I argued.

"It's not me," said Nora.

"Maybe not," I said. "But maybe so."

"Well, I sure as hell didn't know shit," declared Jonathan. He stopped shaking his finger in my face and kept a wary eye on Murphy.

I said, "You'd be the last one to admit it if you did. You hate me."

"I don't hate you," Jonathan snapped. "God, so melodramatic, Stanz. I don't like you very much, true, but I don't hate you. You're not that important to me that I'd hate you."

Murphy snorted derisive laughter that made Jonathan flush. Then, to cover up his humiliation, he stomped out, closely followed by Nora.

"I hope you know what you're doing," Colin Hunter said to me. He glanced at Allerton then back at me before turning to leave. His bond mate hurried after him, nearly knocking over the waiter, who walked in then, bearing a heavy tray full of our entrees.

"There's been a slight change of plans," Allerton told the bewildered waiter, while out in the dirt parking lot the sound of revving engines was plain as day.

# Chapter 19

Murphy was perilously silent in the car on the drive back to the safe house. We raced the sun as it sank into an orange ball of cold fire on the horizon, sending out tendrils of gold and dark magenta to stain the sky.

He'd given me one betrayed look then came the wall of silence.

When he pulled the Prelude into the driveway and parked it behind Kathy Manning's little Jaguar, I was out the door like a shot, but Murphy was faster.

"The three of you planned this shit, didn't you?" He blocked my path so I couldn't escape inside. "When I was out warming up the damn car this morning, the three of you plotted what you'd say, didn't you?"

"I want to go inside, Murphy." I gulped.

"Goddamn it, Stanzie." We stared at each other in the deepening dusk. I thought he might say something else, but instead he turned and stalked into the safe house. I hurried after him, but wasn't in time to stop him from confronting Allerton in the small conference room.

Jason Allerton finished lighting the fire in the grate and rose lithely from his kneeling position.

The glint of a silver chain gleamed around his throat. His bond pendant was tucked beneath his shirt.

Before Murphy could say anything, I said, "We went behind Murphy's back today, Councilor. I don't feel right about that."

Allerton sighed. "We discussed something in private because we knew he would be an obstacle and we didn't have time for obstacles, did we?"

Murphy's jaw began to jut as he bit down on his anger. "You left me out of the plan deliberately. All I ask is that I'm included. Unless you want me out of this particular job. Shall I go back to Boston and wait? To Dublin?"

"Would you actually go?" Allerton radiated disbelief and the faintest bit of exasperated affection.

"Hell, no," said Murphy and Allerton's lips twitched slightly.

"We didn't plan everything out in minute detail, Liam. I gave Constance some guidance and she's the one who took it from there. I was rather hoping she would have shared her thoughts with you on the drive to the funeral home but apparently not."

I bit my lip, remembering the awkward silence in the car.

"Stanzie and I have been having a rough time communicating lately," Murphy said, eyes guilty. "Mostly my fault. Probably all my fault. I'm pretty sure I never gave her the chance today."

Allerton crossed to the built-in bookcases. One shelf had been turned into a repository for bottles of liquor and glasses. He took a decanter of brandy down and poured some into three balloon glasses.

As he handed two of them to me and Murphy he remarked, "I noticed Nora didn't order anything alcoholic at lunch. Your doing, Stanzie?"

I flushed and raised the brandy glass to my mouth.

"Yes, it was," Murphy answered for me. "Those two feckin' idiots were like modeling clay in her hands."

"No," I protested under the admiring scrutiny of the both of them. "I just know them, that's all. I knew what to say because I know them."

"Callie, Vaughn and Peter know them too." Allerton took a sip of the brandy and swirled the rest of the liquid in his glass.

I sighed.

"You were the heart of Riverglow," Allerton said after a moment. "They are a dysfunctional shell of a pack right now."

"Callie's fixated on having a baby, that's why she hasn't talked to Nora and Jonathan before this," I objected. I hadn't been the heart of Riverglow. That was poetic nonsense. And Allerton was not a poetic man so it was doubly flustering to hear something like that from him. "And Vaughn and Peter are fixated on her. She's their bond mate, that's where they should be focused."

"They're Alphas," said Murphy before Allerton could. "Alphas look after the pack, Stanzie."

"You will make a wonderful Alpha someday." Allerton lifted his glass in my direction, as if toasting me, and took a mouthful.

"Murphy's already been Alpha of Mac Tire," I argued.

"You're a new bond mate. You're well within your fertile period. He was a very good Alpha and his time was cut short. I don't think it would be difficult to become Alphas of Mac Tire. Padraic O'Reilly's term is up in a little less than two years. I think it would be relatively easy for you two to take over after him. You could wait another five years, but you'd be on the cusp of infertility then. It might be pushing things, but it could work."

I didn't want to be Alpha. I didn't want that responsibility. I didn't want a baby.

"I want to be an Advisor. I can't be an Advisor and an Alpha," I protested.

"Yes, you can. I can have up to four Advisors. You and Liam would be used sparingly during your time as Alphas." Allerton had an answer for every argument. "Stanzie, if you ever want to be on a Council, Regional or Great, you'll need to be an Alpha at some point. That's how it works." His voice was gentle.

"Council?" I cried. "I'm not Council material. Murphy is, but not me."

Allerton and Murphy exchanged glances while I stood there feeling exposed and idiotic.

"Well, you're his bond mate and Murphy can't be on a Council without being an Alpha either."

"He's been one!" I said.

"We can talk about this another time." Allerton noted the hectic warmth spreading over my face.

* * * *

When I woke the next morning, Murphy was pressed against my back. I could feel his breath on the back of my neck and I knew he was awake. I waited for him touch me so I could melt into him and we could make love and I wouldn't have to think about all the shit that was going on in our lives, but he didn't.

Instead he rolled out of the bed and got into the shower.

Breakfast was a largely silent affair, at least between us. Murphy forked up eggs and sausage, stabbing at them as if they'd personally offended him, while I cut my sausage into little tiny bits and mixed them with eggs and ketchup. I think I ate about four mouthfuls before I gave up and concentrated on my coffee.

Allerton read the newspaper at the table, spreading it on the table next to his plate. I sneaked a peek to see what part he was reading and was astounded to see him perusing the advice columns as well as the comics. He particularly enjoyed Dilbert, judging by his chuckles.

Kathy Manning drank tea and nibbled on toast and peanut butter while flipping through a cookbook. She asked my opinion on several recipes, none of which I gave a shit about but my lackluster responses did not seem to faze her in the slightest.

Murphy's fork clattered down on his aggressively empty plate. He shoved back his chair and left the room, and Kathy looked up from her cookbook to give me a conspiratorial smile.

"If I were you, I'd let him brood alone. Don't chase after him," she suggested.

I considered her words for three whole seconds before I pushed back my chair and left the room.

Murphy was at the window in the front room. He heard me in the hallway and turned his head expectantly but, all at once, I could not face him and kept walking until I found myself at the front door.

Since I had no choice except to go outside unless I wanted to be an idiot and creep back, I put on my coat and unlocked the front door.

Boots crunching on the snow, I made my way down the side path to the driveway where the cars were parked.

Ice coated the windows and both cars were streaked with dried mud and crusted sand from the road. I bet this was killing Murphy, not being able to wash his damn car.

More boots crunched across the snow and Murphy's shadow fell across the hood of the Prelude as he stepped up beside me.

His breath plumed white into the air and neither of us said anything. Stalemate in some half-assed game I was pretty goddamn sure I didn't even want to play.

"Can I have the car keys?" I asked after half a minute of escalating agony. At least it was agony for me; I wasn't sure what it was for him except he didn't like it. Not if his expression was any indication.

Eyebrows elevated. "What for?"

I sighed and tried not to roll my eyes but I don't think I was successful. "Murphy, I want to take a drive."

He opened his mouth three times to say something then closed it again.

At last, he reached into his coat pocket, extracted the keys and handed them to me.

Fuck. He'd called my bluff, the bastard. Now I was committed.

I figured it was only seconds until I'd begin to cry like a goddamn baby the way I always seemed to in times of nervous crisis. Damn it. I had no choice now. The Prelude's lights flashed in response when I pressed the unlock button.

"You're really going to drive?" Murphy tried to sound encouraging but I could hear the doubt loud and clear.

I gritted my teeth and resolutely opened the door. I tried to get behind the wheel but my knees locked rebelliously.

"It looks like you can't bend your knees," he said after a moment. His voice was both ironic and kind, and I winced.

"I can so," I argued. Murphy waited. I took a deep breath, held it, counted to twenty three, exhaled before I passed out and tried to bend my knees again. No dice.

"This is so fucking stupid," I muttered.

"Where do you want to go? I'll drive you," he offered.

"You always drive me everywhere. I want to be the one to drive."

He waited again. He was very patient. My knees were completely uncooperative.

"Oh, fuck." I handed him the keys and all but ran away from the car. Damn thing. My knees worked fine walking away from the driver's side.

"You did try," he said, coming closer to me. He gave me an encouraging smile. "It won't be long now before you're driving, Stanzie."

"Please don't patronize me," I whispered and his smile went away.

"Where do you want to go?" he said after a moment.

"I don't know." I shrugged. "I just want to get the hell away from here."

"Boston?" His laugh was wistful and so was my smile. "Let's just drive," he suggested. So we did.

He drove through Hartford for a little bit but when he ended up on the highway, I abruptly knew where I wanted to go and gave him directions.

\* \* \* \*

The house was smaller than I remembered. They'd painted the shutters black, but they'd been Cape Cod blue when Grey, Elena and I had lived there.

Murphy parked at the curb so that my side of the car had the best view of the house.

The big bay window sparkled in the winter sunshine and I remembered Elena's collection of glass cats. She'd put them all on the little shelves built into the panes of the window glass. They'd all been smashed to hell the day of the funeral. She'd spent her whole life collecting them—since she was five years old. Every birthday, every Christmas, people gave her glass cats.

The wooden box Grey and I had given her when she'd bonded with us had been painted with calico cats. She'd squealed in delight when she'd seen it.

She tried keeping real cats but they always ran away. Cats and wolves don't generally mix.

I sat in the car with one hand pressed to my mouth and stared, while Murphy waited behind the wheel, head bowed a little, allowing me my space and privacy.

When I could talk again, I said, "The shutters used to be blue."

"Yeah," said Murphy. "Things don't stay the same, do they? After Sorcha died, I got an offer for our apartment and that's when I decided to move to Belfast. The company who bought the apartment house wanted it for office space. Tore it all down and rebuilt it. Paddy tells me I wouldn't even recognize it anymore. I can't decide if this is a good thing or not."

"I hate change," I whispered.

"It happens anyway." He switched on the ignition.

I gave him directions back to the highway. There was one more place I wanted to visit.

"I don't think this a good idea," Murphy told me when he realized where we were and why I wanted him to pull over on the off-ramp.

There wasn't a lot of traffic. More than there'd been that night, but there was never that much.

I ignored him and got out of the car.

The guard rail had long since been replaced. The new part gleamed in the winter sun. The small ravine below was a shining, pristine sheet of white tucked into the hill.

During the accident, the Mustang had taken out several bushes and a tree. There had to be a blank spot where they'd been, at least where the tree had stood, but the snow covered everything and made it hard to tell.

It was a deceptively peaceful place. I detected no psychic echoes of Grey's dying agony or Elena's last shriek of terror before her neck snapped.

I looked and looked but could not find the exact spot the car had come to rest.

If it hadn't been so icy, I would have gone down the hill. I did try, but Murphy grabbed me.

"I can't find it. The place exactly," I told him when he wouldn't let go of my shoulder.

"Maybe that's a good thing."

I shrugged. I didn't know for sure. "My cellphone was in my purse. My purse was in the back seat with...with Elena. After Grey died, I left him and went back to the car. I found my cellphone. It worked. Do you know who I called?"

"Grandfather Tobias," he guessed, his face very grim.

I squinted against the blinding sunlight and nodded. "He called the others, Vaughn, Peter and Jonathan. They left Callie and Nora behind. I waited for them to get here and went back and forth between Elena and Grey. Because I didn't want them to be alone. I was talking to myself. Babbling really. Telling myself it was just a dream, a nightmare. But it wasn't. They got here and they saw all the blood on me. It was Grey's blood but they didn't know that. Peter thought I was hurt and he ran to me. Jonathan saw Grey's body and got sick in the bushes. Vaughn found Elena and started to cry. He kept saying, 'no, no, no, not like this, no.'

"Grandfather Tobias put me in Jonathan's car and I lay down in the backseat. I don't remember what happened then except I must have fallen asleep because when I opened my eyes I was at Callie's house, in the driveway. Peter was shaking me awake and we went inside and told Callie and Nora that Grey and Elena were dead. They started screaming and crying and, oh, Murphy, it was a mess."

I stopped talking and looked down the hill again. I still couldn't find the exact spot.

"It's over, Stanzie," Murphy whispered. He tucked a lock of my hair behind one of my ears. "It's the past. Don't let it hurt you anymore. It wasn't your fault and nobody blames you and you can let it go now."

"Can I?" I turned to look at him, at his familiar, attractive face. I wished I could touch him but I didn't. "Someone else was in on it with Grandfather Tobias. I can't let it go until I know who. Not just because Allerton wants to know, not just because the Great Pack needs to know, but because I do. I want to let go, Murphy, and I'm a lot better than I used to be. Look at me, I'm not even crying. Am I?" Amazed, I put a hand to my cheek. It came away dry.

My mouth trembled. "Is that a good thing?"

"It is." He gave me a subdued smile. "Now come on, let's go find someplace and have lunch."

"Is your wolf still awake?" I wondered and his subdued smile became an outright grin.

"He is."

"Want to shift?"

# Chapter 20

*Run, run, run and run more. Friend chases me. I run faster! I want words but I want to run too! Friend chases me. Friend tries to catch me! Me run, fast, fast, fast! White stuff flies up in the air. Paws cold! Cold paws, but me warm. Me...I...I happy! I run! I run fast!*

\* \* \* \*

Jesus, it was cold. I came back to myself in human form, naked and colder than midnight in February.

Murphy was close by and swearing in Irish. Luckily, our clothes were in neatly folded piles right where we'd left them. The first thing Murphy's wolf had taught mine was to remember where we left our clothes and to return there before shifting back. It was a simple, obvious thing, but it was something my wolf was notoriously awful at remembering.

But she had remembered this time. Here was the clearing where we'd shifted near the lot where we'd left the car. It was so cold no Others were around. The parking lot was empty save for the Prelude. One good thing about shifting in the daytime in winter, when it was this cold—the Others stayed away.

Grey, Elena and I had loved this small state park in Manchester and used it far more often than we'd gone to the Devil's Hopyard. That was more for the whole pack, not our triad.

Today seemed a day to go back to old haunts, and I was handling it relatively well. I knew it was because Murphy was with me but I was still proud of myself.

"Jaysus, goddamn, sonofabitch!" Murphy switched to English and half-ran, half-hopped to his clothes and began with his jeans. I swore too and stood on my coat so I could put on my socks. My nipples were so hard they hurt and my teeth chattered so loudly I could barely hear Murphy's steady stream of inventive cursing.

I did hear the crow. It sat in the top of a maple tree about ten yards away from us and it gave a sudden squawk that was just ahead of the shot.

It was enough of a heads up for Murphy. I was slower than he was, trying to fasten my bra. I was struggling with the damn straps when the crow cried out its warning.

The next thing I knew I was flat on the ground, snow crushing up into my mouth and nose as Murphy crawled on top of me and held me down, trying to cover every inch of me with his body.

There were more shots then, enough so I realized what was happening and started to scream. Snow choked me and I bucked and struggled beneath Murphy, trying to get free so I could run but he held me down until he yelled, "Now!" He half dragged me to my feet and we ran like hell for the cover of the maple tree and the trees beyond that one. It was only thirty yards, maybe less, but it seemed a million miles to safety.

A bullet zinged by my head, so close I felt the heat. It buzzed in my ear like a wasp and I screamed and ducked, losing my balance. Murphy had my hand and if not for him I would have gone down, but he held me up and dragged me into the woods.

"Run, just run, keep running," he urged. In human form he could outrun me, but he didn't leave me. He kept behind me, trying to shield me from the bullets in case the person with the gun chased us.

But there were no more bullets once we reached the sanctuary of the woods.

We ran until we couldn't breathe and eventually had to stop, bending double to catch our breath, wheezing, coughing and choking. I was coated with a cold sweat and so scared my brain felt like it was bouncing around inside my skull as if it had been shot out of a pinball machine.

Murphy fell to his knees, gasping, and that's when I smelled blood. His.

"Oh, fuck." I turned to him in horror. Bright scarlet drops of blood stained the forest floor and the clumps of snow that had dropped through the canopy of bare black branches.

"I'm all right," he told me, holding himself as he bent double, trying to breathe.

"Where did you get shot? How bad is it?" I crawled across the ground to get to him.

"Stanzie, it just a graze. My arm." He held his right arm out to show me.

A thin, bloody slash zigzagged down his forearm. He was right. It was just a flesh wound. It was bleeding like a bitch though and I grabbed his hands with mine. Our fingers clutched as we stared at each other.

His brown eyes were glazed with both pain and fear, and I could barely see past the tears in mine. This was my fault. I had planted a seed and it had borne poison fruit.

"We have to get out of here," Murphy told me in a quiet, calm tone even though his chest heaved and his eyes were wild. "Okay, Stanzie? We need to get to the car and get the hell out of here."

"The car?" I moaned. "What if whoever has the gun is waiting in the parking lot?"

"I don't have my coat and neither do you. It's nearly sunset and it's going to go below freezing." His gaze took in my shivering form. I only had on underwear and a pair of wet socks. "We can't stay out here."

"Jesus Christ, let me think. Let me think. I know this place, Murphy. If you let me think I can maybe figure a way out that doesn't mean the parking lot. There are houses nearby. We can go to one and call Allerton. We can't go to the parking lot, can't you understand that?"

"Calm down, Stanz," he said gently, squeezing my hands with his. We were both kneeling in a combination of pine needles, mud and snow. My kneecaps were frozen and he was still bleeding.

We were so absorbed with each other and with fear that we didn't hear the person approaching us from behind until he was nearly upon us and then it was too late to run.

"Liam!" The voice was familiar and had an English accent. Murphy reacted immediately and launched himself at the speaker.

He and Colin Hunter went down hard—a tangle of arms and legs. I leaped to my feet and found a fallen branch. I had this insane idea I was going to brain Colin with it, but Murphy kept getting in the way. Also, I listened to Colin who, in between swearing and punching, was screaming at Murphy that he was trying to help, damn it, help.

Murphy either wasn't listening or didn't believe him.

"I have no gun! I haven't got a gun, it wasn't me!" Colin shouted as he and Murphy thrashed in the pine needles and snow.

What if Colin wasn't lying? Someone else with a gun could be out there and while Murphy and Colin Hunter rolled around on the ground like schoolyard bullies beating the crap out of each other, they were perfect targets. I was an even better one. I shouted at Murphy, trying to get him to stop fighting but he didn't listen to me either. I considered braining him with the branch because by this time I believed Colin Hunter and the sun was sinking and I was getting cold and very scared. But I couldn't bring myself to really do it and cast the branch down in disgust.

Murphy wrestled his way on top of Colin, who was only defending himself and not trying to land punches. That, apparently, registered at last with Murphy, who sat astride him and aimed a fist at his face but did not follow through.

"Liam, goddamnit," snarled Colin. "Listen to me, you bastard. I'm not the one who shot at you. I swear!"

"How do you even know somebody shot at us if you weren't the one doing the shooting, gobshite!" Murphy's Irish accent was thick enough to make me crinkle my brow in confusion, trying to translate, but Colin had no trouble.

"I was sitting in the car park waiting for you two to shift back when I heard the shots. I ran like hell but all I found was your blood and a lot of confused footprints. I think they were yours and Constance's. I don't know who shot at you, and at this point, I don't friggin' care. Let's get out of here."

"How the hell did you come to be sitting in the car park, you lying sack of shit?" Murphy looked as though he wanted to spit in Colin's face, but he didn't.

The setting sun pierced down through the tops of the pine trees and into our eyes and all three of us squinted in protest. I became acutely aware that I had no coat. No jeans or sweater either. Just in the time they'd been fighting it had dropped five or six degrees.

"I was curious when you two sat outside my house staring. I called Allerton and he told me to follow you," Colin explained and Murphy glared at him.

"Your house?" he said. "Your house?"

"He and Devon must be renting it now," I said in a strange voice. It was weird enough to think of other people living there, but other people in Riverglow? It was almost too much.

"Allerton told you to follow us?" Murphy's eyes narrowed.

"You know he's working for him, Murphy," I said softly, reminding him of something we already knew, and Murphy grimaced.

"I want to be one of his Advisors too," confessed Colin.

"Fuck," muttered Murphy. He held Colin down with one hand and searched his pockets with the other. He came up empty. No gun. "You could have ditched it, you bastard. This proves next to nothing."

"Smell my hands. If I'd fired a gun, you'd smell the residue." Colin offered both his hands and Murphy sniffed them. By his expression I knew he didn't smell anything.

"You could have worn gloves and ditched them, ye fecker," he muttered.

"Call Allerton. Ask him if I'm not working for him. Auditioning for the role of Advisor. Like you and Constance must have done at some point," Hunter suggested.

Murphy's lips twitched. He knew Colin was fishing for information and he'd be damned if he'd give him any.

"I know all about the conspiracy," Colin said. "Allerton told me about it. I know Grandfather Mick was the one who set Sorcha up, not you. Not that I ever really believed you did it. I was just so pissed off at the time."

Murphy did spit then, but not directly at Colin. He got to his feet and stalked away as if he couldn't bear to be close to him one second longer.

"You were more interested in being Alpha of Mac Tire than you were of being Sorcha's bond mate," he accused. "Don't think I didn't fucking know that, Hunter."

Colin bowed his head. "Why didn't you tell Sorcha that if you're so sure it's the truth?"

"Nobody told Sorcha anything she didn't want to hear. Besides, she wouldn't have given a shit. She wanted you. She was going to have you. We were a lot alike, Sorcha and I, at least in that respect."

Colin didn't say anything for a moment. "I was that close to being Alpha of Mac Tire. That close." He held his thumb a half inch away from his index finger and laughed a little. "I did like Sorcha, Liam, but you're right. If she hadn't been Alpha of the pack, I would have walked away."

Murphy stood very still, half shadowed by the creeping winter's dusk, but I could still see the sorrow on his face. "I wasn't standing in the way, Colin. You didn't need to give me such grief just because she died."

"I know that now," said Colin. There was just the faintest trace of remorse on his face. "Hell, I knew it then but I was so angry."

"And now you want to be Allerton's Advisor and I'm still the one standing in your way," said Murphy. "Bites, doesn't it?"

Colin shrugged. "Hell, I consider it payback. I'm not your enemy, Liam."

"No, of course not, if I can help you. Not if you can use me to piggyback your way up into position." Murphy flashed him a sardonic grin.

"Look, let's get out of here. Constance is freezing. I think we should take my car."

They exchanged knowing looks and I was confused.

"Car bomb," said Murphy when he saw my expression.

"Are you serious?" I gaped at him. "Nobody in Riverglow knows how to make a car bomb, Murphy. This isn't Belfast. It's Connecticut. Nobody makes car bombs here."

"It's not hard to make a car bomb. Check the internet if you don't believe him," Colin advised. "All we're saying is that we need to check the car out and it's dark and we don't have the equipment."

"How about your car? You haven't watched it every minute. While you've been chasing after us, who's to say the person who shot at us didn't rig your car too while he or she was at it?" I knew I sounded belligerent and defensive, but it was too much to think that someone in Riverglow would resort to car bombs. I was so frigging cold my bones ached. My feet were solid blocks of ice. What did frostbite feel like? Had I been exposed long enough for it to set in?

"Stanzie, what's the harm in playing it safe?" Murphy held out his hand and I took it, although I wanted to run away more than anything else. He put his arm around me and offered me some of his warmth. I leaned into him gratefully.

Halfway back to the parking lot, Colin took out his cellphone and called Allerton. He explained what had happened and listened for half a

*Amy Lee Burgess*

minute before saying, "Right," and hanging up. He looked back at me and Murphy. "He's going to meet you at the Starbuck's on Spencer Street. I'll drop you off."

"Don't you think your cover's blown? Whoever it was who shot at us must know you're here by now," Murphy said with a conversational grin. It was nearly full dark now, but his teeth flashed in the dying sunlight.

"Maybe." Colin didn't seem concerned. "You both take this path to the road and I'll meet you there in five." He kept walking straight while Murphy and I veered right.

"God, I hate that bastard," Murphy remarked.

# Chapter 21

The Starbucks was small and crowded, with squashy armchairs and one long, striped sofa in the back. That's where Murphy and I sat together clutching at double espressos. Mine was sweetened with six packets of raw sugar but it still tasted bitter. I drank it anyway because I was cold.

Colin had retrieved our coats and my clothes and boots from the clearing and they'd been in the backseat of a beat-up Ford Focus that had clearly seen better days. I was half convinced the damn thing would break down on the highway, but it hadn't.

Colin had known better than to try to start conversation with Murphy so he ignored him, but he did try to talk to me. So did Murphy, and I realized belatedly they were both worried about me. I suppose I was a little bit in shock. I'd never been shot at before. It wasn't until we pulled into the strip mall in front of the Starbucks that I realized Murphy wasn't driving. Yeah, I'd fretted about the car breaking down but I hadn't thought about the car crashing because Murphy wasn't driving it. Shock was good for some things.

Murphy saw me grimace at the taste of the coffee. He got up and went to the counter where the sugar, napkins and stirrers were arranged and brought me back several more packets of raw sugar as well as another stirrer.

I dumped three more packets into my cup and stirred. It was better, but still too hot to gulp the way I wanted to.

Just as I reached the bottom of the cup, which was slushy with half-dissolved sugar granules which tasted gritty and sweet on my tongue, Jason Allerton entered the shop.

His commanding presence drew every eye in the place but he ignored everyone except us. Without bothering to get any coffee, he strode across the floor and sat on the squashy armchair to the right of the sofa.

"Constance," he said, his blue eyes worried. He reached out to touch my knee and I realized my jeans were covered with clinging pine needles.

Beside me Murphy was hardly better. He had a bruise spreading beneath the skin of his left cheek and his knuckles were bloody and scraped raw. Pine needles clung to the cuffs of his jeans too.

"I'm all right," I said, because I was. Barely, but I was.

"Happy now?" Murphy asked him with a particularly foul smile. "It's pretty damned obvious the old man had an accomplice, wouldn't you say?"

"I never doubted it," replied Allerton. He patted my knee again then sat back in the arm chair.

"Do you want some coffee?" I asked him. Colin had shoved a twenty dollar bill in my hands as I'd climbed out of the Focus. My purse and Murphy's wallet were locked in the Prelude.

"Here, I'll get you another one," said Murphy, rising to his feet. He looked at Allerton, who nodded. Murphy went to the front of the shop and got in line behind two women who took one look at his face and scrunched closer together for protection. Murphy pretended not to notice, but I could tell it bothered him.

"Who knew you were going to the state park?" Allerton questioned when Murphy returned with two more double espressos. He handed one to me and one to Allerton then went to get sugar and stirrers.

"Nobody that I know of," I responded after thinking for a moment. I pried the lid off my espresso and dumped seven packets of sugar in, one after the other, fascinated by the rush of the light brown crystals as they disappeared into the liquid. "Whoever it was wasn't very good at shooting. They missed. We made pretty good targets too."

Murphy shifted on the sofa beside me, obviously disagreeing with my assessment.

"We were good targets," he said. "I think they missed on purpose."

"A warning?" Allerton lifted his espresso and took a tentative sip because it was so hot. "Why play their hand like that? We had no real proof, only suspicion until now."

"Because maybe it wasn't one of the original members of Riverglow," said Murphy in a hard voice. "Maybe it was somebody new who wants to be an Advisor and thought playing the hero might be his ticket."

I set down my cup and leaned back into the cushions of the sofa. All I wanted was to be far, far away. Without thinking about it, I wrapped my arms around myself.

"Hunter knows how to shoot?" Allerton asked. He was very calm and thoughtful, but a pulse beat visibly in his forehead and I knew he was furious. Whether he was furious at Murphy, Colin Hunter, or just at the situation in general I didn't know.

"He didn't have a gun, Murphy," I felt compelled to point out. Murphy's gaze flicked between me and Allerton.

He sighed. "Easiest thing in the world to ditch it before he got to us. He wouldn't let us come back to the car with him, made us take a different path to the road. That was such bullshit about car bombs."

Murphy had been the one to say 'car bomb' out loud, but I kept quiet. He knew Colin Hunter better than me and Colin had admitted all he'd wanted from Sorcha was a way to become Alpha of Mac Tire. He was clearly an opportunist. But a gun? Shooting at us?

"It's a possibility," allowed Allerton. Murphy smiled darkly to himself and finished his espresso.

"Who does know how to shoot in Riverglow, Constance?" Allerton leaned a bit forward in the squashy armchair and I felt like I always did when he fixed his full attention on me: nervous, awkwardly flattered, pathetic and determined not to let him down. I wondered if he'd been born with this power or had cultivated it through the years.

I said, "Any hunting I ever saw any of them do was in wolf form. Nobody owned guns or talked about them that I can remember."

"You know these people." Allerton's voice was pitched low and his tone was persuasive. I resisted the urge to wiggle in my chair like a puppy who wanted to get down and run around like crazy. "What do you think? Which one of them would have been drawn to the underground movement within the Great Pack?"

"It doesn't even have a name," I burst out. I could not believe I was sitting in a Starbucks discussing my former friends and pack mates like this—dissecting them and their personalities to pinpoint which one

*Amy Lee Burgess*

of them would have been monstrous enough to plot and kill Grey and Elena in the name of the Great Pack. "This conspiracy, this underground movement."

"Would it make it easier for you to deal with it if it did?" Allerton wondered. "We can give it a name."

I shot him a suspicious look.

"Sometimes it's easier to understand something if it has a name," said Allerton.

I thought of my wolf—how she wanted the words for things, the names for the things she'd run by and played with all her life. I was just the same, wasn't I? Wanting to clarify and quantify and dissect and discover.

"It was Vaughn who trashed her house," said Murphy. He flashed me a semi-apologetic smile but he was also bound and determined to speak.

"Because he loved Elena," I objected. "He loved Elena. Why would he plot to kill her?"

"You told me what he said when he got to the accident site," said Murphy. He was sounding more and more apologetic, and he should have been. What I'd told him had been in confidence and here he was spilling it all out to Allerton. But maybe Allerton had the same effect on him as he did on me. People wanted to tell that man everything. They could barely stop themselves.

Despite myself, I conjured up the scene in my mind.

\* \* \* \*

*I stand in the ravine halfway between Grey's twisted, dead body and the ruined hulk of my new gold Mustang GT. Blood drenches me, most of it Grey's, but I do have a cut on my forehead, just beneath the hairline. I have no idea how I got it. I must have hit my head or maybe it was a piece of flying glass. The cut bleeds and sometimes the blood gets in my eye. When it does, the world shifts and turns into a bloody haze, a scarlet-drenched alien landscape as though I am a space traveler on Mars.*

*A car approaches above on the road. Brightness pierces the darkness.*

*The Mustang's headlights somehow still function and they cast a murky glow over the bushes and dirt. Half a tree sticks out from beneath the crushed metal. The other half of the tree still stands, halfway up the hill toward the road.*

*I smell my pack members so I know it is them and not some curious Other. Although the metal guardrail is torn away and there is a gaping hole where it used to be, nobody stops on the road above except for this car.*

*Either they don't see or they don't care. What they can't see is the Mustang. Or me. I have enough sense to stay below with Grey and Elena. It's not like I can leave them anyway. How can I abandon them?*

*Faces peer down at me from above. Figures stand in the broken gap where the guard rail used to be.*

*"Oh. Fuck," says one of them. It is Jonathan.*

*Horror and concern fill Peter's face. He sees me and all the blood. He thinks I'm hurt.*

*"Stanzie, Jesus Christ," he cries and bounds down the hill with his athlete's grace. He is afraid to take me into his arms, afraid he will hurt me. I stand there like a statue. This is bizarre. This is not happening.*

*Vaughn moves next, and propels himself down the hill so fast he pinwheels his arms for balance. He says a name, over and over again.*

*Elena's.*

*Jonathan follows more prudently. His very caution undoes him and he falls onto his ass once, then again, and finally slides the rest of the way down.*

*He wanders over to where Grey's body is stiff and twisted, mouth and eyes open.*

*His own eyes widen. He claps a hand over his mouth and staggers off into the bushes. Retching noises. I see Peter cast a disgusted, angry look in his direction before he looks back at me. Peter's face softens. Tears gleam in his eyes. Trickle down his cheeks.*

*"Stanzie," he says again. I don't say anything.*

*"No, no, no!" A keening wail from the back of the Mustang. "No, not like this! Not like this!" Vaughn sobs the way men do when they have lost everything. It sounds like he is being torn apart from the inside out and is powerless to stop it.*

*Up above on the road, Grandfather Tobias waits and watches. He is too old to come down the hill. Or so I think then.*

\* \* \* \*

"Maybe the old man lied to him and told him it wasn't going to be Elena. Maybe he told him it was going to be you and Grey and then he'd get Elena."

I stared at Murphy in absolute horror. That was diabolical.

"Grandfather Tobias wouldn't do that. Lie? And then when Elena died, why would Vaughn not say something?"

"He was compromised. In too deep."

I shook my head stubbornly.

"Vaughn loved Elena and if she'd died and he thought Grandfather Tobias was lying to him, he wouldn't have cared about compromising himself. He tore my house apart. Why direct his rage at me and not Grandfather Tobias? No, Murphy, not Vaughn."

"Jonathan then." Murphy switched gears faster than a race car driver. "He wants power and relevance and maybe the old man said he'd get both under the new regime."

"Jonathan is not sly enough to keep something like that up. He'd brag and tell at least somebody," I protested.

"He told Nora. Yeah, she lost her baby, but maybe that plus the weight of Jonathan's treachery drove her to drink. She did pull away from him. I know her type. Adoring. It would take a lot for Jonathan to tumble from the pedestal she put him on."

I winced a little. Was I the adoring type too? Murphy spoke so scathingly.

"You could make a case for anyone in the pack, couldn't you?" I was both fascinated and repelled.

"Sure," he agreed at once. "It's easy. And there's one we haven't discussed, which is maybe someone in this pack just plain out believes in the cause. Like the old man. Maybe they didn't care about incentives. Peter, for instance. Very old-fashioned, very loyal."

"He puts spiders he finds in the bathtub into the back yard. He opens windows to shoo flies back out. He would never have conspired to kill Grey and Elena!"

"Maybe Tobias didn't tell him about that part of it—the killing part—until he was already in."

"And Callie?" My eyes burned but I was damned if I would cry. "She's very traditional and loyal too. But she would never kill her own pack members. I know her. She was my best friend next to Elena. This is ridiculous, Murphy. None of them would do it. I can't believe it of any of them."

"Stanzie, someone shot at us this afternoon," Murphy reminded me. There was blood on the sleeve of his sweater. What if the bullet had gotten him in the back? In the head?

I kept my head very still and my eyes fixed on the clock on the wall behind the barista's head. If I blinked I'd cry.

"We can go now." Allerton patted me on the knee. He and Murphy looked at each other, as though silently agreeing between them I'd had enough. I felt so weak and so stupid. But I had definitely had enough.

\* \* \* \*

Slicked with sweat, heart pounding, I screamed myself awake, my fingers clutching at my throat.

Murphy was lucid and sitting up beside me in less than three seconds, remarkably calm for being jerked out of a sound sleep.

He put his arms around me and rocked me, whispering something in my ear I couldn't understand because it was in Irish. It sounded so nice, whatever it was.

"Our bond pendants," I choked out, my fingers still clutching for the missing necklace around my throat. "We left them in the glove box. In the car. It's bad luck to lose your bond pendant!"

"We haven't lost them, Stanzie," he told me, his arms strong around me. "We'll get them back tomorrow, I promise."

"The bullet could have killed you." I whimpered. "You could have been killed and I sat there in that Starbucks and argued with you about how my friends wouldn't do something like that. When it had already happened! Oh, Liam, I'm sorry. I don't know what I would do if something bad happened to you. Please don't let something bad happen to you!"

"I'll try my best," he vowed. "I don't want anything to happen to you either, you know."

"How could it with you around? You got on top of me. You got shot because you covered me, used your own body as a shield. That was stupid, you know."

"It's hard to think with bullets zinging around your face," he teased. "Does it still hurt? Where you got shot?"

He switched on the bedside lamp and showed me his arm. An angry red line zig-zagged down his forearm. Above it, on his bicep, was a puckered scar in the shape of a bite. My wolf's legacy. Now he'd have another scar because of me.

"I didn't get shot, Stanzie. It grazed me, that's all. You see?"

I nodded, but I was far from placated.

"Drink this." He handed me a glass of water and I gulped most of it down. My stomach gurgled and he laughed.

"You're hungry." He handed me a butterscotch square. Kathy Manning had been baking again. She'd left a plate of them in the bedroom for us.

"You eat something too," I said and so he took one and we had a midnight picnic in bed together.

"Jaysus, that woman can bake," mumbled Murphy around a huge mouthful.

I laughed and waited for Murphy to swallow before breaking off a piece of my butterscotch square so I could feed it to him with my fingers.

He ate it then he kissed me. I tasted butterscotch and his breath—a tantalizing combination.

Midnight picnic forgotten we collapsed together onto the mattress. Murphy filled my ears with a singsong string of Irish as he deftly removed my pajamas and I tore off his.

I wrapped my legs tight around his waist, and closed my eyes as he thrust deep inside me. There was desperation to our passion that night we'd never experienced before. Getting shot at proved to be something of an aphrodisiac. It almost made it worth it. Almost.

* * * *

The car was where we'd left it in the parking lot when Murphy and I returned the next day with Kathy Manning. Instead of her sporty green Jaguar, she drove a sleek black Lincoln Town Car.

The Jaguar was in the parking lot when we pulled in off the rutted, rural road that dead-ended at the entrance to the park. It was parked prudently far from the Prelude, although judging by the open doors, trunk and hood of the Prelude, it had been an unnecessary precaution.

"No car bomb," I said. The Town Car's windows were tinted and, sitting in the back seat, I felt like a rock star being ferried from my hotel to a gig even though I supposed rock stars rode in limos.

I'd been a baby about Kathy driving but she hadn't given in to me. She'd just smiled and told me to sit in the back and buckle my seat belt. I really did feel about five years old around her, like she was my mother or something.

I could tell Murphy wanted to argue with her but she hadn't given him the opportunity. She was good, but then she was a Councilor. She'd told him to buckle his seat belt too and help her with the GPS navigation system.

"I know where we're going." I'd pouted from the back seat. "Murphy does too. We were there yesterday."

"Indulge me," said Kathy as she'd settled herself behind the wheel. Pulling down the sun visor, she'd examined her appearance and rearranged a few stray locks of hair before pushing the visor back up.

In her dark-green DKNY pantsuit and forest-brown woolen coat, she was the quintessential New England upper middle class young matron. Tiny pearl studs adorned her ears and a strand of bigger ones encircled her throat. If she wore her bond pendant, it didn't show.

Her shoes were nice—brown, flat ballerinas with gold buckles on the toe. Gucci. Too bland and conformist for me, although before Murphy I couldn't have hoped to afford them. It was beyond my comprehension to fathom why anybody would wear ballerina flats in this weather. The parking lot at the state park had been plowed once during the beginning of the storm but it was hardly clear. Her shoes could be ruined if she walked through snow in them. Maybe she didn't care. Maybe she had a closet full of shoe racks in a Rhode Island mansion in Providence.

My own boots were black—a pair of Guess ankle boots loaded with unnecessary but fabulous buckles, lined with red-and-black plaid flannel and imminently suitable for snow. They were kick-ass cute.

I'd admired them as we traveled because I couldn't look at the way Kathy Manning drove. She was a fiddler. She'd fiddled with the radio station then switched to the CD player. Then she'd switched songs. Then the entire CD. She'd rummaged in her purse for a stick of gum then her cellphone. The third time she went for her purse Murphy had picked it up and all but thrown it into the back seat with me. He'd been watching me turn progressively paler despite the allure of my boots.

When she'd started texting as she drove that did it. He'd blown up and declared that she was either going to drive or she was going to blather on with her friends, not both, so make up her mind. If she preferred to text, she'd better pull the damn car over and let him drive. If she was hell-bent on driving, she'd better put the goddamn phone down now.

After casting him an amused smile, she'd put the phone down. She'd managed to hit send before she did so and, a moment later, a reply bleep shattered the simmering silence and Murphy had sworn in Irish.

"Do you mind telling me what that says?" Kathy had asked sweetly and Murphy's face went apoplectic. He'd almost been rendered speechless but managed to snarl, "I fucking do," which had only made Kathy laugh.

"I'm trying to make sure my son is going to school. He has this annoying tendency to skip. He's seventeen and thinks he knows everything."

"Takes after his mother," Murphy had grumbled and Kathy laughed again.

"Your son goes to a public school? With Others?" I'd asked, fingers clenched, eyes fixed on my boots.

There had been a beat of silence because apparently nobody had expected me to be able to talk past my panic.

I had been panicking a little. I was sweating and my heart thumped uncomfortably in my chest. On the plus side, we were nearly at the park and were still alive, so we'd had that going for us.

"We home schooled until he was in the third grade but after that he wanted to go to public school and so we let him. It's been great for him. He has tons of friends and lots of self-confidence. Along with an annoying tendency to skip now that he's a senior and thinks he's a big shot." Kathy had looked at me in the rearview mirror while she talked, hardly keeping an eye on the road.

I felt the panic claw at my stomach and wished like hell she'd look at the cars in front of us. They had all been moving fast, but what if there was a sudden stop or some black ice?

"There's a small pack in Houston called Dark Bayou and a little girl named Mindy went to the public school there. One night her father was in a hot tub and a grandmother in the pack brought him out a beer. Spiked with sleeping pills. When he fell asleep, she held him under the water until he drowned." My voice had been matter of fact and clinical but Murphy half-turned around in his seat anyway and had given me a concerned look.

"Constance, not all grandmothers and grandfathers are part of the conspiracy. I trust the ones in my pack." Kathy's tone had been slightly condescending and dismissive.

"I trusted the one in mine too." I had shrugged.

"So when you and Murphy have a child, you're not going to let him or her go to public school because you're afraid of the grandmothers and grandfathers?" Kathy had wondered.

"I don't want a child," I'd declared mutinously. Hurt washed over Murphy's face for a split second. He'd thought I didn't want his child.

"I've never wanted a child," I had clarified. "If Grey, Elena and I had ever gotten to be Alphas of our pack, she was the one who was going to have a baby or at least go off birth control. I was going to stay on it."

"Grey and Elena knew this?" Kathy had been fascinated.

"Of course. It's not a big thing, Kathy."

Her smile said otherwise and I felt my face warm with humiliation and growing wrath. I hated to discuss children with women of the Pack. They never understood my position.

"You're afraid to have a baby, aren't you?" Kathy had guessed with an astuteness that made me squirm against the leather seat.

"I'm not scared," I protested, but I could tell she didn't believe me.

"So it's not just the conspiracy, it's all your life, this fear. You've let fear rule your entire existence, haven't you? You never developed your wolf because you were scared. You don't want a baby because you're scared. You look at a grandmother or a grandfather and you're scared. So tell me, Stanzie, all this fear, has it ever stopped the bad shit from happening anyway?" Kathy had tried to meet my gaze in the rearview mirror again but I stared at my boots. All at once, they'd seemed far less cute than they used to be.

# Chapter 22

Murphy took me aside after we parked the damn car. Kathy strode on ahead to get to Allerton, who stood by the Prelude with two other Pack. From the distance I didn't recognize them, and assumed they must be from one of the New England packs or maybe New York—people with experience as far as car bombs or explosives were concerned. That even such Pack members existed made me want to cry. When had we become so violent? Had we lost our way, or was this normal?

"She was too hard on you." Murphy held onto my arm even though I tried to get free so I could follow her. I didn't want to have this conversation with him.

"Maybe you're being too easy on me," I argued when it was clear he wouldn't let go. I stopped trying to get free and faced him. "I hid behind Grey and Elena, and I'm hiding behind you, and she's right, I am scared of too many things. I always have been."

"You do not have to have a baby," he told me in a very gentle tone. He looked so understanding and approachable. I knew I could touch him if I wanted. I knew he would take me in his arms if I wanted him to and I did want him to—so much it physically hurt. I stood my ground.

"When we're Alpha, you can stay on birth control," he told me.

"No!" Frustrated tears blinded me until I blinked them away. "No, Murphy, I can't. Not only is that against everything the Alpha system stands for, it's not fair to the woman who might have been Alpha instead of me, who might lose her chance at having a baby because I was Alpha during her fertile period and she wasn't. I can't do that. In Riverglow I could have done that. Elena was there, for one thing, but I can't deprive someone of a potential child just so you and I can become Councilors.

No. If we're Alpha, we'll have a baby. Or at least try to have one. Or I don't want to be Alpha."

"Maybe I don't want to either," he countered and I shook my head violently.

"No! You want to be a Councilor. You are not going to let me and my fear take away that potential too. No. This has been going on too long! I'm not going to let fear rule my whole life anymore!"

He didn't say anything, he just looked at me.

"I know you like to play the protector, but it's going to get old and then you'll resent and hate me," I predicted.

"I'm not playing anything with you," he said, his eyes flashing. "I'm telling you, you don't have to do all this shit just for me. That what you want counts too, that's all I'm saying!"

"Allerton's waving us over. I think we can leave. I want to drive back," I cried.

He swept a frustrated hand through his hair. "Damn that woman! You do not have to do everything all at once. You do not have to face every single goddamn fear you have in one damn day, Stanzie! We were doing fine and then we had to come here and now you're letting that bloody busybody woman lecture you. You're letting Allerton's expectations get to you. You're letting that old man scare you from the grave and you think you have to do all this shit on your own when you don't have to. It was you and me before. Why should that change?"

"I hide behind you!" I shouted. "I hide! And you're letting me! I think you get off on it, you like the chase, and right now you're chasing my fears but I'm the one who has to do that, not you!"

He let go of my arm and before he erased all the expression on his face, he looked vulnerable and lost. Unsure. All his usual confidence destroyed.

I left him standing there by the Town Car and stomped my way across the icy parking lot to where Allerton, Kathy and the two strangers stood by the Prelude.

"Everything all right?" Allerton asked me and I nodded, too strangled by emotion to speak. "I'll give Liam the keys. The Prelude is fine, Constance."

"I'll take the keys." I found my voice somehow and held out my hand. After a moment, Allerton put them in my palm.

"Thank you, Ray. Thank you, Noah," he said, addressing the two strange men. One was balding and verging past middle age, the other young, around my age. Possibly grandfather and grandson. Now that I was closer, I knew their faces from Regionals, but I was pretty sure I'd never spoken to either of them. My wolf had kept me isolated from most of the men in other packs. While I'd sometimes participated in the Great Hunts, I'd never shifted with anyone outside Riverglow. When I'd been first bonded to Grey, I hadn't wanted to, and after we'd been together a few years all of New England and upper-state New York knew about my wolf. Opportunities to shift with men outside my pack had noticeably dwindled. No one wanted to babysit when they shifted.

The younger one gave me a knowing stare and a surge of humiliation burned in my gut. Next the asshole would make a comment like *How's the wolf these days, Stanzie?* Or *Seen any good trees lately?* That was a particular favorite. Everyone in the region knew how much my wolf loved to run so that the world became a blur of speed and motion. They thought they were so goddamn clever. I'd show them someday when my wolf was normal just like theirs.

Abruptly, I became aware of my clenched fists and forced my fingers straight.

The older one nudged the younger and they faded back to a small red pickup which belched blue smoke from the exhaust pipe when the engine roared to life.

We watched them drive away then Kathy and Allerton began to pick their way carefully across the snowy expanse of the parking lot toward the Town Car and the Jaguar.

Kathy got into the Jaguar and drove off. Allerton got behind the wheel of the Town Car.

Murphy stared across the lot at me, the wind tumbling his hair across his forehead then he got into the Town Car and slammed the door shut so I couldn't see him anymore.

I waited until the Town Car was gone out of the lot before I turned back to the Prelude. Now I would stop being such a goddamn baby and take some control of my life.

The hood and trunk had been closed but I checked them both anyway. All I needed was for either of them to pop open when I was doing fifty miles per hour. I checked the tires too. I knew I was procrastinating but I couldn't help it. I took my time examining the car, not letting myself acknowledge I was only trying to delay getting into it.

Even though I knew there was no bomb, the idea of one sat like a malignant tumor at the base of my brain, flooding my body with random bursts of terror.

It couldn't have been more than twenty degrees, but I could feel cold sweat trickling down the back of my neck.

"I can do this." I spoke the words aloud to see if they gave me courage. Except that I sounded so scared and shaky it was a joke.

My hand reached for the door handle three times before I made contact and then it was a good minute and a half before I could bring myself to open the damn door.

Above the keening of the wind I could hear my own frightened, shallow breathing. I wished Murphy were there with me. Then, for having that traitorous thought, I took the heel of my hand and slammed it between my eyes hard enough to make my head swim.

"Baby," I spat at myself. "Coward. Pathetic fucking freak."

Yelling at myself, I got behind the wheel. One of my feet hit the brake pedal and I froze. My mind blanked. I didn't remember how to drive. I didn't remember my own goddamn name.

The keys were heavy in my fist. I couldn't make my fingers uncurl and I sat there for five minutes staring at my own hand, the car door yawning open, wind whipping inside, as icy, slick sweat trickled down my back.

*"The Comet or Blue Moon, Grey? Which club do you want to go to?"*

I heard my own words echo in my head from a night two and a half years in the past. I could see myself sitting behind the wheel of the Mustang in my little black dress and my gold spike-heel sandals. I could smell my perfume. J'adore. Four parts Dior, six parts unique Stanzie. I could see Grandfather Tobias scooting underneath the car on the little board on wheels he kept in the garage. The car was jacked up off the ground so he could fit and the gold paint on the car shone with a metallic brilliance in the August sun. I could see his work boots and the cuffs of his faded jeans as he tampered with the brake line when I thought he was just checking everything out. I could see Grey sitting beside me with his hair pulled back. His black t-shirt was tucked into his black jeans. I could see

Elena in the backseat in her white mini dress and white sandals, the ones that had ties that twirled around her shapely calves and knotted just below her knee. I could smell her perfume too—Estee Lauder's Pleasures, the scent she always wore in the summer.

Their faces were bright and clear in my memory today. No fading. No blurring. They were as plain and in focus as if they were really sitting in the car with me.

"*Fuuuck!*" I screamed, pounding on the wheel with both my fists. "*Fuuuck!*"

I fumbled open the door and got the hell out of the car.

My purse was in the trunk. So was my cellphone. After retrieving both, I leaned back against the bumper and stared at the cellphone. I put it down on the trunk and pulled my glove off with my teeth. My right hand still clutched the keys and wouldn't uncurl.

I picked up the phone in my left hand and scrolled through my contacts until I got to Murphy's name.

"Epic fail, Stanzie," I whispered before I pressed *send*.

Twelve seconds later I heard a cellphone ring from the glove compartment.

Swearing, I disconnected and shoved my cellphone back into my purse. Murphy's phone, muffled by the glove compartment, stopped its goddamn noise.

I got back into the car, the passenger seat this time. I could breathe again and I took several deep breaths before I opened the glove compartment.

Hidden under Murphy's cellphone, the insurance papers, owner's manual and maintenance receipts were our bond pendants. Curled up in little chain link balls beside each other. His chain was longer, with bigger links. Mine was shinier.

The wind rocked the car then it came inside. Along with Murphy. I couldn't look at him, I was so ashamed. I wasn't sure how long I'd been sitting in the passenger seat staring at our pendants but something told me it had been awhile.

"I actually did unbend my knees. I was sitting where you are for a little while anyway," I whispered when he didn't say anything. "I just can't unmake my fist." I lifted my right hand, still clenched, and waved it for emphasis. "The keys are there."

"See, progress," he said, a smile in his voice.

I didn't answer.

"Someday, Stanzie, you're going to drive this car. You'll be ready. You're doing really well, you know, better than you think."

"Bullshit. Every week you ask me if I want to drive and every week I laugh at you and say no way. I let you do all the driving and I hate it when other people drive. I get so scared when other people drive me."

"But not when I do?"

I shrugged. "No. You, I trust."

"You didn't in the beginning. That first time you got into a car with me, you wouldn't fasten your seatbelt, remember that? And then when you finally did, you spent the whole drive between the chateau and Paris with your hands clutched into fists, knuckles so white it hurt me to look at them. Stiff and upright in your seat, just this side of panic. And every time you'd get into the car with me at first, you'd start to tense up before we even unlocked the doors. And again with the clenched fists and the stiff body. I used to stop every ten miles just so you could get the blood circulating through your fingers again."

"I remember you stopping, but not my clenched fists." I stole a look at him.

He was smiling at me, his face so kind. "I know. You hated every minute in the car the first couple of weeks. But you got in the car and you did it. And now it's gotten to the point where you're still anxious, but I can go two hours now without stopping instead of fifteen minutes. And the first time I asked if you wanted to drive, you shut down for an entire hour. You didn't talk, you didn't look at me. You just shut down. Now you laugh at me when I ask you. You've come a long way, honey, and you don't see it but I do. You think everything has to happen all at once in a big rush or it doesn't mean anything, it's not real, but that's not true. It's one step at a time, Stanzie. You don't have to do it all at once. And look at you, today in the car with Kathy? She drove like a lunatic on purpose and you handled it. If that had happened three months ago you would have been crying and begging her to let you out of the car, you know that? So stop beating yourself up."

"We were all the way to the Starbucks yesterday before I realized you weren't driving," I offered and his smile got bigger.

"Yes, exactly. You see?"

"I was too scared of being shot at to be scared at driving in a car," I sighed. "I just traded one fear for another."

"People can't be scared of multiple things at the same time? You handled the car yesterday, Stanzie. You handled being shot at too."

"Ha. I woke up screaming in the middle of the night. Delayed reaction," I said.

He sighed.

"Sorcha died falling down the stairs. I don't see you scared of staircases now. But if she'd been my bond mate, I'll bet I'd be afraid and have to live on the ground floor, take a Valium if I need to step up more than three stairs at a time. I'm a coward, Murphy."

"No, you're not. I didn't fall down the stairs with Sorcha, did I? You were in the car. You were in a terrible, terrible accident. You were with your bond mates when they died. You saw it all. You heard it. You smelled it. You touched it. And you got fuck all for support after it happened. From anybody. Not your bloody ex pack, not your birth pack, you had no friends or anybody at all. And you were alone. All alone. I've never been that. I moved to Belfast, sure, but I had friends from Mac Tire visiting me all the damn time. Ringing me up, dropping by all the way from Dublin, emailing me, everything. My mother was there for me and me da too. They wouldn't let me be even when I begged them, when I screamed at them.

"So don't you tell me you're a coward, Constance Newcastle, because you are not. You've got your fears and you're facing them. You push yourself too hard is what you do. Push and get frustrated and it kills me to watch you doing it. I want to help. I want to be there for you and now you're thinking you're hiding behind me and you're going to push me away but I'm not going to let you, so you'd just better give it up, okay? You push me all you want but I'm not going anywhere."

For once the waterworks didn't start. My eyes remained dry. I felt hollow and yet strangely heavy and weighted down all at the same time.

"You forget. Everyone blamed me for Grey and Elena. Nobody but Colin Hunter blamed you for Sorcha. Why should anyone have bothered with me if I really had been at fault?"

"For one thing, you weren't, and nobody stuck by you. I would have. Even if you had been guilty. People make mistakes. All the time they make them. And if they're smart enough, they learn from them and go on. Say you had been drunk that night and you lost control of that car and drove off that embankment. Do you think every pack in the world would have cast you out?" Murphy's voice was passionate but so was mine when I said,

"You don't kill Pack!"

"Not deliberately, but sometimes shit happens." Murphy sighed in frustration. "There was this woman in Mac Tire once. The Alpha before me. She had a little four-year-old daughter who liked to play with everything but her own toys. This woman was well aware of that. She smoked cigarettes. Can you guess what happened? That little girl found her mother's matches one morning before anybody else in the house was up. Set herself and the house on fire. She died, the father died, the mother, she lived. Do you think Mac Tire kicked her out?"

I shrugged.

"It gets worse. They had a party the night before. That's why she left out the matches. She was drunk. She admitted that to the Council. She thought about cleaning up before going to bed but was too drunk. She passed out in the bathroom which was near the back door and the only reason she didn't die in the fire too."

I shook my head. I didn't want to hear it.

"The Council judged her guilty of gross negligence, Stanzie. Left the punishment up to the Alphas. You know what we did?"

"Let her stay in the pack," I whispered to get him to shut up.

"Yes, we did. Sorcha and I," he said with a bleak smile. "She bonded with a duo. Her best friend and her bond mate. Last I knew she was teaching art to the kids in the pack."

"She didn't get punished at all?"

"Oh, yes, she did. She had to give up smoking. Hasn't gone near a cigarette since. Wonder why?"

I pushed hair out of my eyes with my free hand.

"So, okay, Mac Tire is a forgiving pack, and you were a benevolent, generous Alpha. Maybe in Ireland pack members can forgive shit like that, but this is New England."

"You can talk, talk, talk all night long about how you deserved it and I'll never agree. You were fucked over, Stanzie. It's okay to be mad about it. I mean really mad about it. Not pretend mad to get the guilty person to admit he or she was in on it with the old man."

"Is that what you think I'm doing? I was angry at Grandfather Tobias. I was mean to him when I gave him the poison. And I don't forgive him, that wasn't an act. I don't," I cried.

"Good! Good for you. But are you doing it for yourself or for Grey and Elena?"

"What's the difference? And, anyway, Murphy, you're a hypocrite because *you* blame yourself for Sorcha's death. You don't forgive yourself for not being there."

"Maybe," he allowed. "It seems sometimes like it happened to somebody else, not me. I'm actually kinda happy lately. I want to let it all go, let it be in the past."

"Me too," I admitted, not looking at him because I felt so guilty. "You're good to me, Murphy. Thank you."

"We're bond mates." He reached into the glove compartment and took out his pendant.

"And friends too," I added, my voice trembling.

"Yeah, and friends," he echoed, but he sounded sad, just like me.

\* \* \* \*

Halfway back to the safe house, my cellphone chirped. I had the ring tone set to the sound of crickets. It reminded me of the woods and being my wolf.

"Stanzie, Councilor Manning gave me your number." It was Callie. She tried to sound bright, but I heard the weariness behind it. "What are you and Liam doing for lunch? Do you want to come over?"

"Lunch?" I repeated, probably sounding stupid.

"You haven't eaten yet, have you? It's just eleven. Nora and Jonathan stopped by for coffee and I thought maybe you and Liam would like to come over too. Nothing special, just sandwiches and chips. I've got a bottle of Chianti. You still like Chianti, don't you?"

"Sure," I said. "We can come over, Callie. It's good timing. Murphy and I are going back to Boston soon. Maybe tomorrow, definitely by Sunday." This, of course, was wishful thinking, but it was also calculated.

"I thought you were going to try to find out Grandfather's Tobias's deep, dark secret?" Again she tried for light, again she failed.

"Nah, I give up." I didn't have to try to sound tired.

"That doesn't sound like you. Normally, you're a bulldog when it comes to things you've made your mind up over," she teased. "It was Vaughn's idea to invite you. Isn't that funny? I think he has something to tell you."

For a moment I thought she meant he was going to come out and confess he'd been Grandfather Tobias's accomplice but then I wondered if she meant he was going to tell me he trashed my house.

Or maybe Jonathan or Nora had skillfully suggested she invite us over. Only Jonathan wasn't that skillful. If Nora wasn't drunk, she might be.

Or maybe I was paranoid.

"We can be there in about twenty minutes." I calculated, taking a look at where we were on the highway and figuring out how far we were from the exit we needed.

I hung up and told Murphy we had a lunch invitation.

Suspicion dawned in his eyes and he frowned for a moment as he debated what to do. "Call Allerton and let him know, will you, love?"

Allerton didn't say much. He did tell me he hoped we had a good time and that he wanted to hear about it when we returned. And that Kathy Manning was making brownies.

"Jaysus, Mary and Joseph, I won't be able to button my pants if she keeps doing shite like that," Murphy remarked. I couldn't help but laugh just a little.

# Chapter 23

Callie, Peter and Vaughn lived in a small three-bedroom ranch house with a finished basement level.

They did their entertaining in the basement. Callie had never much liked the kitchen and they'd made the dining room into the third bedroom.

Technically each of them had a bedroom, but Peter never slept in his, so his room was the smallest.

The dining room was Vaughn's hideout. There was an actual door into the hallway, but just an archway into the kitchen. He'd strung up a beaded curtain and it was another reason Callie liked entertaining in the basement. She hated that curtain.

It was pretty psychedelic. Bold blues, swirling reds, deep purples, eye-popping yellows. The peace sign picked out in black beads was the *piece de resistance*, though.

There was no bathroom in the basement and, after two glasses of Chianti and half a glass of mineral water, I had to go.

I trudged up the stairs, leaving Callie, Vaughn, Jonathan, Nora and Murphy below. I attempted to be quiet because Peter was sleeping off a migraine. He got them sometimes, usually in the winter. I remembered that.

Callie's basement brought back lots of memories.

The rag rugs on the floor, the fireplace heaped with logs, the blue recliner that could fit two people if they squished.

It had never seemed shabby before but today it did. It had never seemed claustrophobic either, but I was glad to escape to the top level. The windows were small and narrow, casement windows that cranked open and, even then, not all the way. Not that they were open in this winter weather.

Callie had covered them with dark brown curtains, which added to the smothering effect.

I hated that basement room. I realized it as I flushed the toilet and examined my face in the spotted mirror above the sink.

The bathroom was very clean, but still dingy, because everything in it dated back to the 1980s. I guess people who lived on retail salaries couldn't have Kohler fixtures and Italian ceramic tile.

"You're spoiled, Stanzie," I told my reflection. I might be wearing a twenty dollar sweater, but my boots had cost two hundred and fifty dollars and I'd plunked down my debit card without blinking when I'd bought them in Manhattan.

I don't think Callie had spent two hundred fifty dollars on any item of clothing she'd ever worn in her entire life.

The towels on the rack were cheap and fraying, although I'd bet she hadn't owned them more than a few months. I was used to the plush luxury towels found in boutique hotels.

The shower curtain was cheap too—bright see-through plastic with huge red-and-yellow flowers that almost but not quite matched the towels and bath mat.

I had on a pair of sapphire earrings Murphy had put into my Christmas stocking. Real sapphires. Not chips, not synthetic, not glass or crystal.

The only real gems Callie owned were the ones in her bond pendant—a tiny emerald, an even smaller diamond and a garnet.

My blond hair was long but expertly styled. I'd spent a hundred dollars at a salon in Beacon Hill on New Year's Eve so my hair would look nice for dinner. Then I'd gone and shifted in the woods. By the time I'd shifted back, the elegant updo had bits of leaves and grass stuck in it. Half the pins had been gone, most of it straggled down my back in a blond snarl that had taken me half an hour to comb through.

"Spoiled, spoiled, spoiled," I told myself and nearly kicked down the door to get the hell out.

Once in the hallway I wrinkled my nose. I wasn't the only thing that was spoiled. Either the garbage needed taking out or there was something bad in the refrigerator.

I started to tremble for some reason and went into the kitchen to see if I could track down the smell and get rid of it. It was making me sick.

The psychedelic beaded curtain was pulled back and looped over a hook in the wall, exposing most of Vaughn's room.

It was relatively neat for a man's bedroom. The bed was even made. The bed consisted of a mattress on the floor covered by a bright blue comforter. A wide bookcase took up most of the floor space. The shelves were piled high with books and papers and magazines.

There was also a cat. A pretty glass cat. A cat I recognized. The last time I had seen it, shining amber in the slanting summer sunlight, it had been perched on the window sill in my house next to a blue kitten with a glass ball of yarn.

This cat sat up with her tail curled around her paws, her face tilted as if she pondered something deep and metaphysical.

If I'd ever needed proof that Vaughn had trashed my house, here it was. And he didn't even bother to hide it. The cat was now a paperweight on his bookcase. Instead of sitting in a window, she sat on top of the latest three issues of *Penthouse*.

Elena would have been pissed.

"Elena would have been pissed." I reached out to snatch the cat off the magazines.

"I know," said Vaughn from behind me. He'd come into the room silently. I'd only figured out he was there the split second before I reached for the cat.

"*Penthouse*, Vaughn?" I turned around, cradling the cat in both hands and gave him a scornful, outraged look.

He shrugged. "I can't stand *Playboy*, sorry."

"You stole this." I shook the cat in front of his face and wished that smell would go away. "What is that smell?"

"I don't know. It's rank, isn't it?" Vaughn wrinkled his nose and we both looked around his room, but it wasn't coming from here. It wasn't coming from the kitchen either. He gave a little shiver and his face was foreign to me at that moment. Here was a man I'd played duets with on Saturday afternoons, a man I'd laughed and joked with, slept with, commiserated with when he'd told me he'd loved Elena. But after two and a half years he was almost a stranger and everything that had come before seemed like a mirage or suspect memories. Maybe fantasies or dreams. Not reality because reality was standing right in front of me with a blank expression and no connection to me whatsoever.

"It was supposed to be me and Grey who died, right? And then you'd get Elena? Is that how Grandfather Tobias told you it would go? Is that why you helped him?" My voice was flat, but I was shaking. I almost dropped Elena's cat but managed to hang onto her.

Vaughn stared at me for an excruciating moment. A pulse beat thickly in his throat.

"You're fucked in the head," he eventually said. Malevolence gleamed in his small brown eyes. "It was an accident, Stanzie. The old man made a mistake. Now you're saying not only did I cover it up, I helped him do it on purpose? Fuck you. I loved Grey like a brother. I loved you, you idiot. I would never have hurt either of you. Even to get Elena. I would never have covered anything up and let you take the blame. You go to hell."

I stared at his unfamiliar face and it all at once swam into focus. I knew him. And what's more, I believed him. I totally and completely believed him.

"But you know who did help him, don't you?" I accused next and he let out a desperate laugh and swept a hand through his tangled brown hair.

"You're fucked in the head," he said again, but there was no conviction.

"It's all right, Vaughn," said Callie, pulling the beaded curtain closed as she entered the room. "You can tell her."

"Callie," whispered Vaughn. His eyes begged her to stop talking, stop walking, but she did neither.

"This was going to be the nursery," said Callie, looking around the room and laughing a little.

Her ethereal features seemed to glow with the fervor of her dreams. She was never more beautiful or terrible.

Her strawberry blond hair flowed down to her shoulders, a mass of loose, beautiful curls.

"I thought it would be convenient near the kitchen. I could sing the baby to sleep when I did dishes or when I was cooking dinner." She shook herself out of her daydream and smiled.

I took an involuntary step backward and hit the bookcase. There was nowhere to go.

"You weren't the only one who visited Grandfather Tobias, Stanzie. He always liked you best, but he could talk to me. Tell me how he really felt. You were too innocent, too naive, but not me."

She smiled again. Her hands were clasped behind her back, which made her look as if she were a sweet innocent maiden posing for a picture. If anyone ever looked naive it was her. Except for her eyes. They knew darkness.

"Callie," Vaughn tried again, shaking his head, and I realized he didn't know anything. He hadn't known anything until now when it all fell into place for him. "Callie, I loved her. I loved Elena. Tell me you didn't...you didn't have anything to do with it. Tell me!"

She flashed him a look of pitying contempt. "He tampered with that car on purpose. It was no accident, Vaughn, and I knew about it. I'm the one who suggested they get her a car for her birthday. Don't you remember? Elena and Grey came over one night for a beer and we were talking about what to get Stanzie for her birthday and I said a car. Stanzie's always wanted a Mustang, and you laughed because you didn't think Elena and Grey could afford that but then you never paid much attention to how much money they had and how poor we were. As long as we had enough for beer and your fucking *Penthouse* subscription, you were cool, right?"

"Callie," Vaughn croaked. His eyes were pools of utter horror. He remembered the conversation, I could see it. "Why?"

"Why?" Her pretty mouth twisted and made her look like a harpy, not a woman. "Why? Why do you think, Vaughn? Nora and Jonathan couldn't be Alpha forever, could they? And who would be next in line after them? Here's a clue—not us. Not unless..." She grinned and Vaughn moaned.

"You did it so you could have another shot at having a baby?" Aghast, he gaped at her. "You helped murder Elena and Grey so you could have a fucking baby? Callie, you can't have a baby. All you have are miscarriages! You fucking killed them so you could have six more miscarriages before you turned forty-five? Are you fucking serious? Are you fucking standing there telling me you murdered Elena and Grey for that and that old man helped you?"

"Maybe the next one wouldn't have miscarried," Callie argued and Vaughn moaned again. "But now because Stanzie had to come waltzing back into our lives and stir everything up, I won't have the chance, will I?"

She transferred her dark blue gaze to me. "You were supposed to die too in that car crash. He said you all would. And then you had to go and walk away without a scratch and I had to work Jonathan up into a frenzy about you being drunk and that damned old man wouldn't help me at all. I had to do it all myself. You were supposed to die with them, Stanzie. You weren't supposed to suffer the way you did. I never wanted that. You're my friend and I didn't want you to suffer."

"Are you fucking kidding me?" Vaughn gasped. "Oh my God."

From the hallway, we all heard the basement door rattle. It was locked. More rattling then pounding. Callie ignored it, but waited for Vaughn and me to look at her again.

"I don't like people to suffer. I'm sorry, Vaughn, about this. I knew you'd get over Elena once we were Alpha again and you needed to focus on me. I was right too. I wish you'd stayed downstairs with the others. I didn't want you to see this." Callie smiled at him wistfully.

"If you don't like people to suffer, why didn't you think about me or Peter before you did this? This is going to destroy him, you know that? He worships you, Callie." Vaughn had tears in his eyes now, but he wasn't crying yet.

A soft smile made Callie's face radiant.

I already knew, but it took Vaughn a moment to catch up, and even then he wouldn't let himself believe it.

"Where's Peter? Where's Peter, Callie?"

"In the bedroom," she said, still smiling.

The pounding got louder. It sounded as though someone was throwing himself at the door with all his strength.

Voices were calling now too. Callie's name. Mine. Two male voices, one female. The more they shouted, the more Callie smiled.

"That door's solid oak. The bolt's new too," she remarked with a self-satisfied sigh.

"What did you do to Peter, Callie? Oh God, what did you do?" Vaughn was crying now, huge tears slipping down his cheeks that he ignored as he pleaded with his bond mate.

"He had a headache," Callie said with a dreamy expression, although there was also grief. "So I gave him something to make the pain stop."

Vaughn shook his head then shook it again harder. It was easy to identify the smell now—now that we knew what it was.

Callie gave me a beatific, conspiratorial smile, as if we were accomplices together.

"Just like Stanzie gave Grandfather Tobias something to stop the pain. The pain of living. Right, Stanzie?"

She looked back at Vaughn. "You didn't buy that whole we'll exile him to Florida act, did you? Wasn't it convenient how he died before he got there? Stanzie knows just how convenient, doesn't she?" Callie turned to me again and I stood there.

"You didn't have to kill Peter," I said and Vaughn let out a hoarse cry because I'd said it out loud and he wasn't ready to hear it yet.

"Yes, I did. He worshipped me and he would never have understood why I did what I did. I didn't want him to ever know and now he never will."

"We need to go back downstairs, Callie," I said. "I'll get you something to drink and we can work this out, okay?"

Callie laughed at me. "Work what out, Stanzie? I'm not going to be tried by the Council. I'm not going to wait around to be executed like Grandfather Tobias. I played and lost and I'm going to end this whole thing my way. It doesn't matter, because Peter is dead and I don't have a baby. I have nothing. So don't worry, Stanzie, I'll get what's coming to me, but I'll do it my way, not yours."

She pressed the gun she'd been holding behind her back to her pale forehead.

"I thought I could kill you and Liam yesterday but I didn't have the guts," she told me, her eyes locked to mine. "But I have the guts to do this."

She pulled the trigger.

Blood, bone and brain matter exploded in all directions. Most of it hit the ceiling, but enough of it ended up on me and Vaughn to make us both cry out and throw our arms up to protect our eyes. Only it was too late.

Callie's body crumpled to the floor. Her dead fingers tightened convulsively around the trigger of the gun but it didn't go off again.

The solid oak basement door splintered and I could hear Murphy screaming my name. I couldn't move. I couldn't even lower my arms at first.

There was a blur of color and motion in the kitchen and the beaded curtain broke, cascading beads every which way. Some of them rolled into the pool of blood gathering beneath Callie's ruined head. I could see it, so I must have lowered my arms, only I didn't remember doing it.

Even as Murphy jerked me into his arms, I kept my face turned so I could watch the multi-colored beads roll into the blood.

He was crying and he held me so tightly I couldn't breathe. It hurt but I didn't try to get free. I just wanted to watch the beads in the blood.

Somehow I still had Elena's cat in my hands. It rubbed against Murphy's thigh. My arms were trapped against my sides because I couldn't move, he held me so tightly.

Jonathan took one appalled look and rushed off to the bathroom, hand over his mouth.

When I heard him retching, I remembered how he'd thrown up in the bushes when he saw Grey's dead body. He was such a wuss.

Nora flattened herself against the wall, her eyes huge. She stuffed one fist to her mouth but she didn't cry, scream or puke. I think she would have fallen if not for the wall.

"Vaughn," I said. Only I could barely recognize my own voice. It didn't seem to be coming from my body for one thing.

I forced myself to stop looking at the beads and blood, and turned my face in Vaughn's direction. Only he wasn't there. The hallway door was open. It had been closed before.

"Vaughn," I said again. I struggled to be free of Murphy's embrace and he let me go, although clearly he didn't want to.

Carefully skirting Callie's body and most of the blood, I followed Vaughn's bloody footprints down the hall to the master bedroom.

The smell was bad and it got worse the closer I got to the door.

Inside the room was dark save for the light that came in through the hallway.

Vaughn knelt by the bed, head down, crying.

Peter lay on his back, one arm across his chest.

*Amy Lee Burgess*

His skin was waxy gray, but his eyes were closed. He even seemed to be smiling a little.

His chest was bare and toned. His bond pendant gleamed from around his throat.

He looked as if he were only sleeping. Because I was Pack, I could smell death way before decay set in.

Peter had only been dead a few hours. Three at the most. Rigor mortis hadn't even set in yet.

I knelt beside Vaughn and put my arms around him, drawing him close.

He buried his face in my neck and cried so hard I had to use the bed to brace us or we would have fallen over.

I was numb, but a part of me relived the terrible moment just before I'd fully comprehended Grey and Elena were really dead. Vaughn was in that same moment now and he would crash into the horrible next phase of his life soon. A life filled with hopelessness and betrayal. And worst of all, he'd be alone where no one could quite reach him.

Even though I'd experienced the same hell, it wouldn't be enough to bridge the gap, but I held him anyway. No one had held me, but I would hold him. Maybe, just maybe, he wouldn't feel quite as alone as I had.

Murphy's shadow fell across us and I looked up to see him staring down at Peter.

"Mother of God," he said, his face grim. He took out his cellphone and called Allerton.

Twenty minutes later the clean-up began. It didn't take long to remove the bodies and scrub the floors, walls and ceiling clean, but I only had to close my eyes to make all the blood come back. There was no industrial-strength quick-cleanser to scrub out the memories.

\* \* \* \*

We stood in a circle in the same clearing we had four days earlier. The same people, only now, two of them were reduced to ash inside ceramic urns.

Callie's was black, Peter's cobalt blue.

Vaughn had carried them both as we'd walked single file through the woods. Some of the snow had melted between Grandfather Tobias's funeral and this one, but not much. I'd walked behind Vaughn because he wouldn't let anyone else near him.

He hadn't talked much since he'd watched Callie blow her head half off. Any talking he'd done had been to me and that had been mostly monosyllabic. He ate only what I put in front of him, drank only what I poured for him, slept in the same bed with me, holding onto me as if I could save him from the nightmares he suffered. When he woke screaming, I was there. I tried to make him feel safe but I don't know if I did.

Kathy Manning made him cookies, pies and all his favorite food but he didn't seem to taste any of it. She watched him eat, her elfish brows knitted as she schemed her next tempting meal or baked good. She was determined to get through to him with food.

Allerton let him alone, but he watched. That man always watched and he missed nothing.

Murphy was a saint, not the least bit jealous or impatient. He sat with Vaughn and me all day long. He talked, told Vaughn about Sorcha. Things he hadn't even told me yet, he told Vaughn, and I heard them for the first time too.

Vaughn didn't say anything, but I think he listened. When Murphy left the room, Vaughn would follow him with his gaze and when he returned, Vaughn seemed to relax maybe just a little.

I wasn't sure he'd carry the urns but he took them from Colin Hunter's hands in the parking lot in front of the Devil's Hopyard.

Colin and Devon were Alphas of Riverglow now. Vaughn couldn't be Alpha without a bond mate. He couldn't even stay a member of Riverglow unless he bonded within the next three months. I somehow doubted he gave a shit, but he would, eventually. At least I hoped he would.

Now we waited in a circle around Vaughn, who stood in the center with both the urns.

Vaughn's gaze met mine and I nodded encouragement. I wanted him to say what he wanted to say. It didn't matter if it was angry or mournful, hateful or wistful. I just wanted him to speak from his heart.

Very carefully he put Peter's urn down on the forest floor at his feet. He held Callie's urn in both hands and, for a moment, I thought he might smash it down to the ground and stomp on it and that would have been all right too, but he didn't.

He took the top off the urn and reached in for some of the grayish-white cremains.

Saying nothing, he sprinkled in a circle around himself, careful not to get any on Peter's urn.

They'd been bond mates for almost two decades. They'd always been a triad. Peter and Vaughn had grown up together in the same birth pack. They'd been inseparable since they could walk. Peter had been older by only a year.

They'd met Callie at a Regional in Maine when Vaughn had been sixteen and Peter and Callie had been seventeen. They'd bonded four years later at another Regional, this one in Connecticut, and they'd formed Riverglow with Jonathan and Nora.

They'd been Alphas of the pack for seven years before Jonathan and Nora took over.

When Grey and I had joined, they'd been Alphas. The transition to Jonathan and Nora had happened the same year Grey and I had bonded with Elena.

Vaughn had spent more than half his life with Callie and he had nothing to say at her funeral.

Reverently, he picked up Peter's urn and removed the top. He had to stand very still for a moment before he brought himself to take a handful of the cremains.

"My brother," he whispered, a cheated smile flashing across his face. "I try to tell myself that this is the way you'd have wanted it. That you wouldn't have wanted to know the truth. Died loving her as much as you always and ever have. I've been telling myself that for days now but I don't think I believe it. Maybe that's why I've been left behind because I don't believe in anything." He closed his eyes and a flock of starlings burst from the tree tops and swirled together high above his head. I could hear their flapping wings, the muted flutter of their rapid heartbeats before they were gone, as if they'd never been.

"Goodbye," said Vaughn and he sprinkled Peter's ashes in a circle around himself.

He came to stand beside me and I took his hand. He leaned against me for comfort but kept his eyes fixed to the center of the circle.

One by one people stepped into the center of the circle. Everyone had something good to say about Peter. Jonathan cried. Nora didn't. Today she did not smell of alcohol, only perfume.

Murphy said things in Irish for Callie but he spoke English for Peter. He said, "Of everyone in Riverglow, you tried to make it right and, at least with me, you did. I would have been proud to call you friend if time had allowed. You'll be missed, Peter Gardiner, of that I have no doubt."

Then it was my turn and I had to let go of Vaughn's hand to step into the circle.

I picked up Peter's urn first and, although I told myself I wouldn't cry, I did.

"There's a lot of things to remember about you, Peter," I said when I could. "But I'll always remember you're the one who showed me how to put ketchup on my eggs."

Nora started to laugh a little then even she began to cry.

"You made the best breakfasts in the world, but they were always just a little bit better with lots of ketchup."

Even Vaughn smiled then and I sprinkled some of Peter's ashes around in a circle, remembering him standing behind the stove in the kitchen Callie had never liked, spatula in one hand, beer in the other because, just as much as ketchup, Peter had loved beer with breakfast. Of course by the time all of us had rolled out of bed the morning after shifting and gotten our bleary asses to the table, it had been past noon so it wasn't so much breakfast as brunch.

I remembered the handful of times Peter and I had gone to bed together—how he would pick me up in a bear hug and nail me against the wall, my legs locked around his waist as he told me how goddamn hot I was and I'd be reduced to shivering jelly, secretly wishing Grey would do me against the wall like that but he never had.

My eyes shut, I let myself think about Peter for a moment. I hoped like hell he wasn't walking like Grandfather Tobias, that he wasn't still lingering like Grey and Elena had for me. *"I'll watch over Vaughn,"* I whispered inside my head to him, not knowing if he could hear, but compelled to say it anyway. *"You go ahead and I'll take care of him, Peter, I swear."*

Callie's urn wasn't heavy but it seemed to weigh a ton in my hands. It was mostly empty by now because I was the last inside the circle.

At first I didn't know what to say, if I could say anything, if I'd be like most of them who'd gone before me, who hadn't said anything, but had simply sifted her ashes through their gloved fingers and walked away.

But the words suddenly came to me and I spoke them aloud in a voice that was steady and determined. "I'll remember you too, Callie. I'll remember you and hope for myself that I never want something so much that I forget what I already have."

Vaughn bowed his head. Devon Talbot stood beside her bond mate, tears coursing down her cheeks. Colin Hunter nodded and looked across the circle at Murphy, who stared at me.

I stared back, while above our heads the starlings swirled out of the tree tops and darted in and out of the branches before flying away to find a quieter roost.

# Meet the Author

Why do I write? Since I was a child I've sent myself to sleep by planning stories. It took me until I was ten to figure out I needed to write them down as well as imagine them. After that, I tortured my friends reading them all aloud and if they were nice to me, they got a character named for them. Yeah, okay, I usually killed them off, but every story needs some dramatic tension, right?

Nowadays I only kill off purely fictional characters who may or may not be based on hot Hollywood actors. Unlike my friends, they never complain.

I grew up in Connecticut and the towns and parks mentioned in this novel are all real, although I've taken certain liberties with some of them. I live and work in Houston these days, but New England remains a limitless source of inspiration.

I'm fascinated with the concept of shapeshifting and what a person might discover about herself if she could find and release the wolf within. Stanzie's continuing story is my exploration as much as it is hers.

Amy's Website:
http://amyleeburgess.blogspot.com/
Reader eMail:
Amyleeburgess99@gmail.com

Turn the page for a special excerpt of Amy Lee Burgess's

# Hidden In Plain Sight

*As Stanzie discovers her wolf, she learns being herself is more danger-
ous than ever.*

Where is Bethany Dillon? The seventeen year-old girl is missing from
the Maplefair pack and Constance Newcastle--Stanzie--and Liam
Murphy must find her. Fast. A serial killer still has not been caught.
Bethany could have run away, or killed herself. But no one in her pack
seems to know the truth. Or, they're just not telling.

Constanceís knack for uncovering secrets leads her into peril, and to
save Bethany, she must break every rule. She risks losing everything,
including Liam...and her life.

*On sale now!*

# Chapter 1

*I follow Friend in the woods. Trees can be woods. Trees can be oak. Can be willow. I like willow trees. They pretty. Both words for the same thing. My head is so big with words. But many words left to find. When will I? Friend wants to run and play but there are words I do not have. Friend run fast, I run fast. I scared to be just me in the woods. I scared I need word I not find yet. I scared. I wish I had word for why but that one hides. All words hide. I find. Dig up from inside my head, from ground, from sky. Words hide but I find. I find them all. Then I not scared no more.*

\* \* \* \*

The day after shifting into wolf form could be rough. It depended on how much water we drank before we shifted and if we were stupid enough to drink alcohol.

Murphy and I hadn't planned to shift, it had happened organically after a bottle of white wine and two hours of intense sex. Vaughn had gone out drinking at the pubs on Beacon Street and we'd had the condo to ourselves for a change.

It had been Murphy's idea to shift. The wine had been my idea. Sex had been a mutual decision.

It was April and spring had definitely sprung in Boston.

The three of us sprawled on a wooden bench beneath a willow tree on Boston Common. The branches dipped into a small pond where four ducks quacked indignantly to cover up their innate fear of us. We were Pack and they knew it, although in human form we wouldn't touch them. Wolf form? Yeah, they would be smart to avoid us.

Vaughn had his long legs stretched straight out in front of him as he consumed a foot-long hotdog smothered in chili. The smell of it nauseated me, and I tried to breathe through my mouth to dilute the scent.

On my other side Murphy watched joggers run past. One girl was seasonally optimistic in a pair of bright red shorts with white piping. Her legs looked cold to me but Murphy obviously found them attractive. He tracked her with his dark eyes but then I noticed him grin because he was aware I watched him do it. I swore that man loved to fuck with me.

I stretched my legs out and ignored him. They ached like a bitch. I sucked water from a huge plastic bottle but it was too little too late. A limping retreat back to the condo seemed more and more likely.

Vaughn ignored the jogger. He ignored all the Others—regular humans. He semi-ignored us too, but only because he was so engrossed in his damn chili dog.

"That's disgusting." I was unable to keep silent anymore. "How can you eat that, Vaughn? It smells awful."

"But it tastes great," he said around a mouthful.

Murphy chuckled and I wanted to elbow him in the ribs but I was too sore.

The three of us idled in the spring sunshine, happy despite all the bullshit that had taken place three months previously when Vaughn's bond mates had died.

Callie had shot herself in the head when it had become clear she would be exposed as a conspirator in the underground movement within the Great Pack that attempted to scare us all back to the old ways. She'd murdered their bond mate, Peter, with a fatal dose of narcotics that he'd thought had been pain medicine for a migraine. She hadn't wanted him to know she'd helped murder my bond mates, Grey and Elena, in a rigged car crash nearly three years ago.

Vaughn had been left behind. He and I had both watched Callie kill herself and still had nightmares about it. After their funeral, Vaughn had come to stay with me and Murphy in Boston. He'd left Riverglow, but he wasn't in exile. As soon as he found a bond mate he could rejoin a pack, but it had been barely three months and a new bond mate was probably the furthest thing from his mind.

Murphy and I belonged to Mac Tire, the largest pack in Great Britain. Technically, we were supposed to live in Dublin, but our Alphas, Padraic O'Reilly and Fiona Carmichael, had given us leave to stay in Boston while Murphy and I worked on my wolf.

My wolf was not as evolved as others. I'd kept her deliberately childlike and free, but now I sought for her to catch up with everyone else. It had proven to be a long and difficult process. Paddy and Fee had nearly lost patience with us, and now we had Vaughn as another excuse to avoid going to Dublin. I was in no rush to see him leave, although I wished his suffering would ease. I hated to see him grief-stricken and in pain.

I heard him sometimes through the bedroom wall. Heard him jerk awake with a strangled scream. Heard him swear. Sometimes he punched the wall. Sometimes he cried. The nights where he cried I got out of bed and went to him and he clung to me like a child.

He hadn't cried in nearly three weeks, and I hoped the worst was over.

Vaughn wadded up the remains of his chili dog and tossed it and a bunch of paper napkins into a nearby trash can.

I reached up to touch the soft leaves above my tilted face. I was worried about my wolf. Since Vaughn had come to stay with us, Murphy and I rarely found the opportunity to have sex, let alone shift. Last night my wolf had been stubbornly reluctant to come out. For the first time since we'd started to shift together, Murphy had finished his transformation before me. Then my wolf had spent the entire time on a search for words for different types of trees. No playing. No fun.

The willow leaves were soft as they brushed my face. "My wolf knows willow tree. She knows oak and birch and maple too."

Murphy gave me a look that on anyone else's face I would have called infatuated, but since it was Murphy who looked at me, I didn't know what precisely to call it.

Maybe the infatuation was for my wolf. That made more sense anyway.

I glanced at my watch. "It's nearly two o'clock. Kathy said she'd get to our place around two thirty, so we'd better start getting back."

Tortured resignation stole over Vaughn's face. "Oh, Jesus, I forgot she was coming."

"How can you forget lemon squares?" Murphy demanded, in shock. "Or brownies. Or those goddamn delicious cookies with the stupid name?"

"Snickerdoodles," I supplied. Murphy snorted the way he always did when someone said *snickerdoodles*. He thought the word was funny, but what was really hilarious was the way he snorted laughter every single time he heard it. And the way he wolfed them down almost without chewing.

"That woman is weird. Always smiling. Does anyone ever have anything that good going on that they'd smile like that almost every single second?" Vaughn said *smile* the way most people would say *cockroach*.

"She brings baked goods. She can come in clown face with a rubber nose that squeaks for all I care as long as I get something good to eat." Murphy seemed transported at the thought of all the possibilities.

"That's not all she brings," I remarked and Vaughn shuddered.

"Oh, hell, she's not bringing Whatshername again, is she? Mona? Monica?"

"After the way you treated her, not likely. Your rudeness knew no bounds, Vaughn," I scolded.

Vaughn extended his middle finger in my direction. "Why does that woman want to set me up? I am not interested in bonding with anybody who's in the same pack as her. I'd have to see her smiling all the goddamn time if I joined her pack."

"Get used to it, mate," advised Murphy. "For three years people kept trying to set me up before I finally got cornered by Stanzie."

"Asshole, I did not corner you," I mumbled under my breath as Vaughn burst into reluctant laughter.

"Sure you did," Murphy teased. "There I was, Vaughn, minding my own damn business at the first night banquet at the Great Gathering, and who comes waltzing over to my table on the arm of Councilor Allerton but the woman sitting between us today. And Allerton, wasn't he the last one in a long line of busybodies who relentlessly tried to pair me up with somebody? And her in this red dress looking so beautiful I couldn't even swallow my wine."

"You knew then you wanted to bond with her?" Vaughn didn't know the story. He wasn't aware of the conspiracy within the Great Pack. He thought Callie had done what she had solely to recapture Alpha status within Riverglow so she could have a baby. There was no reason for him to know about the conspiracy, and I wasn't about to add to his already heavy burden of grief and betrayal.

"Hell no, I ran the other way." Murphy grinned broadly, and when I stuck my tongue out at him, he winked.

"You were obnoxious."

"Didn't I know I was destined to bond with the woman the first time I saw her?" Murphy let his Irish accent show more than usual and I tried not to grimace because he was so full of shit. He put on a show for Vaughn but it hurt my feelings because I secretly wanted him to be telling the truth. Somewhere along the line over the past six months with this man, I'd fallen in love. His heart, however, still firmly belonged to his dead bond mate, Sorcha. It didn't mean he wasn't fond of me, devoted even, but of course I wanted more.

"You're so full of Irish blarney, Murphy."

The skin around Murphy's eyes crinkled when he smiled at me. "You don't believe me?"

"Not one word."

He gave me that damn infatuated look again which about drove me mad. "You should, because I'm telling you the truth."

Our gazes locked and I felt a strange clutch at my heart. "We'd better go if we want to be back before Kathy gets there."

My muscles gave a protesting twinge as I rose. I gulped down water in the hope it would do me some good.

Murphy, damn him, did not seem sore at all, even though he'd drunk as much wine as I had. Of course he was taller and heavier than me, but it still did not seem in the least bit fair.

* * * *

Our cheery yellow, two-family condo was in the Brighton neighborhood of Boston. Ours was the upstairs unit.

Kathy Manning stood by the front steps and we saw her when we rounded the corner of our street.

Although she was at least fifty years old, because she was Pack she didn't appear to be much past twenty-five, thirty tops.

Dressed in a pair of cream tailored pants and blazer with a turquoise blue shell top beneath it, she fiddled in her oversize brown leather Coach bag. Her shoes were plain caramel Gucci flats with cute little leather bows on the toe. A gold tennis bracelet gleamed from one wrist, and her bond pendant hung from a fine link gold chain that encircled her throat. A Macy's shopping bag rested at her feet, which made Murphy's eyes gleam. He obviously hoped the bag contained something edible and sweet.

She was aware of us the moment we turned the corner even though we were still more than half a block away. Aside from a slight stiffening of her body, she ignored us and continued to poke around in her bag.

As we approached, she stopped rummaging in her bag and straightened. She gave us all one of her bright smiles and I was reminded of an elf. Barely topping five feet, she had short, pixie-cut brown hair and slanted gray-blue eyes. Her makeup was minimal yet effective.

"Hello, Vaughn." She singled him out, much to his dismay.

"Councilor Manning."

"Vaughn, dear, what can you tell me about Maplefair? There's a situation brewing there and unfortunately Vermont's Regional Councilor has just moved up to the Great Council and somehow I've been asked to handle things. It's rather awkward for me at the moment because I don't have an Advisor since mine was voted Alpha of our pack last month."

She flashed a smile at me and Murphy because we were Advisors to Councilor Jason Allerton. He served on the Great Council which oversaw the entire Pack and also the Regional Councils across the world. She was also Allerton's mistress and had, for some reason, decided to watch over the three of us.

"Why ask me about Maplefair? I haven't belonged to that pack in twenty years." Vaughn's tone was suspicious and Murphy gave him an interested look.

"Well, you were quite close with the pack's Alpha female at the last Regional, weren't you? I thought you might still be in contact." Kathy's smile was bright and innocent.

Dull spots of color burned Vaughn's cheeks. "It was two Regionals ago, actually, and all we did was hunt together. We're not exactly best buds, Councilor."

"Call me Kathy," she invited with a coquettish toss of her head. Vaughn gritted his teeth.

"You initiated her wolf years ago, didn't you?"

"Oh, for Christ's sake. What is this? So I initiated her wolf and I went on a Great Hunt with her fifteen years after that. What are you trying to say? I don't stay in touch with her. I don't stay in touch with anyone in Maplefair." Vaughn's fists clenched and Murphy took a step closer to him, disturbed by the tension. Whether he meant to protect Kathy or form a united front against her I wasn't sure.

I tried not to gape. Vaughn had hunted with Jossie Wilbanks? Since when? After he'd initiated her wolf, Jossie had thrown herself at him, intent on persuading him to sever ties with Peter and Callie so he could bond with her. He'd wanted no part of that.

Jossie and I had been good friends when we were teens, but things had gotten weird between us after the initiation of her wolf. She'd been determined to bond with Vaughn, and I'd been mortified at the brazen things she'd done when it was clear he wasn't interested.

Then I'd met Grey. We'd joined Riverglow and Vaughn became my pack mate. Jossie had tried to use my access to Vaughn to her advantage and I'd been caught in the middle.

We'd had a huge fight when I'd bluntly told her it was never going to happen between her and Vaughn. A year later she'd announced her intentions to bond with Nate Carver, who was a fifth-generation member of Maplefair, Vaughn's birth pack.

When I'd accused her of bonding with Nate only because he was Maplefair, we'd had another huge falling out and she hadn't spoken to me for a long time.

Out of the blue one year, she'd sent me a Christmas card and we'd patched things up as best we could—mostly through the mail.

Through it all Vaughn had refused to have anything to do with her.

Yet he'd hunted with her? Slept with her at a Regional and shifted with her? That was quite a reversal, and he was defensive as hell about it.

My mind boggled.

Kathy picked up the Macy's bag and handed it to Murphy. When we went inside, Vaughn trailed behind us.

Murphy made coffee while I set out a plate of the baked goods Kathy had brought us.

"Snickerdoodles," I called over to Murphy, who threw me a delighted grin over his shoulder as he juggled the good cups and saucers. Normally we used mugs, but we knew better when Kathy Manning visited.

Vaughn slouched in the chair farthest from Kathy's. After we'd all consumed cookies and coffee, Kathy set down her cup and looked between us all.

"Stanzie, I'd like you and Liam to pay a visit to Maplefair. The situation I mentioned needs resolution and it's time the Council stepped in."

"The Regional Council can't resolve it?" I was confused.

"As I said, the New England Regional Council is in a bit of a flux state at the moment. There are some gaps that need to be filled in the ranks.

"One Council member has recently resigned due to age. Another was tapped to serve on the Great Council. Their Advisors no longer serve obviously. Because of this situation in the Regional Council and because I'm currently between Advisors, Councilor Allerton has offered me your assistance. You'll report to me and if necessary the Great Council will be brought in. I'm hoping it won't be. I'm hoping Bethany will come back or least be found, but that remains to be seen I suppose."

"Who's Bethany?" I sat up straight in my chair.

"Bethany Dillon. She's seventeen, and she's been missing since Thursday."

"She ran away?" Murphy leaned forward. He'd been blissed out on a sugar high, but now the conversation had drawn him in. "Is she fighting with her parents?"

Kathy sighed and picked up her coffee cup but didn't drink from it. "They say not. They say she's been withdrawn and moody lately but they put that down to the fact she hasn't been allowed to see her boyfriend. He's in the pack too. He's nineteen. In view of what happened at the Regional Gathering, they've been kept apart as much as possible."

I bit my lip. "What happened at the Regional?"

"Oh, what normally happens. A group of teenagers got together and shifted during the Great Hunt the way they sometimes do no matter how you guard against it. It happened that way to you didn't it, Stanzie? You shifted at a Great Gathering when you were a teenager, right?"

I flushed with remembered embarrassment.

"Bethany and Cody say they are in love and want to bond, but they'll have to wait until they reach majority," Kathy said.

"So why keep them apart until then? What difference does it make? Now that they've shifted, why not let them be together?" I knew I was advocating pack heresy. Pack generally shifted the first time between seventeen and twenty, but we were supposed to be initiated by an experienced member of the pack in order to develop our wolves. Shifting for fun with lovers came later.

Kathy gave me a measured look from beneath half lowered lashes. Once again she resembled an elf—enigmatic, all knowing and nearly impossible to relate to.

"It makes a big difference to their wolves, dear. No one is telling them they can't see each other—they aren't supposed to shift together. The boy, Cody, is willing to work with an experienced partner, but Bethany is being stubborn."

This conversion veered way too close to my own experience and I fervently wished we could talk about something else, but of course we couldn't.

"Well, he didn't disappear too, did he? They didn't run away together?" Murphy asked.

"No," answered Kathy with an elegant lift of her shoulders.

I took a deep breath. "Are you sure Bethany wasn't pregnant?"

Kathy gave another graceful shrug. "Her mother said she got her period after the Regional."

"I don't see why she would run away without him," I insisted.

Kathy nodded. "I know. This is a troubling situation. That's why the Council wants to look into it."

Then, with a devastating directness that took my breath away, she said, "You know it's no shame to admit you got pregnant at that Great Gathering, Stanzie."

"What the hell are you talking about?" My mouth hung open and I closed it with a snap. "We're talking about Bethany. You said she wasn't pregnant. Why are we talking about me? What does that have to do with anything?"

"I was just trying to piece together why you are so afraid to have a baby," Kathy mused. "I just wondered if having to have a discreet abortion after sneaking out and shifting with another teenager has created this silly fear of yours."

Murphy's face darkened at the word *silly* but he didn't say anything. Probably because I was so betrayed and pissed off I didn't give him a chance.

"Kathy, you're wrong. I did not get pregnant after I shifted. Besides, the grandmothers gave us all something horrible-tasting to drink after we shifted back. All the girls. My father was right there to force me to drink it. They said it would most likely prevent conception and I had to drink that shit for a whole week. Paul made me drink it for two just in case." My mouth twisted at the remembered vile taste. "Didn't they make Bethany do the same damn thing? I thought it was de rigueur in cases like that."

"Yes, I believe they did. Also, as I said, her mother has reported she did get her period after that. No one is saying she got pregnant at the Regional. She's either run away or maybe she's hiding in plain sight somewhere within her pack. She may have had an accident or killed herself in a lonely field. She may have taken a bus to New York or even here to Boston. There's a lot of things that may have happened and for her sake I hope we find the truth."

She and Murphy both continued to stare at me. I felt flushed and guilty even though I had no reason to be ashamed. Vaughn stared at me and I was sure he wondered whether I'd told the truth.

"Honestly, I didn't get pregnant. I've never been pregnant."

"Your fear of having a baby, Stanzie, has to come from somewhere." Kathy's voice was warm and soothing as butterscotch but I wasn't lulled by the false sweetness.

It was truly amazing how this woman took every opportunity to wave my fears in front of my face as if we stood in a bullring and I had hooves and a fucking tail while she sported a toreador's outfit and a red cape.

We were supposed to be concentrating on the missing girl, not some phantom pregnancy in my past. Vaughn opened his mouth as if to argue, but closed it again. I knew damn well what he thought because we'd been pack mates for a decade and he knew how I felt about babies. Yet I could tell by his expression he still wondered if I'd gotten pregnant the first time I shifted. So did Murphy. Goddamn Kathy Manning. Goddamn her.

"You're a Regional Councilor. You should know all the nasty secrets of the New England area packs. I don't have a nasty secret about being pregnant, Kathy."

"Your birth pack is extremely reticent and close-minded. There's hasn't been a member on either Council or even an Advisor from Mayflower for years." That fact seemed to puzzle, even exasperate her. "These cases are supposed to be brought before the Regional Council. At the very least we're supposed to be notified."

"Well, Maplefair notified you," I tried to bring the focus back to Bethany.

"Yes, Jocelyn and Nate brought it to our attention right away." Kathy nodded. "You and Liam will be staying at their house in Easton. They're restoring the most adorable rambling old farmhouse and are expecting you tomorrow afternoon."

Murphy shifted in his seat, a look of protest spread across his face.

"We haven't said we'd do this yet," he objected softly.

"Councilor Allerton offered me your services, remember?" Kathy swept on as if Murphy hadn't spoken and he rolled his eyes. "Jason's attending to some personal business at the moment, but you can call him and confirm that if you doubt my word."

Murphy grumbled something under his breath, which Kathy ignored with her usual serenity.

"Hopefully, this situation won't take long to resolve and you can return here. Although I would think Dublin might be nice this time of year. Isn't that so, Liam?" She turned her gaze in Murphy's direction.

He blew out his breath gustily. "We're well aware of our pack obligations, Councilor Manning, thank you just the same for the reminder."

"I know *you* are, Liam." Kathy's voice oozed sympathy and I could almost hear his teeth grind. I kept my gaze fixed on my coffee cup.

After she dabbed her mouth with her napkin, Kathy rose gracefully to her feet. Murphy was on his half a second later. I didn't bother to get up. My head was full of memories of the past.

* * * *

*"Oh, god, Rudi." I am scared because my body feels weird. Something is wrong. My face burns, my skin itches. A strange pressure builds inside me and it needs to be released. Now.*

*Rudi's face in the moonlight is unearthly and beautiful. He is so perfectly gorgeous—everything Wes Hanover is not. But I can't concentrate on Rudi's face or Wes Hanover's either. Pain, shocking and bright, stabs me.*

*I can hear the others in the cane field. One of them howls. It is not a human sound, but that thing within me howls back, ripping me to shreds in the process.*

*"Rudi," I cry, aware that he is on all fours and his back is arched like Halloween cat's, but his face is not feline. It is lupine. It is...wolf.*

\* \* \* \*

Vaughn's chair scraped against the laminate floor and tore me away from the memory. I watched him walk out of the kitchen as Murphy's footsteps sounded on the stairs. I shoved my own chair back and retreated into the living room.

\* \* \* \*

Murphy found me and sat next to me on the sofa. He took one look at my face and knew something was wrong.

"You thinking about Rudi?" He was so damn perceptive. Too damn perceptive sometimes.

I nodded and he put an arm around my shoulders.

"I'm sorry, honey."

The last time I'd seen Rudi Grunwald, his eyes had been empty. Dead. Just like him. Murdered by a Paris grandmother—another casualty of the conspiracy. All because he worked in the world of the Others and had made name for himself in technological circles. He drew attention to himself instead of existing in the shadows where the Pack had lived for millennia.

"I'm so happy with you, but I wish he weren't dead." If he hadn't died at the Great Gathering, I would be in Germany now with Rudi's pack. We'd be bonded. I couldn't imagine life without Murphy, but it wasn't fair Rudi was dead.

Murphy played with ends of my hair. I'd put it back in a messy bun, but some of it had escaped. I thought of us the night before, of him above me in the bed, how he'd felt inside me, his expression as he'd concentrated and tried to hold himself back so I could come first. Love rushed through my veins and I smiled at him.

He gave me another infatuated look and my smile faltered.

"Why do you look at me like that?" I couldn't help ask.

Wistfulness replaced infatuation. "You don't like it?"

"I don't understand it." He loved Sorcha even though she was dead. Why did he look at me the way he did? I was his bond mate and he was devoted to me, but what he felt for me couldn't touch what he'd felt for her. Already I suspected my love for him went even deeper than what I'd felt for Grey. Which confused and terrified the hell out of me because I'd loved Grey so much and when I'd lost him, my whole world had crumbled. I didn't ever want to feel like that again. I didn't ever want to be so vulnerable, so wrapped up in another person that I exposed myself to potential devastation. But I had the sinking suspicion it was way too late.

"It's simple really." Murphy took a deep breath and for a moment I swore I saw fear in his dark eyes, but then he smiled at me. "Stanzie, I—"

Vaughn's bedroom door slammed. Murphy and I both jerked and the moment between us shattered.

Vaughn stalked into the living room. He saw something on our faces and drew up short, his smile nervous.

"Sorry. I didn't mean to interrupt. I just wanted to tell you that I'm coming with you to Vermont tomorrow."

Murphy regarded him silently for a moment. "You know the girl? Bethany?"

Vaughn grimaced. "She's seventeen and I left the pack twenty years ago. Does it seem likely that I know her?"

"Precisely my point, Vaughn."

"I knew her mother. Gina Dillon. She's about ten years older than me and she initiated my wolf. Is that a good enough reason maybe?"

Murphy sighed. "Sorry. I didn't know that."

Vaughn shrugged.

"We're staying with Jossie and Nate," I reminded him. "You gonna be all right with that?"

"Sure, why not?" The challenge in Vaughn's eyes was unmistakable. "Jossie's the one that spent years chasing me, not the other way around, remember?"

"I remember," I agreed. "I also remember you did a lot of running away."

"Oh, fuck you." His mouth tightened. "It was fifteen fucking years ago, Stanz. She's been happily bonded with Nate for over a decade. Stop living in the past."

"Whose idea was hunting together at the Regional?" I wondered.

"What is this third degree bullshit? Is it because I'm not a goddamn Advisor? I'll keep out of your way, I swear. Why do you have to be like this?"

"I'm just amazed that after running away from her as fast you could fifteen years ago, you went and slept with her at a Regional. It doesn't make any sense."

"You weren't there. Why is it a crime if two people decide to let bygones be bygones? And it's not like we fell into bed together. It was a hunt. There's a little bit of a difference. It was a chance to—I don't know—put it all behind us. She's not eighteen years old anymore. She's the Alpha of Maplefair. She's long since gotten over me."

We glared at each other. Neither one of us would look away.

"Are you two actually fighting?" Murphy sounded a little incredulous.

"No!" Vaughn broke eye contact and flushed. "Stanz? We're not fighting, are we?"

He sounded so forlorn I was ashamed of myself.

"No, I'm sorry. I'm confused. I missed a lot the past couple of years, I guess. It's none of my business anyway. I'm defensive because I'm used to being dragged into the middle of it with you two. She never really forgave me for being on your side."

"You weren't on my side, you were my pack mate. You had my back." Vaughn came to the sofa, dropped to his knees and buried his face in my lap. I stroked his long, dark hair.

"You always have my back, don't you?" His voice was muffled and contrite.

"Always," I vowed. Murphy put his arm around me and I let my head drop to his shoulder. Vaughn shifted so he sat on the floor, against our legs. We rested together companionably, so comfortable conversation was irrelevant.

www.ingramcontent.com/pod-product-compliance
Lightning Source LLC
Chambersburg PA
CBHW020804250626
47155CB00003B/1205

* 9 7 8 1 6 1 6 5 0 8 5 3 1 *